Blood Trail

C. M. Sutter

AUTHOR'S NOTE

ABOUT THE AUTHOR

C. M. Sutter is a crime fiction writer who resides in Florida, although she is originally from California.

She is a member of over fifty writing groups and book clubs. In addition to writing, she enjoys spending time with her family and dog, and you'll often find her writing in airports and on planes as she flies from state to state on family visits.

She is an art enthusiast and loves to create gourd birdhouses, pebble art, and handmade soaps. Gardening, bicycling, fishing, and traveling are a few of her favorite pastimes.

C.M. Sutter

http://cmsutter.com/

Contact C. M. Sutter - http://cmsutter.com/contact/

Blood Trail
FBI Agent Jade Monroe - Live or Die Series, Book 2

Recently released prisoners, Gary Rhodes and Leon Brady, need a new enterprise to keep them in cash. The thriving human trafficking business seems like an easy gig—snatch and grab unsuspecting teenage girls with the help of their own girlfriends, Claire Usher and Hope Daniels. Because the two spoiled rich girls are easily bored, risks are taken, and mistakes begin to happen.

FBI agents Jade Monroe and her partner, Lorenzo DeLeon, along with two other seasoned agents are tasked to South Dakota and Wyoming, where a handful of girls have been snatched without a trace or a single witness.

As days pass and the FBI closes in on the culprits, the kidnappers panic and victims begin to die. With only one girl left to deliver and the FBI hot on the kidnappers trail, a harrowing chase ensues through Colorado's backcountry. The FBI needs to stop them before the last girl dies or possibly disappears forever.

See all of C. M. Sutter's books at:
http://cmsutter.com/available-books/

Find C. M. Sutter on Facebook at:
https://www.facebook.com/cmsutterauthor/

Don't want to miss C. M. Sutter's next release?
Sign up for the VIP e-mail list at:
http://cmsutter.com/newsletter/

Chapter 1

My frustration was mounting. I pounded the steering wheel and checked the time on the dash. I was going to be late for work—I had no doubt—and it certainly wasn't the first time. Twice before, in as many months, I'd arrived late to our St. Francis headquarters.

"Damn traffic jam!"

As I closed in on the bottleneck, I saw flashing red and blues—it was an accident and a bad one. The chances of someone texting while driving were high since the roads were clear and it was a sunny September day. There was no reason for that four-car pileup other than negligence.

I pressed Renz's name on my infotainment center, and the phone rang on his end.

"Good morning, Agent Monroe."

"Morning, Mr. Sunshine. How is it fair that you have a fourteen-minute drive to work and mine is an hour?"

"What exactly are you asking? Are you trying to justify the reason you aren't here yet and I'm walking into our office as we speak?"

"I guess. There's a crash on I-43 south, and the traffic is

at a standstill. I'll be passing it any second, but it's pushed me back a solid fifteen minutes. I'm sorry, Renz."

"Don't tell me. Tell Taft. She's your boss."

"I'll have to start leaving my house even earlier since nobody can predict accidents."

"Nope, you sure can't. So now what?"

"Now I walk in late and apologize to everyone for disrupting the morning update meeting after it's already started."

"I'll let Taft know you'll be a few minutes late. I can always bring you up to speed on whatever you miss."

"Thanks, partner." I tapped the screen and ended the call. With my blinker on, I squeezed into the bottleneck, which had diminished from a four-lane freeway into a one-lane path. I fell in line with the cars trying to make their way around the bumpers and broken glass on the road. As the highway widened again, I gunned my Mustang—I needed to make up time.

The guard lifted the gate and waved me through once I arrived at our headquarters along the shores of Lake Michigan. I parked in my assigned spot, crossed the asphalt to our back door, scanned my ID badge, and stared into the retinal reader, then after that door opened, I still had to enter my PIN on the next secured door. I powered through those steps in a matter of seconds then rode the elevator to the third floor, where our offices were located.

After dropping off my purse and briefcase, I sucked in a calming breath, grabbed a pen and notepad from my desk, and headed to the conference room. I was sure I would get the stink eye from Taft, and I deserved it. I had to do better.

I knocked and entered. To my surprise and relief, five people were in attendance. I would only be humiliated by half our staff.

"Jade, nice of you to join us." Taft tipped her wrist. "It's twenty after eight."

"I'm so sorry, Maureen. There was a pileup on the freeway. I'll make sure to leave the house even earlier going forward."

She gave me a curt nod and continued with the meeting as I took my seat.

"As I was explaining to the rest of the team, Tommy and Fay left for Casper, Wyoming, yesterday morning. Word from the local police, who reached out to us, is that two friends, Gary Lee Rhodes and Leon Brady, former prisoners at the state penitentiary in Rawlins, Wyoming, may be up to no good again. They each have a laundry list of offenses, but both served their full sentences—five years—for statutory rape and were released back into society last month. Gary still lives in Wyoming, and Leon moved to South Dakota, yet we were told that they've recently been seen together."

"Where were they originally from?" I asked.

"They grew up in Gillette, Wyoming, as neighborhood friends. Both men were nineteen by the time they began their sentences, and both are twenty-four now, pushing twenty-five. Back then, anything they got into was because Gary put the bug in Leon's ear. According to this police report, he has always been the instigator in their hijinks, except a good number of those hijinks were illegal. The underaged girls were also from Gillette, and even though they were sixteen at the time, they dressed and acted like they were twenty-one."

I huffed. "As if twenty-one is even old enough to think logically. Their brains aren't fully developed until they're twenty-five."

Maureen agreed. "True enough." She ran her finger down the report. "They lived within a few blocks of each other and hung out at the same community park where all the high schoolers and older kids went, so they were well acquainted."

I went on with my questions. "Is Gillette a small town?"

"Not particularly," Renz said. "About the same size as Houma, Louisiana."

I remembered Houma well from a case we worked several months back. "So, if the guys served their time and were released, then what raised a red flag? Are they under suspicion of something else?"

"According to the Gillette police chief, it's a long story. Both girls involved in their initial sentence come from affluent families, and both were horribly spoiled—given everything they wanted—and still are, by the sound of it. The parents were the ones who pushed for the maximum sentence for Gary and Leon, and with their local connections, it got passed through. In Wyoming, the legal age of consent is seventeen, and anyone over the age of eighteen who has sex with a sixteen-year-old, is committing statutory rape, even if the sixteen-year-old consented. The parents believe the girls could very well be with Gary and Leon. The police chief said the parents have been a thorn in his side since the men were released from prison, but because the girls are now legal adults, there isn't much the parents can do."

"But they still want to control their daughters?"

Renz looked my way. "That seems to sum it up."

SSA Kyle Moore took over. "The police chief has known both Gary and Leon their entire lives and said anything is possible with those two, especially if they put their minds together and act as a team."

I waited for further details.

Maureen continued. "Supposedly, the girls have disappeared. They're both twenty-one, but according to the parents, neither girl mentioned leaving town. They've just up and vanished, and they don't respond to phone calls or text messages. Because the credit cards used by the girls actually belong to the parents, they were able to see where they were used. Hope Daniels's card was used to buy diesel fuel at a truck stop in Schaeferville, South Dakota, just three days ago, and on that same date, Claire Usher was spotted at the counter in a truck stop along I-25 in Glenrock, Wyoming. She paid for snacks and thirty gallons of diesel fuel. The problem is, both girls own cars that take regular gas, and neither vehicle has a thirty-gallon gas tank. Law enforcement agencies in both areas, at the request of the Buffalo Police Department, checked video footage from those truck stops, and neither vehicle owned by the girls showed up at any pumps or parking spots. What did show up in both locations at the pumps on record were two similar white cube trucks without any identifiable features."

I held up my hand. "Wait a minute. Where is Buffalo, and why is that town in play?"

Kyle responded by saying the girls had recently moved to Buffalo, where they rented a lower duplex together.

I wrote that down.

Renz took the reins. "Like I said before, the parents are concerned that the girls are with Gary and Leon."

"So?"

He continued. "They believe it's by force."

I pulled back. "How can that be, when Claire Usher went inside alone to pay for the fuel and snacks? She easily could have asked somebody to call the police on her behalf."

"That's true," Maureen said. "On the other hand, Hope swiped her credit card at the pump, so we don't actually have footage of her being alone inside the truck stop she was at."

"What about the drivers? Did they ever get out of the vehicles, or were the girls there by themselves?"

Kyle answered. "Both girls climbed into the passenger seats before the trucks drove out of camera view, so no, they weren't alone, but we couldn't see either driver or the plate numbers on the vehicles."

I rubbed my chin. "But back to my initial question—so what? Maybe it's just sour grapes on the parents' part. They don't want to admit, if it's the case, that their daughters actually like Gary and Leon and want to hang out with them. Do we have a reason to think something illegal is going on? I assume the men can't go far since they have to meet with their parole officers every so often, right?"

Maureen continued. "That's correct, but their offenses weren't nearly as serious as someone who lands in federal prison for a capital crime. They may only have to meet their parole officers once a month or even less."

"But can they legally leave their state of residence without notifying their parole officers?"

Maureen tapped her fingers on the report. "I'd have to find out about that. Every state's requirements are different depending on the offense. Still, the local police think there's cause to worry, and that's why I've sent Tommy and Fay to Casper ahead of you and Lorenzo."

"We're going to Casper too?"

"No, actually you two are going to Rapid City, and here's why. Apparently, Hope and Claire aren't the only ones who have gone missing since the release of both men. Interstate 25 goes from Las Cruces, New Mexico, north through Casper to Buffalo, Wyoming, where it ends. Interstate 90 goes from Seattle to Boston but also intersects in Buffalo as well as Rapid City, South Dakota."

I raised my right brow. "So Gary lives in Casper. Leon lives in Rapid City, and two major interstates go through those cities and meet in Buffalo, where the girls who did live in Gillette just rented a duplex together? That's either quite the coincidence or a well-planned idea, but for what purpose?"

"We don't know yet," Maureen said, "but teenage girls who live in small towns along both interstates between

Casper and Rapid City are starting to disappear."

"Hmm… but why does law enforcement think Gary and Leon are involved? I assume the interstates passed through those towns long before the guys were released from prison."

Maureen chuckled. "Well, that *is* true, but the guys had no particular reason to choose to live in the cities they did. They don't have family there, and the same holds true for the girls moving to Buffalo."

Renz spoke up. "There must be a reason they all wanted to distance themselves from family. Gillette to Casper is around a two-hour drive, the same distance from Gillette to Rapid City. The girls live the nearest to their hometown, with Gillette being an hour drive from Buffalo."

I raised a curious brow. "But still a world away from their parents, if that was their intention."

Maureen continued. "I agree. Checking further, the police said that neither Gary nor Leon were home on the dates the girls were spotted at truck stops. Police stopped at both residences, banged on the doors numerous times, and nobody ever answered or was seen coming or going. They don't have a legal reason to question the men, and I wasn't told what excuse they intended to use for being there, but three days went by before the guys returned home. Gary was seen taking out his trash a few days ago. How they traveled isn't known, since neither of them have a car registered in their name. As of yet, the girls are still a no-show in Buffalo, but that in itself isn't a crime."

"Uh-huh." I took notes as Maureen spoke. "What type

of homes do Gary and Leon live in?"

Renz answered. "Gary lives in a dumpy apartment on the southern outskirts of Casper, and Leon is renting an equally dumpy studio apartment on the north side of Rapid City, but neither left prison with more than two hundred dollars on their person."

I was still confused. "So somebody is funding their living expenses?"

"It appears that way since they don't have jobs yet," Kyle said.

"Obviously, we have no witness accounts of Gary and Leon abducting people. They'd be back in prison for life and we wouldn't be having this discussion if that were the case."

"Unfortunately, that's true, Jade," Maureen said.

"So, what is local law enforcement doing in the individual towns where the teenagers have gone missing?"

Maureen passed a copy of the most recent police report filed by the Buffalo Police Department across the table to me. "The usual. Looking at street cams, interviewing neighbors, talking to friends and family, and asking about school interactions with bullies and the like. We're tracking Claire and Hope's credit card transactions, but so far nothing has come up at all for box truck rentals or given us an indication that either girl is supporting Gary or Leon."

I glanced at the sheet. "Why did the Buffalo Police Department only make the move to contact the FBI?"

"The case was passed to us because the abductions, all in a relatively short time frame, came from neighboring states," Maureen said. "We're assuming the abductions are all connected and the people who are committing those abductions are crossing state lines. Four of the teens are from Wyoming, and two from South Dakota. In all honesty, I'd say the push for our involvement came because Claire and Hope live together in Buffalo, and even though they're of legal age to come and go as they please, it's their parents making all the noise."

Chapter 2

Claire twisted her long blond hair around her finger as she video chatted with Gary that morning. "This is sooo boring."

"Tough shit. Nobody said what we're doing was supposed to be like a day at Disneyland. I thought you wanted to make a boatload of cash, get out from under your mom and dad's thumb, and earn your own money. If you don't, they'll run your life forever. They dangle those Benjamin Franklins in front of you like fish bait, give you credit cards to use, and pay all your bills, then you comply with whatever they tell you to do to keep the bucks rolling in. They hold that shit over your head twenty-four seven."

"Fine!" she sniped. "No reason to bring up my entire life. I know how manipulative my mom and dad can be— I'm living it," she whined into the phone. "I'll admit, it's been easy money though."

"I know how hard it is being you, Claire," Gary said with thick sarcasm, "but it's time to get out from under their control. Don't you want to call your own shots?"

"Yeah."

"What? I didn't hear you. Say it louder."

"YEAH! Did you hear me that time?"

"Don't get pissy with me. Pick us up at the bus terminal in Denver. The bus gets in at three o'clock, so don't be late."

"I won't. Just so you know, Hope said she's bored too."

"I really don't care. You two want the big bucks, and the system we just started is working fine, so do your part, shut up, and deal with it."

"Okay, okay. I'll see you at three o'clock. No need to yell at me."

"Don't be late either." Gary hung up and immediately dialed Leon. "Hey, bro, we're on for later, so hit the road now. Drive the beater to Cheyenne's bus station, and get on the bus going to Denver. Your bus leaves Cheyenne station at one twenty-five, so don't miss it. That delivery is going to land us a decent amount of money."

Leon grunted into the phone. "I'd much rather drive Hope's car. It's more reliable."

"Have you painted it and swapped out the plates?"

"No, I don't have the money to buy paint."

"Then you aren't driving it anywhere until that's done. Get the money from Hope tomorrow. Pretty soon we'll be able to drive luxury cars, so be patient. Don't mess this up, and don't miss the damn bus. My bus gets in about ten minutes before yours, so I'll be waiting inside the terminal for you. Make sure to leave the beater parked in the bus station's lot." Gary clicked off the call and cursed the fact that he had three whiners to deal with.

Somebody has to take charge, and God knows that person

has to be me. If I left it up to those three idiots, we'd all be in jail.

Gary made the call to Charlie, his contact who lived west of Denver. He waited as the phone rang four times in his ear.

"Yeah?"

"It's Gary."

"You have the merchandise?"

"I have three items now, and if I'm lucky, I may be able to score another one by the time we meet up later." He listened through ten seconds of silence before he got a reaction.

"Okay, we'll meet just outside Central City. Take I-70 west out of Denver, and before you reach Idaho Springs, you'll exit right onto Central City Parkway. Follow that road into town. Pull over by the Gold Nugget Café, and call my number for further instructions. Understand?"

"Yes, I understand."

"Good. What time should I expect your call?"

After calculating the time frame in his mind, Gary suggested five o'clock to be on the safe side.

"Then I'll be waiting for that call."

The phone abruptly went dead. Gary gave the screen a glance then shook his head. "Such a warm and friendly guy. Asshole."

Gary thought back to Willis Johns—the con he befriended in prison who got the ball rolling for him. Willis was a hardcore criminal who was serving a fifteen-year term for interstate transport and sales of minors. He'd received a lesser sentence for ratting out the higher-ups, which landed him in a state penitentiary instead of a federal prison, and for half the term. He'd insisted on being put in the witness protection program after he fulfilled his sentence as part of the deal, and it was approved.

Those five years behind bars had taught Gary a lot, and with the few names Willis had given him, he made contact once he was on the outside. He promised to do the heavy lifting and prove his worth if they gave him a chance. Charlie Dunn was his contact guy and who Gary would pass the merchandise off to. The way Willis explained it was that Gary would never meet the actual people in charge beyond Charlie, who was only a middleman. He would never advance through the ranks, and he would never amount to jack shit. He would be one of the people making the deliveries. He would earn good money, and if he kept his mouth shut and his eyes open, he would do well financially. He remembered Willis's words, "Don't get too full of yourself or too greedy, because you'll surely be busted or killed if you do."

Gary would heed those words, and with last week's first delivery being a huge three-thousand-dollar success, he intended to play by the rules. He just had to make sure Leon, Claire, and Hope did too.

Chapter 3

Our instructions were to fly to Rapid City's regional airport, grab a rental car, and drive into town to meet up with the police chief, Tony Franklin, and the deputy sheriff of Meade County, Ben Tilley. Both departments and Casper PD had already been briefed by the Buffalo Police Department's chief, Roger Worth, in regard to the teenagers who had gone missing.

We were supposed to spend the rest of Monday being briefed and all of Tuesday conducting interviews with the missing teenagers' families, followed by visits to the crime scenes where the girls were abducted. Our FBI colleagues in Casper had already been briefed yesterday and would begin the interview process immediately since more teens had been abducted from Wyoming than South Dakota.

Renz and I gathered our bags and headed to Mitchell International Airport, where we were scheduled to set to the sky at ten a.m. sharp. We each had a folder containing contact names for every police station we would be dealing with as well as the names, ages, and town residences of every teen who had gone missing and their parents' names, home addresses, and locations of abduction.

An hour later, after boarding our jet and taking to the sky, I settled in with paper and a pen at my side and began reading every police report and witness statement taken at the site of the abductions. After that, I read through what the police departments nearest the abduction sites did in regards to their own investigations.

Renz and I would work the South Dakota abductions. Tommy and Fay were deep into the Wyoming cases, and we would meet in the middle in Buffalo on Wednesday.

After reading the police reports, I learned that the South Dakota teens were taken from a camp ground and an RV park.

"Hmm… an RV park and a campground are probably the easiest places to snatch teens from."

Renz looked up and lifted his reading glasses. "Why do you say that?"

I double-checked the girls' ages. "They're fifteen and sixteen, the worst ages since they aren't kids, yet they aren't adults either."

Renz chuckled. "I have a fifteen-year-old niece, and she definitely thinks she's an adult."

"Exactly my point, and the last place they want to be is anywhere with their parents. Hell, at that age, I didn't want to be around my mom and dad or my younger sister, Amber. I could easily see a fifteen-year-old wandering off by herself because she's already pissed that she has to be there. Maybe the abductors befriended her, offered her beer or something like that, then caught her off guard and snatched her. It can't be a coincidence that the girls were taken from an RV park and a campground. Those places are isolated, to a degree, and they don't have security cameras for the most part unless they're by buildings. Mix all that together, and you've got a great kidnap cocktail."

"Damn, Jade. You've really got a way with words."

I grinned. "Thanks."

"But—"

I rolled my eyes. "I should have known a *but* was coming."

Renz waved off my skepticism. "What I was going to say is that your theory isn't bad, *but* let's not get ahead of ourselves. What we envision isn't always the reality. The campground and RV park could be packed with people. They might have dozens of buildings, and the campsites might be right on top of each other. Maybe those places aren't as rural or isolated as you think."

"Or maybe they are."

"We'll find out everything once we arrive, talk to the cops, then go to those sites tomorrow. We'll see exactly where the campsites were and where the girls were last seen, then go from there."

"Sounds like a plan." I glanced at my phone. "How long before we land in Rapid City?"

Renz tipped his wrist. "We should be on the ground by twelve forty-five, so we have another hour and a half. Might as well sit back, relax, and enjoy the view."

After skirting around a wall of black rain clouds and heavy turbulence that detoured us a bit, we landed safely in Rapid City at one o'clock.

We deplaned after waiting for the door to be opened and the jet's stairs to be lowered. As I crossed the tarmac and walked into the hangar, I breathed in the fresh air and looked to the sky. The sun was out, and it was a comfortable sixty degrees. I thought back to our time spent in Houma, Louisiana, and smiled, thankful for the current weather in Rapid City.

Our rental car awaited us, and all we needed to do was sign the paperwork. Renz took care of that while I checked the city map for our hotel location. Tory had booked our rooms at the Mountain View Inn, six blocks from the police station but the best hotel in town.

I led the way with my phone's GPS as Renz drove the ten miles to downtown Rapid City. We gave ourselves fifteen minutes to check into our hotel rooms, freshen up, then head out. I made the call to the police station during our drive and told them to expect us by two o'clock.

"Not a bad vehicle." I gave the new Chevy Tahoe a once-over.

Renz gave it his own approving nod. "That's one good thing about having a lot of rental cars to use during our cases. We can weed out the ones we don't like and put check marks next to the ones we do so when it comes time to trade in our own vehicles, we have decent options."

"True, but I doubt that Tory is going to reserve us a sports car."

Renz laughed. "Yeah, what's up with you and hot rod cars?"

I shrugged. "I can get to the bar faster than you and your Volvo wagon."

"That's only if we were going to a bar."

"We will someday, and it won't be one that's attached to a hotel in a distant city."

We arrived at our nicely appointed hotel at one forty, checked in, and headed down the left hallway to our rooms, numbers four and six. Inside room four, I hung the few outfits I brought then headed to the bathroom, where I washed my face and brushed my teeth and hair. Within ten minutes, I was out the door again.

I read the latest headlines in the newspaper that sat on the coffee table in the lounge area while I waited for Renz. The article showed that nobody had been apprehended yet in the two abductions at the RV park in Blackhawk and the campground just outside Sturgis.

I always had a secret desire to visit Sturgis and partake in that biker-rally phenomenon, but it wasn't the right reason or the right time of year to indulge in something like that.

"Ready?"

I looked up to see Renz walking toward me.

"Yep, just reading the headlines in the local paper about the kidnappings."

He raised his brows as he held the outer door open for me. "Yeah, anything of value in the article?"

"Not that I got to. It just said that nobody had been apprehended yet."

We crossed the parking lot to the Tahoe, and Renz clicked the fob. We climbed in, and he continued with the conversation.

"We'll learn a lot more between today and tomorrow."

Five minutes later, we reached the police station and parked in front of their brick building. At the long counter near the back wall, we showed our credentials and told the desk sergeant that Chief Franklin and Deputy Sheriff Tilley were expecting us. He gave us a nod and made the call.

Within seconds, a pleasant-looking man came out to greet us. He appeared to be in his early forties and had buzz-cut blond hair and a blond goatee. He wore stylish glasses and a wide smile. He reached out and shook our hands. "Agents, I'm Chief Tony Franklin. We're so lucky and appreciative to have your help with these disturbing abductions. Please, right this way." He pointed down the hallway. "Deputy Sheriff Ben Tilley is waiting in the second room on the right. His insight will be more than beneficial as we sit down to go over the details."

Renz thanked him. "That's perfect, and we appreciate the fact that he drove down here to meet us."

Chapter 4

We entered the conference room and were introduced to the deputy sheriff. The Meade County Sheriff's Office was located in Sturgis, but the RV park abduction took place only a few miles outside Rapid City.

"Agents Monroe and DeLeon, this is Ben Tilley, the deputy sheriff of Meade County. He has been leading the investigation in the abduction of Tracy Bast and Jillian Nance since they went missing."

I nodded. "Great, and I'm sure you have a lot to share with us."

Ben Tilley responded. "Even though the RV park in Blackhawk is right on the border of Rapid City, this is Pennington County not Meade County. The abduction still took place in my jurisdiction, which means all incidents pertaining to it come to us. So for the two teenagers who have been abducted, other than the first responder statements and eyewitness accounts, you'll be dealing directly with me. Because you flew into Rapid City and the police department is a convenient place to conduct business, I thought it better to meet you here." He turned to Tony. "Because of the proximity of the RV park to Rapid City, I'd venture to say Chief Franklin would probably hear a lot more chatter about the incident than I would up in Sturgis."

"Makes sense, and every bit of information passed on means more people for us to talk to. Sooner or later, we'll get the tip we're looking for," Renz said.

After we took our seats, I pulled the reports, two notepads, and two pens out of my briefcase. I slid one folder to Renz. "These reports were emailed to our headquarters this morning before we left Milwaukee. Has anything changed in the last few hours?"

"Not to our knowledge," Tony Franklin said. "At least no new evidence has come in, and no new abductions have been reported today."

"That's good news, so we can put our focus on what we do have and know. Two girls have been abducted from South Dakota and four from Wyoming in the last two weeks, which is a startling amount. We have two other agents on the ground working the cases in Wyoming. They arrived in Casper yesterday. They'll work their end until Wednesday, and we'll do the same here, then meet in Buffalo. You have both been briefed on the possibility that these abductions are coming from an organized effort of two men who have recently been released from prison, correct?" Renz looked from Tony to Ben and back to Tony.

"We have," Ben said. "Does real evidence point to them, or is it just speculation at this time?"

"Definitely speculation," I said. "It's more of the

coincidental timelines, the possible players who could be involved, and the locations that cause us to lean toward them. Of course, that information came from the Buffalo PD at the request of the parents of two young women, now of legal age, who had previous relations with the men. They've gone missing, but at this point we don't know if they were abducted or are deliberately out of touch with their families. The backstory of those young ladies leads us to believe they're missing on purpose and are tired of controlling parents inserting themselves in their lives."

Renz spoke up. "Yet we aren't ruling out the possibility of those women being involved, if the abductions were actually at the hands of Gary Rhodes and Leon Brady."

"Who interviewed the families and got a timeline of events from them?" I asked.

Ben answered first. "Since the Blackhawk RV park is in Meade County, it was one of my deputies who was dispatched to the scene."

I flipped through the report pages. "A Deputy Tim Jenner?"

"That's correct."

"Is there a chance of meeting with him tomorrow at the RV park to have him walk us through the area where Jillian was last seen?"

"Sure thing. I'll arrange it for whenever you want to meet up with us."

Renz brought up that the Nance family lived in Rapid City. "That has to create a sticky situation, doesn't it? Jillian's family lives in Pennington County, but the abduction took place in Meade County."

"We have no issues working hand in hand," Tony said.

"Why would the family travel five miles from home to go to an RV park?" I asked.

Tony continued. "I asked that very question myself. I was told that the family just bought the RV, so they wanted to take it out for the weekend to get the feel of a real camping experience rather than sleeping in it overnight in their driveway. According to the mom, Jillian was furious that they wouldn't let her stay home alone from a week ago Friday through last Sunday. The abduction took place sometime Saturday afternoon after a heated argument between the dad and Jillian. They didn't call the sheriff's office until nearly dark. They figured she was just blowing off steam and wandering around the area. They assumed she would come back long before sunset, but she didn't."

I shook my head. "Nobody knows when something that seems off turns into a real situation. It's completely understandable but unfortunate. I imagine, with the sun going down, there wasn't much time to look for evidence before dark."

"That's correct, Agent Monroe, and there was also a thunderstorm that night. Any physical evidence like tire tracks or signs of a scuffle that may have been there would have been washed away. We combed the entire park and yelled out her name but never got a response. We had six deputies out searching that night along with the father but didn't have any luck. We also spoke with other campers, but nobody saw an altercation or an abduction. We ruled out an animal attack the next day when we didn't find evidence of blood or torn clothing anywhere in the park."

I tapped my pen against my notepad as I thought. "Give us an idea of the topography. Is the area heavily wooded?"

"Not at all. More like open plains with stands of pine trees scattered about, and the interstate runs parallel to the park."

"How close?" Renz asked.

"Probably a half mile away, but campsites are farther in so you don't hear the constant hum of cars and semis."

"Okay, and what about the campground where Tracy Bast went missing?"

Ben fielded that question. "That's more in my own backyard and just a few miles west of Sturgis. If the abduction had happened along the interstate in August during the bike rally, I'd be inclined to say somebody who was up to no good had a hand in it, but the timing is off. Most folks at the bike rally are there for the experience and a great cross-country ride, but I can't say that's everyone's intentions. Regardless, if the same thing is happening as far away as Casper, Wyoming, it wouldn't likely be bikers committing the crimes."

I had to agree. "Are plenty of people still tent camping around Sturgis in September?"

Ben nodded. "Yep, a lot of diehards who like the great outdoors. They'll camp beyond the first frost and even into early winter. The campground Tracy went missing from has a bit more tree cover than the Blackhawk RV park but still has plenty of open space where one would see or hear an abduction taking place. Somehow those girls were snatched up without a single person noticing."

I sighed. "That's what worries me. The abductors have a method that works for them, nobody notices, and the interstate is usually less than a mile away."

"What did the family say the situation was in Tracy's case?" Renz asked.

"Nothing out of the ordinary. She went out to walk the dog and never returned. The dog found its way back to the campsite about an hour later, dragging the leash behind it, but no Tracy in sight."

"Where is the family from?"

"Bear Butte, less than ten miles east of Sturgis. South Dakota has a lot of open land, and the majority of the towns are along highways and interstates. Most everywhere else is wilderness."

"Got it. So both girls disappeared without a trace, and nobody saw or heard anything?"

"It appears that way, Agent Monroe," Ben said.

"Okay, as long as we're in Rapid City right now, I'd like to call on Jillian's family and get their account. Sometimes people's recollections change after a few days, and we'd like to make sure what they remember today is the same as what they gave as their statement last week."

"Sure thing. I can arrange that as soon as you like," Tony said.

I thanked him. "Now would be good."

Chapter 5

So far, the plan was going without a hitch. Both men were on busses—Gary on the one from Casper to Denver and Leon on the bus from Cheyenne to Denver. Gary had made the call to Leon earlier to make sure he was actually on the bus and it was en route. Now it was up to the girls to arrive at the bus station on time to pick them up and to have the merchandise ready for delivery later that day.

Hope and Claire had one box truck, and the other sat at a storage facility in Schaeferville. It would be used once the four of them set out again for the next delivery. The sides of both trucks would be covered with magnetic advertising decals, which would get swapped out with a different decal for every use. It was Hope and Claire's responsibility to have their truck already set up with the magnetic ads on the sides.

Gary dozed off during the ride but woke to the hiss of the air brakes as the bus pulled into Denver's bus terminal and parked. He gathered his backpack from the bin above his head and stood in line to exit the bus. After entering the terminal, Gary found a spot to sit with a view of the incoming busses, where he would see Leon arrive from

Cheyenne. He checked the time on the oversized digital wall clock. Leon's bus should be there in six minutes. Gary glanced across the terminal to the sandwich kiosk then back at the clock—he had just enough time to grab something to eat. He crossed the marble floor and snatched a prepackaged turkey sub and a bag of chips, then went to the cashier to pay.

"I'll take a medium soda too." He pulled out his wallet. A tap on his shoulder startled him. Gary spun to see Leon standing at his back.

"Chill, dude. Jesus, you nervous about something?"

"No, and keep your voice down. I wasn't expecting you for another five minutes, that's all. Grab something to eat. We got two hours before we're supposed to meet up with Charlie."

With their bags slung over their shoulders and their food in hand, the men walked out to the parking lot.

Gary set his food and bag on the brick retaining wall and shielded his eyes as he scanned the lot from left to right. "Where the hell are they? I told Claire she better not be late, damn her."

"Traffic maybe?"

"My guess would be more like uncooperative passengers."

Leon frowned. "I thought they were supposed to keep them sedated."

"They are, but Claire and Hope are both twenty-one, cell phone addicts, and can't remember instructions from one minute to the next. I swear they're going to be sold, too, if they don't get their shit together."

"Calm down, man. We have plenty of time before we're supposed to meet Charlie." Leon set his meal on the brick wall, too, then leaned against it.

"Right, but I was hoping to pick up another passenger on our way. Don't forget, anyone under seventeen is worth a hell of a lot more than the ones over that age. If they're minors, somebody is likely looking for them, which means more risk to us but more money to us as well."

Leon rubbed his hands together. "Lately, all I dream about is money. Fancy cars, jewelry, flashing cash around, and going on trips."

Gary smirked. "Don't forget what my buddy Willis told me."

"Yeah, yeah, 'Don't get ahead of yourself, and don't get greedy. You'll either end up in prison or dead.'"

"Exactly, and we've already been to prison." Gary took the last bite of his sandwich and pointed his chin toward the parking lot entrance. "That's got to be them turning in."

A large white box truck with the words "Guido's Gourmet Pizza—Our Own Slice of Italy" with a fake phone number and address written across the sides in magnetic letters pulled into the parking lot, stopped, and idled.

"Come on. That's them. Claire knows better than to get close to any buildings with outdoor cameras. You circle left and climb into the passenger seat, and I'll go right. I'm driving."

They stayed out at what Gary felt was a safe enough distance from the cameras and approached the box truck. Hope waved out the window.

Gary cursed under his breath and stepped up his pace.

I swear I'm going to jack her up. I told them a hundred times to stay low-key. He reached the driver's door and jerked it open. "Climb into the back, both of you."

"You could at least say hi," Claire said.

"Hi, now get your asses in the back."

Leon climbed in on the passenger side seconds later. "What was the holdup?"

Hope poked her head into the walk-through opening between the seats. "One of the little bitches back here was giving us trouble."

"What kind of trouble?" Gary asked.

"I don't know. She was shaking really hard."

Leon spun in his seat. "What the hell does that mean? Was she having a seizure?"

Hope shrugged.

Gary pulled out onto North Broadway and continued south to West Colfax, which ran parallel to I-70 west. Already pissed off, he yelled at Leon, "Climb into the back, and see what's going on with that girl!"

Leon entered the enclosed box area of the truck.

From the driver's seat, Gary listened to the conversation between Leon and Hope.

"Which girl was shaking?"

"The one with the long black hair."

Gary called out, "What's going on back there?"

"Son of a bitch, Gary, she doesn't have a pulse."

Leon and the girls slammed against the sides of the truck as Gary made an abrupt turn into a strip mall's parking lot.

"What the hell do you mean she doesn't have a pulse?" Gary killed the engine and climbed into the back. "Get out of the way!" He knelt at the girl's side, pulled the tape from her mouth, and saw that she'd choked on her own vomit. She was dead.

"I thought I told you two to take care of these girls until we handed them off to Charlie. Why did she puke?"

Claire tried to backpedal. "You told us to keep them drugged so they'd stay quiet. Maybe she had an allergic reaction or something. It's Hope's fault. She was supposed to keep her eye on them."

"She's dead for God's sake! *Maybe* you gave her too many drugs so you wouldn't have to bother with her."

Hope stomped her foot. "She was resisting us a lot—much more than those other two."

"I should beat your ass." Gary raised his fist, but Leon grabbed his hand.

"Enough already! From now on, we'll just keep them in restraints and tape their mouths," Leon said. "They don't need to be drugged."

Gary looked around the back. "We need to set this up better back here, but first we have to dump her and find another girl. I told Charlie we had three ready for delivery." He glared at Claire and Hope. "If you want freedom from your parents' control, you better toe the line. Another mistake like this, and you'll both be out on your asses. Understand?"

Claire stared at the floor. "Uh-huh."

"Hope?"

"Yeah, yeah, I understand."

"You damn well better. If we don't find another girl to deliver before we get to Central City, you'll both go without pay. Maybe you will anyway as a lesson."

Gary climbed back into the driver's seat, pulled up a map on his phone, and looked for a remote location on the way to Central City where they could dump the dead girl, but before they left Denver, they would have to pick up a replacement. They had an hour to spare, and they had to take advantage of every second. Gary exited Colfax and drove up and down the surface streets for twenty minutes.

"There." He pointed out the windshield. "Those two will do just fine."

"But there are *two* of them. How the hell are we supposed to get them both in the truck at the same time?" Leon asked. His frantic voice had gone up a full octave.

"You and I are going to grab them and toss them in the back. We don't have a choice. If we only grab one, the other can identify us and the truck." Gary drove past them and parked a half block ahead. He jerked the shifter into Park and climbed through the opening behind the seats. "I want both you girls to get out, and as soon as they get close to the rear of the truck, I want you to strike up a conversation with them about how to get to I-70. Leon and I will take it from there." He jabbed the air with a threatening finger. "Don't screw it up either." Gary watched out the side mirror until the girls were within fifty feet of the truck's rear then climbed into the back with Leon. "You two get out, and you better play up the questions like you're Academy

Award-worthy actresses. Now go! We're going to jump out the back and snatch them as soon as we hear you talking to them. It'll be to your benefit to pitch in when we need help too."

Leon added to that comment. "Yeah, like club them over the head once we get them inside."

Claire and Hope exited the truck.

With his ear pressed against one of the back doors, Gary heard them talking to the girls on the sidewalk. "Got the zip ties and tape ready?"

Leon pointed to both items lying on the floor next to the doors. "They're ready to go, and so am I."

"Okay." Gary lifted the door latch then the handle. He looked at Leon and nodded. "Go!"

They bolted from the back of the truck and saw all four girls together on the sidewalk. Gary jerked his head at Claire, and with a hard shove, she pushed one of the girls toward Gary. Hope did the same with the other one, and within seconds, they were both at the mercy of the men. Gary and Leon grabbed them, tossed them in the back, and set the attack into motion. Claire and Hope jumped in and closed the doors behind them.

"Bring us the tape and zip ties!" Leon yelled.

Hope and Claire did as instructed, and with the girls pinned to the floor, the men straddling their backs, their wrists were bound behind them while Hope and Claire quickly silenced their screams with tape.

"Okay, that's done!" Gary wiped his brow with the back of his hand. "I need to get us out of here now. You three secure them to the restraints along the walls with more zip ties. Make sure they can't budge, and make sure you don't have tape over their noses. Dead girls don't bring in money." Gary climbed through the opening, jumped into the driver's seat, and barreled down the street, following the signs toward I-70 west. He jerked his head to the right when Leon climbed into the cab and plopped down in the passenger seat with a grunt. "Everything under control back there?"

"It's all good. Now let's dump the dead girl before she starts to stink."

Chapter 6

Chief Franklin had an officer escort us to the home of Bill and Peggy Nance. They lived in a typical middle-class neighborhood on Adams Street in a well-kept home. We parked along the curb behind Officer Talbot's squad car and walked to the front door with him. The Nances were expecting us.

Mr. Nance, or Bill, as he insisted we call him, offered us the couch to sit on in the living room. Peggy joined him minutes later, then a child—who appeared to be around seven—peeked around the corner.

"Lanie, go play in your bedroom. We have grown-up things to discuss with these agents," Peggy said.

The little girl looked at me with sad eyes. "Are you going to find my sister?"

"We're going to do our best to make that happen, sweetie," I said.

Peggy waved her off. "Now go on. This won't take too long." Peggy waited until Lanie walked away before she spoke again. "She's been scared to death since Jillian went missing. She has nightmares nearly every night."

"We're sorry to hear that, ma'am," Renz said.

"Peggy, please call me Peggy."

Renz nodded. "I'm sure you've given your statement to a half dozen people by now, but we'd like to hear it in your own words. Other girls have gone missing in the last few weeks, and although we don't have solid proof yet that the cases are connected, we're leaning that way."

Peggy buried her face in Bill's shoulder. "It's been over a week, and we're no closer to finding her than we were then." She wiped her eyes and looked at her husband. "Are you going to give the accounts, or should I?"

"Go ahead until Saturday, when Jill and I started arguing, then I'll take over."

I pulled out my notepad and waited. Renz asked Peggy to begin with the day they left for the RV park.

"That was a week ago Friday. Jill was so angry that we wouldn't let her stay home alone." Peggy looked from Renz to me. "But she's only sixteen, and well—"

"Well what?" I asked.

"She hasn't been entirely trustworthy in the past. We've had problems with Jill, so I told her absolutely not. We weren't going to allow her to stay home alone from Friday night until Sunday afternoon. But now in hindsight—"

Bill put his arm around his wife. "Honey, we had no way to know the outcome of the weekend. You can't carry the blame for her disappearance."

"Then why do I feel so guilty?"

I had to keep her talking. "Peggy, please continue with Friday, when you left home."

She nodded. "I'm sorry for getting distracted."

"No worries," Renz said.

Peggy continued. "Jill screamed at both of us for being unfair. Teenagers have a real knack for laying guilt on parents. We did our best not to engage, but she was so belligerent. She even yelled at Lanie for no reason whatsoever. We got to the RV park, set up the trailer, and Bill made a campfire dinner. Lanie loved it, but Jill marched off. She came back an hour later, went inside the RV, and didn't talk to us for the rest of the night."

Bill took his turn. "The next day—Saturday—she continued with the silent treatment. She stayed in the RV and texted with her friends all day long. Finally, I had enough. I ripped her phone from her hands and told her she couldn't have it back until we got home. She was to act like a family member and have fun with her little sister—even if she had to fake it. That's when she stormed off for the last time"—Bill's voice cracked—"and we haven't seen her since. I checked her texts but there was nothing earth shattering in her messages. She told her friends she hated camping and that was about it."

"That's a heartbreaking story," I said.

"If only I would have let her keep her phone, maybe she could have called for help, or there's the chance the cops could have tracked it. Something! Damn it, it's all my fault."

"We've been through the what-if scenarios many times with families. Usually if the perpetrator finds a phone on their captive, they destroy it immediately, toss it to the side, or turn it off. Even if she'd had it, the chances of it doing her any good are truly slim."

Bill shook his head. "Was that supposed to make me feel better?"

I gave him a half smile. "No, but you might find some comfort in knowing the truth."

Officer Talbot took over. "Meade County Sheriff's Office got the call several hours later, and they took over the investigation because it's their jurisdiction."

"Got it." Renz looked from Peggy to Bill. "Do either of you know about problems at school, bullies, or anyone who took issue with Jillian?"

"Not at all," Peggy said. "Honestly, the only people who probably fought with her was us. I swear, kids hate their parents until they're in their twenties. After that, and once they're on their own, they realize just how good they had it."

"I imagine that's true in a lot of families," I said.

"So, what happened after you called 911 and the deputy arrived?"

"Deputy Jenner showed up first and walked the park with us as we explained the situation. We only had a few hours before dark, so he made the call and got five more deputies out there. We combed the area and talked to the other campers but got nothing. Jill stormed off, nobody heard or saw anything, then poof"—he emphasized the *poof* with his hands—"she was gone. More deputies and some of the campers helped search the next day, but we found no signs of her, a scuffle, blood, or clothing anywhere."

I nodded then turned to Officer Talbot. "Has Meade

County kept you abreast of their investigation? Do they have any clues?"

"Sorry, but they don't have any leads. Jillian's face was aired on the news three times over the last week, but no reliable tips have come in."

I let out a hard breath. "Okay. Tomorrow we'll be going to the site to look things over with Deputy Jenner. Another girl was abducted near Sturgis last week and several more in Wyoming. City and county law enforcement agencies have been actively working the cases. We just arrived today, and we have two more agents working the Wyoming side of the investigation. It's going to take some time to connect all the dots, but we intend to give it everything we have."

Bill furrowed his brow. "So more girls were kidnapped? Why?"

I had my own theories although nothing had been substantiated yet, but by the expression that took over Bill's face, I knew he was reading my thoughts.

"Jill wasn't kidnapped because somebody wanted to do her harm or demand a ransom, was she? She was kidnapped to be sold."

"Bill, at this point it's too early to know anything for sure, but we have state troopers watching the interstates, county and city officers watching towns and rural areas, and the FBI is covering South Dakota and Wyoming with feet on the ground. We'll get to the bottom of this. All we ask for is some patience on your part."

They held tightly to each other, thanked us for our visit, and showed us to the door.

I gave Peggy my card. "Please, contact us if anything comes up."

They promised they would, and we returned to the police department.

Ben Tilley had gone back to Sturgis and left word that Deputy Jenner would meet us at the Blackhawk RV park tomorrow at nine a.m. At that point, we didn't have anything else to discuss about the case with Tony, since he wasn't actively working the Meade County abductions. We did want to review all felony activities that had taken place in Pennington County over the last five years to see if a connection could be made to the abductions or if any local felon raised a red flag.

After we checked out the Blackhawk RV park with Deputy Jenner the next day, we would continue north to Sturgis, check out that abduction site, speak with Tracy's parents, then meet up with Ben Tilley again.

Chapter 7

Once Denver was in the rearview mirror, Gary sucked in and blew out a few calming breaths. "Claire, come up here. I need to talk to you."

She poked her head through the opening. "Yeah?"

"Explain that broken taillight to me, and choose your words carefully. I can smell a liar a mile away."

She stuttered as she began. "Um, wait what? A broken taillight?"

"You get one chance to answer honestly."

Hope yelled from the back of the truck, "I'll tell—"

Leon spun in his seat. "Hope, shut up! Gary isn't talking to you."

She grumbled and went silent.

"I'm waiting, Claire."

"Okay already. I didn't know it was broken, and that's the truth. I parked on a residential street so we could get some sleep, just for an hour or so, but when it was time to leave, I backed into a driveway to turn around." She began to whine. "You know I can't see shit through those side mirrors—"

"What happened?"

"I hit the car that was parked in the driveway, but I took off right away. It wasn't like anyone saw us. It was the middle of the night for God's sake."

Gary cursed. "You better hope to hell this doesn't come back to haunt us. Where were you when that happened, and where were you going?"

"We were passing through Cheyenne on the way here, to Denver."

"So it happened in a residential neighborhood in Cheyenne in the middle of the night?"

"Yes, sorry. I don't like driving this big truck."

"Go sit down. I have to think about things." Gary continued on and had to focus on his driving. He watched for sideroads that would exit the interstate and take them deep into the backcountry. He needed to make sure the coyotes would make short work of the dead girl before any hiker caught sight of her. Gary turned off the interstate at Evergreen Road and continued north for several miles. A sign that read Rushing Brook Canyon Road caught his eye, and it sounded intriguing. He cranked the wheel and made a hard right onto the dirt road. Claire yelled that she'd just slammed against the opposite wall in the back.

"Shut up, hang on, and keep your eyes on those new girls. We'll be stopping in a few minutes to dump the dead one." Gary continued deeper into the rugged backcountry and hit every bump and pothole on that one-lane road.

Leon watched out the window. "Don't get yourself into a spot where we can't turn around. We have no idea where this road goes or if it ends without warning."

"Yeah, you're right. Let's get out and see what we've got." Gary pressed the brake pedal and shifted into Park, then killed the engine and waited for the dust to settle.

"Where are you going?" Hope yelled as they opened the doors and climbed out.

"To look for a good spot around here, so stay put for now."

The men walked the outer edge of the road, where a deep ravine lay directly to their left.

"Be careful. The rocks are loose," Gary said as they peered over the edge.

"Yeah, but around loose rocks is a good place to dump a body. Hikers wouldn't go down there."

"That's true." Gary looked ahead down the road. "I don't see a place to turn around though. The road is too narrow."

"Let's get rid of the girl then continue on until we see a side road or a spot wide enough to turn around. We need to get back to the interstate pretty soon, so we can't go much farther."

"Okay." Gary walked to the back doors, lifted the latch, and pulled them open.

Hope and Claire squinted from the sun blasting in. The new girls squirmed and moaned through the tape.

Claire kicked one in the hip. "Shut up. I've listened to whiny bitches for days, and I'm getting tired of it." She and Hope jumped out and stretched. "Ahh… fresh air."

Gary tipped his head toward the bound girls inside.

"Come on. Let's get this over with."

The men disappeared for a minute into the dark box of the truck. They came out carrying the dead girl—Gary with his elbows locked under her armpits, and Leon grasping her ankles. They placed her on the edge of the road and removed what remained of the tape and zip ties. Gary balled it up and threw it back into the truck.

"Double-check her pockets before we toss her over the edge."

Leon jammed his hand into every pocket and gave Gary a nod. "She's good to go."

"Okay, we're going to swing her a few times then let go. We need her to fall deep into the ravine so we have to put all our effort into it."

"I'm ready whenever you are."

Gary grabbed her by the wrists, Leon took her ankles, and they swung the girl back and forth.

"Let go now!"

On the third swing, they released her. She hit several boulders before she rolled down the hill.

Gary inched ahead carefully and peered over the edge. "See anything?"

Leon shielded his eyes and looked down. "I don't see shit except for a lot of trees and rocks."

"Then we're good." Gary jerked his chin toward the trees. "Everyone go take a piss, then we've got to get back on the freeway."

Several minutes later, Gary found a turnout a mile farther. "Finally!" With some back and forth sawing maneuvers, Gary was able to get the truck facing the way they'd come. "Now we've got to make up time. I'm supposed to call Charlie in twenty-five minutes."

Leon grinned. "He'll give us a pass. Hell, we're bringing him an extra girl he wasn't expecting. That's another thousand bucks in our pocket and who knows how much more in his?"

Gary tapped the steering wheel as the truck barreled forward and the rear tires kicked up dust. "What I'd like to know is who the actual broker is and how much money he's making on every girl. It's got to be at least five grand."

"Yeah, wouldn't it be sweet to be in his shoes?"

Gary's mind raced. "It would be damn sweet. When is your next meeting with the parole officer?"

"Next week, then it goes monthly."

"Same here, and after that, we're going to step up our pace."

Chapter 8

We'd gone through the Pennington County reports but didn't find a single felon who had tendencies to commit kidnapping or anyone who had in the past. With that angle leading nowhere, we packed up and said goodbye to Tony Franklin. After supper, we would touch base through video chat with Tommy and Fay to get and give each other updates on the investigation.

We would stay the night in the Rapid City hotel, spend tomorrow in the field, then grab a hotel in Sturgis for that night. Wednesday we would meet Tommy and Fay in Buffalo, but I had something to suggest later, during our video chat.

"What do you want for supper?" Renz asked as we climbed into the Tahoe.

"Mmmm—steak comes to mind. I guess, out here in God's country, I'm envisioning a longhorn steer."

"I'm pretty sure that's more of a Texas phenomenon. Here in South Dakota, I believe bison is popular."

"Really? Okay, I'm game. I'll see what steak joints I can find near the hotel that serve bison." I checked every four-star restaurant within five blocks of the hotel. It would be a nice night to walk there and back. "I found one that has great reviews. It's called Jerome's Grill."

"Sure. How far is it from the hotel?"

"Only three blocks."

Renz lowered the driver's-side window and stuck out his hand. "Damn nice night for a walk."

I laughed. "That's exactly what I was thinking."

Later, after a delicious bison steak and mouthwatering sides at Jerome's, I was happy to walk off the meal and dessert I'd just eaten. Back at the hotel, I powered up my laptop in a seating area near the bar. Renz had called Tommy after we'd left the restaurant and told him we would be video calling them at seven thirty. We still had ten minutes before the call.

Renz tipped his head toward the bar. "Want something to drink?"

"I'd love a glass of wine, but I better stick to coffee. I don't want the others to think I'm taking my job lightly."

He waved off my comment. "I can guarantee you they aren't going to think that, and as a matter of fact, I can damn near guarantee you that Tommy will have a beer at his side."

"You sure?"

"One hundred percent. We are human, you know."

I smiled. "Okay, a glass of Cab sounds good."

"Coming up."

I watched as Renz walked to the bar. He and I were perfect partners, and as much as I missed Jack and J.T., my former sidekicks, Renz was a great guy, mild mannered, and as smart as a whip. I was happy that Maureen paired us up, and in my opinion, we were a good match. Renz returned to our table with two glasses of wine.

"Thanks, partner. We have a couple of minutes before the call. I've organized our notes and have paper and pens ready to go."

A minute later, an invite link came through my email to join the meeting. I clicked on it, and within a few seconds, we saw Fay's and Tommy's faces on the screen.

"Hey, guys," I said. "Hope you've had more luck than we have today. We haven't learned anything more than what was in the report filed by the Meade County Sheriff's Office."

Tommy began with what they had. "We've talked to all the parents of the missing girls, and needless to say, they're devastated. Nobody knows anything, but it's not uncommon for parents of teenagers to be absolutely clueless. Kids that age don't share information with authority figures, especially their own moms and dads. It seems that every teen disappeared right from their own neighborhoods, but the exact location of where they were when the abduction took place is unknown. We have a general area, and that expands five blocks out in every direction from their homes. We've interviewed their friends, too, and walked the neighborhoods, but came up empty."

Fay took her turn. "One thing that's interesting, though, is the call that came into the Cheyenne, Wyoming, police department four nights ago. It was a disturbance call from a homeowner in a residential neighborhood, and when the police arrived, they found the homeowner's car sitting in the driveway with the rear end damaged. Pieces of a taillight from the assumed hit-and-run vehicle were lying in the driveway. The police bagged them, and the homeowner filed an insurance claim, but it wasn't until yesterday that anyone actually took enough interest in the pieces to look up the serial numbers imprinted in the plastic. Sounds like the insurance company was asking about it. It turns out that type of taillight comes from a 2005 box truck. Of course, we looked over those truck stop videos again but couldn't make out if either white box truck had a broken taillight or not."

I rubbed my chin. "That *is* interesting. So the truck was in a residential neighborhood in the middle of the night and was—what—turning around?"

"Probably. Those box trucks don't have windows in the back doors, so the driver has to rely on the side mirrors. I could see how an unexperienced driver may have backed into something," Tommy said.

Renz took his turn. "So where exactly is Cheyenne?"

"Cheyenne runs along I-25 and is about halfway between Casper and Denver."

"Then where is Cheyenne in relation to Glenrock, where Claire was spotted paying for gas?"

Tommy shook his head. "Not that close—two hours away, but Casper, where Gary lives, is only a half hour from Glenrock."

"Hmm… I wonder if that's a coincidence or not. Where

are those trucks coming from anyway? They aren't parked at anyone's homes."

"Good question, Jade," Fay said.

"If the truck with the broken taillight was one of those white box trucks that we saw Hope and Claire getting out of, then where the hell were they going? We know there's a connection between the men from Casper to Rapid City and abductions took place along that route, but south of Casper?" I asked. "If that vehicle is actually using the interstate and we know what time that police report came in, we might catch it passing a plate reader somewhere. We'd have to know where the nearest readers are in both directions out of Cheyenne though."

"Not a bad idea, Jade," Tommy said. "We'll absolutely check that out."

I continued. "Not to change the subject, but we have to pass through Gillette on our way to Buffalo on Wednesday. In my opinion, it would be worth our while to pay all the parents a visit."

"I agree," Fay said. "We need to know more about the four of them, plus we need to know how those girls have access to money other than through credit cards."

Tommy took his turn. "Tomorrow, besides learning more about the police report and plate readers, we're going to get in touch with both men's parole officers. I want to know how often they're supposed to report in and what their schedules were from the minute they were released from prison. The times when they were home and when they weren't might be based on those parole meetings."

"Good plan. Let's touch base again tomorrow night. Sounds like we'll all be busy during the day," Renz said.

With the time for our next video chat planned, I logged off. Renz and I each had another drink, then we parted ways at our rooms.

Chapter 9

Leon whistled as they climbed back into the truck and set off for the return trip to Denver. "Damn, that Charlie is a scary dude. Did you see how hard he punched that girl after she bit his hand?"

"I thought Charlie demanded the merchandise be in good condition when we make the delivery. He said his people don't want banged-up girls, and that's why we can't slap them around," Hope said.

Leon continued. "He'll likely have to hold onto her for a while until her bruises go away. I'll tell you one thing, I for one, don't want to get on that guy's bad side."

Hope laughed. "That's because you're a chickenshit."

Gary looked back at Hope, shook his head, and groaned. "That was the wrong thing to say."

Leon spun in his seat and slapped Hope across the face, bloodying her lip. She fell backward into the box of the truck. Claire cursed Leon and flipped him the bird.

"Shut up, Claire!" Leon snarled then looked at Gary. "Whose idea was it to let these bitches tag along?"

"Mine, and they serve a purpose, so deal with it. We'll

make a lot more money with four people working instead of two. Being chicks, they're easier to control, and we've known them for years. They're trustworthy."

Leon looked over his shoulder and glared at Hope. "Maybe so, but this one has a smart mouth. The next time you call me a chickenshit, I'll break your jaw. Understand?"

Hope nodded. "Yeah."

"Say you're sorry."

"Sorry, Leon."

"That's better." Leon relaxed as he pulled the stack of cash out of the envelope and counted it for the third time. "Damn, I could get used to this."

Gary snickered his response. "That's our intention, as long as nobody screws it up."

Hope grabbed at Leon's hands. "I want my share." She pulled back when Leon fanned the money in her face.

Gary jerked his head to the right. "What the hell is that supposed to mean? You two don't get a share this time. That'll teach you not to let girls die. We'd have another thousand bucks to split up if it wasn't for your stupidity and negligence. That's not to mention pissing off Charlie because we reached Central City late. You're lucky I made up a bullshit story about having to change one of the tires. If he knew we had to dump a dead girl, we'd lose this gig for sure."

Leon huffed. "And that's if Charlie was feeling generous. Chances are, we'd all be tossed into a ravine, too, since dead people don't talk." Leon looked over his shoulder at the girls. "Charlie's no joke, and it would benefit you both to remember that."

Gary tipped his chin at Leon. "Put the damn money away, and make yourself useful. Reserve two rooms for the night at a motel near the bus station."

"Yep, on it."

They were on their way back to Denver. They would get rooms for the night then part ways the next morning. Leon and Hope would board the bus from Denver to Cheyenne, pick up the beater, and drive back to Rapid City. Gary and Claire would head for Casper in the truck. With the pizza delivery decals still on the sides of it, Gary felt safe enough to be on the interstate during daylight hours. Once they arrived in Casper, the truck would go into the storage garage until the next round of abductions. They had another delivery scheduled in less than a week, and the pizza decals would be swapped out with different ones.

Forty-five minutes later, Gary parked in an all-night lot across the street from the Mile-High Manor, a two-bit motel only a block from the bus station.

Hope groaned after they entered the building. "Come on. This place sucks. Let's get out of here, and I'll put the rooms on my credit card to make up for our mistake."

Gary grabbed her arm. "Not happening. I've told you both no more credit card use since I'm sure your folks are monitoring every transaction. If you need to take cash advances, that's fine, but no more swiping cards, and you better not be doing it behind our backs. We're making enough money now that everyone can pay their fair share in cash."

She jerked away from him. "All right, already, geez."

Leon looked back before walking up to the counter. "And this is where we're staying tonight, so deal with it."

After checking in and dropping off their bags, the four of them went to the diner across the street from the motel. During that dinner hour, they discussed the next round of abductions. So far, the two deliveries they'd made to Charlie came from towns along the I-25 and I-90 routes between Casper and Rapid City. Continuing that same route was too dangerous since Gary was sure state troopers had begun patrolling those interstates more than usual. It was time to mix things up. They would go over other options once they were back at the motel, but one truck would leave from Casper, and the other from Schaeferville, South Dakota. Each time the haul would get bigger, and their income would grow faster.

They ate dinner and walked back to the motel. The Cheyenne bus was scheduled to leave the station at seven fifteen a.m. the next day. That night, they would make tentative plans for the next round of abductions then leave Denver first thing in the morning.

Chapter 10

After breakfast, we checked out of our hotel and were off to the Blackhawk RV park for our nine a.m. meeting with Deputy Tim Jenner. We would listen to his account of that day then walk the area. Jillian had been missing for more than a week, and it was unlikely that any of the campers who were there a week ago would still be there that morning, yet my intentions were to talk to the current campers and ask if anybody had been trolling the campground who didn't seem to be staying there. If suspicious-seeming characters were roaming around without an RV or a designated campsite, it would be imperative to find out why.

We waited in our vehicle at the park entrance, and at three minutes before nine, a Meade County deputy sheriff's car pulled up next to ours and lowered the passenger-side window.

"Agents DeLeon and Monroe?"

"That's us," Renz said. "Deputy Jenner?"

The man tipped his head. "Follow me. I'll take you to the campsite the Nances used."

The site was occupied by a different family, so we parked

along the road. Deputy Jenner climbed out of his car, shook our hands, and went on to explain that RV site forty-seven was the one that had been occupied by the Nance family. It was deeper into the park and near a hill of pines that almost beckoned people to come explore. In the distance, I saw the interstate with cars zipping by, but as far away as they were, the sound was only a low hum and nothing that would interrupt the peace and quiet at their campsite. I wondered how the alleged argument between father and daughter went over in that seemingly serene location.

"Deputy Jenner, were there occupied campsites all around the Nances'?"

"There were, Agent Monroe."

"And all the people were interviewed?"

"Absolutely. Other than hearing the argument between Mr. Nance and Jillian, then seeing her storm off in that direction"— he pointed toward the pines—"there was no indication that anything else was wrong. Nobody heard her yell for help or saw a suspicious vehicle barreling out to the highway—nothing. She just walked away and never came back."

Renz pointed toward the trees with his chin. "Can we take a walk?"

"Sure thing, sir."

We reached the hill of pines several minutes later. From our elevated position, we could see the entire park with all the roads that went to different campsites.

"One way in and out that turns into six different roads."

"Yep, with campsites on both sides and right next to each other," Jenner said.

I frowned. "As pretty as it is up here in the trees, down there doesn't remind me of any childhood camping experiences that I recall."

"No, ma'am. It's more like a trailer park in the country if you ask me."

Renz did a three sixty. "There aren't any amenities here, but maybe that's what people like. No Yogi Bear stuff, just wilderness with an interstate a half mile away."

"Maybe the kidnappers liked it too." I noticed campsites farther back, and if the perps had been there, chances were, they saw everything going on below them. They would also see if someone was walking their way. "The kidnappers could have pulled in here to take a break, saw an opportunity with Jillian, snatched her up, and casually left without drawing any attention to themselves."

"That is possible," Renz said, "but wouldn't they need a way to draw her in?"

"Sure, but if they're who we assume they are, what sixteen-year-old wouldn't think it's cool to be with young men and women in their twenties? When I was that age, I would have thought I was hot stuff to hang out with older people, especially if they seemed rebellious."

Renz rolled his eyes. "I guess, and you may be onto something, Jade. The kidnappers could entice the girls with beer, booze, cigarettes, or weed. Who knows? I'd venture to say most teens would go for it though."

I turned around. "Let's head back down. I'd like to speak to a few of the campers before we leave."

Back at campsite number forty-seven, I asked

neighboring campers if they'd seen any unusual vehicles or white box trucks come into the RV park, but nobody had. We thanked them and left, then followed Jenner back to the interstate and headed north to Sturgis.

Tracy's parents agreed to meet us and Deputy Jenner at the campground. I appreciated their offer since it would save us time by not having to drive out to their home in Bear Butte, east of Sturgis. Deputy Sheriff Ben Tilley said he would be there too.

Once again, introductions were made, and we were shown the site that the Bast family had chosen for their camping experience. Their account of the events were exactly like what was on the written report. Nothing varied, was added, or taken out.

They explained that it was Tracy who was the main caregiver of the family's Jack Russell terrier, Riley, since it was Tracy who'd begged for a dog.

"That afternoon, Tracy took Riley for a walk, just like she'd done every day. She'd walk the park with him after breakfast, usually at nine in the morning and again late in the afternoon. If the dog needed another walk after dark, we'd go out as a family," Mrs. Bast said.

I glanced over the report. "And you guys were here for how many days?"

Mr. Bast responded. "A week. It originally was meant to be five days, but once Tracy disappeared, it was hard for us to leave. We hoped she'd somehow wander back."

Ben Tilley took over. "Our deputies and volunteers walked the entire park. We had the Meade County helicopter go over twice with heat-seeking radar, but we came up empty. Tracy wasn't anywhere in the area."

I wasn't surprised, and I was sure the purpose of those box trucks was to snatch and go. The girls were long gone, but to where, we still didn't know.

We thanked the sheriff's office for their help and gave the Bast family as much hope as we were comfortable giving. We didn't want to make false promises, and if the missing girls had actually been sold off to an underground organization, finding them would be nearly impossible. I was more than familiar with the statistics, and they were horrifying. Eighty percent of abducted kids were over the age of twelve, and in the United States alone, a child went missing every forty seconds.

Renz and I drove into Sturgis and had lunch. As we sat at a table at the far end of the room and quietly discussed the case, we reviewed the information we had and who we'd spoken to so far.

I rubbed my forehead as I gave Gary and Leon some thought. "Why can't we haul them in for questioning or have them followed? It seems like that would end the abductions quickly, or am I missing something?"

Renz somewhat agreed with my theory. "That would seem like a logical remedy, but nobody has witnessed them doing anything wrong. As of last month, both men have completed their incarceration and paid their debt to society. They're hopefully law-abiding citizens, and until we can prove they aren't, we can't harass them simply because they were once in prison. We need hard evidence against them and possibly Claire and Hope too. Also, keep in mind, that the small fish will eventually lead us to the big fish."

I was shocked. "What exactly are you saying?"

"Like I said, we need hard evidence implicating them, like actually catching them in the act. We can use that against them and hope they tell us who the big players are or, depending on Taft's recommendation, follow them to the drop-off location. Chances are, that person is just a middleman, then we keep going up the ladder, get the Justice Department involved, and try to find out where the kids are held until they're sold."

My mind was reeling. "I can't imagine what those kids must be going through, Renz. Isn't it more important to shut down the abduction right out of the gate?" I thought back to my early years at the Washburn County Sheriff's Office and the case against Matt and Jeremy—the brothers who kidnapped girls and kept them in cages in their basement. They sold them on the black market through the dark web to the most vile men from every walk of life. I had to shake those thoughts out of my head and focus on our current case.

"Jade, if Gary and Leon are involved in trafficking teenagers and we take them in, they'll be replaced within minutes by someone else chomping at the bit to take over their positions. As low-level as they are, and without undeniable proof that we can use to scare the bejesus out of them, the abductions will continue without the slightest hiccup in the process. We need the big dogs, and my guess is we'll have to go through a half dozen other people to get to them. It's highly unlikely that Gary and Leon even know who they are."

"Then what difference do they make?"

"We have to get the goods on them with real proof, follow them with the girls to the next-tier guy, and go from there."

I let out a long sigh. "I feel like we're in a holding pattern until tomorrow when we convene in Buffalo. Why don't we knock out the visits with the parents now and get that out of the way?"

"Not a bad idea, but I'm not sure we want to show our hand to Gary's and Leon's folks. We don't even know if their parents have contact with them on a regular basis, but if they do, we don't want them to warn the guys that the FBI is sniffing around. On the other hand, Claire's and Hope's parents are the hovering ones. They'll tell us everything they know about their daughters, and that information should prove helpful."

After lunch and two cups of coffee, I suggested we forgo the hotel rooms in Sturgis. "We'll be passing through Gillette tomorrow anyway. Why not get a room there and save ourselves needless hours of driving back and forth?"

"Good idea."

Renz waved down the waitress and asked for the check. I tossed a ten on the table and gathered my purse and briefcase, and we were on the road five minutes later.

I climbed into the passenger seat and buckled up. "Gillette is an hour and a half away. I'll make the calls while you drive."

Chapter 11

I called Hope's mom, Diane, and she offered to contact Claire's parents on our behalf since Claire's and Hope's families were close friends and had been for years. Diane suggested we come to her home and said she would make sure that Mr. and Mrs. Usher were there as well. Not only would that allow us to talk openly and candidly, but it would also give us the opportunity to run ideas by both sets of parents at once.

After thanking her and saying they should expect us around two p.m., I ended the call.

As Renz drove, I stared out the window. I'd loved road trips for as long as I could remember. During my years as an FBI agent, I'd traveled all over the country, and that would be my dream under different circumstances. The rolling hills, tall trees, and ragged sandstone formations of South Dakota were beautiful and a sight to behold.

If only we had time to tour around, but I know better— someday, maybe.

I sighed as I enjoyed the view.

"You seem relaxed." Renz looked over and gave me a smile.

"I am and would love to pitch a tent, build a campfire, and watch the stars all night, but that'll have to wait for another time. Right now, I need to fire off a text to Fay." I lifted my phone from the cup holder, tapped Fay's name, and told her about our change of plans, and that we would be getting a hotel in Gillette that night. I also said we would be on the road for the next hour, so if they needed help with anything, I would be able to work from my phone. Several minutes later, a return text came in. I read it as Renz drove then paraphrased it for him.

"Fay sent the contact information for John Moretti, the parole officer for Leon Brady. He's located in Rapid City, so that will definitely have to take place via phone call. She asked if we could take care of contacting him and said that they'd already stopped in the office of Ken Demmler, Gary's parole officer in Casper. Apparently, she and Tommy are swamped right now and would appreciate the help."

"Yeah, go ahead. Make sure Mr. Moretti emails you copies of every appointment Leon has attended and the dates for his appointments through the end of the year."

"Got it." I reached over the seat, grabbed my briefcase, and pulled it to me, then took out a pen and notepad. I would use the briefcase as my tabletop for writing purposes.

I made the call to John Moretti and told him who I was and what I needed. My notes already showed that Leon's prison release date was August 13, but up to that point, I didn't know who he'd been assigned as a parole officer. Mr. Moretti told me that Leon had had his introductory meeting with him on August 20, after he'd had a physical address to put on record. Since then, Leon had had two appointments, both of which he'd attended. They'd been on September 5 and September 12. He had one more scheduled for September 29, then they would go monthly for six months. If he remained out of trouble during that period of time, his meetings would end, and he would go forward as a man completely free of all legal restraints. He would be a regular member of society, like everyone else. I gave Mr. Moretti my email address, asked for all Leon's records and appointment dates, thanked him, and shook my head as I hung up.

Renz gave me a side-eyed glance. "What?"

"Leon must put on the good-boy show every time he meets with Mr. Moretti."

Renz laughed. "Yeah, just like every ex-con who meets with their parole officer. Don't worry about it. If Leon and Gary are doing what we think they are, their freedom is going to be short-lived."

"I need Fay to email me the dates of Gary's meetings. We'll compare his to Leon's then compare both to the dates girls have gone missing. With any luck, those dates should help us put the nails in their coffins."

"Yep, and maybe in Claire's and Hope's too."

I tapped off a message to Fay saying I'd spoken with John Moretti and had him email me every appointment he'd had and had scheduled for Leon. I needed Fay to do the same with Gary's dates. I would compare them and the dates the girls went missing when I had my computer set up later.

My phone buzzed two more times—one from Fay saying she would email me everything we needed and the other from Diane Daniels, who said the meeting was all set with Claire's parents. Both couples would be waiting for us at the Danielses' home.

"Good, everything is set. Now we just have to get to Gillette, and after we talk to the parents, we'll check into a hotel and compare all the dates."

We arrived in Gillette without a single hiccup on the interstate. Diane and Mike Daniels lived along the Bell Nob Golf Course, and I directed Renz to the address. He pulled up to the curb in front of an expansive log home.

Renz whistled as he ducked his head and looked out the passenger window. "This is it, huh?"

"According to the address she texted me, yeah." I chuckled. "Apparently, she knows how to make money."

Renz huffed. "I'd probably give the credit to the hubby, but that's just my opinion."

I climbed out with my briefcase in hand. "Is being a chauvinist still a thing?"

He shrugged as we walked up the paved driveway, past a gold Mercedes sedan, and to the front door. Renz clacked the doorknocker, and we waited.

I heard what sounded like heels tapping against the floor as the person approached the door. I assumed it would be Diane who would answer. I looked down at my shoes still coated in dust from walking the campground.

"Damn it." I leaned over to wipe them just as Renz spoke up.

"Too late." He pointed at the doorknob as it turned. "Hurry, stand up."

I quickly righted myself and tried to look like an FBI agent—whatever that might be.

A fortysomething woman with a stylish haircut, wearing false eyelashes, and dressed in what looked like a designer pantsuit pulled open the door, introduced herself, and welcomed us in.

Diane led us into an enormous family room, where three other people sat on couches opposite each other with a giant redwood coffee table separating them. Introductions were made between us and the other three. Diane's husband, Mike, stood and shook our hands, as did Laura and Adam Usher.

Diane shooed the cat off the couch. "Guido, scram. Please, Agents DeLeon and Monroe, have a seat. May I offer you something to drink, sparkling water maybe?"

"That sounds delicious," I said. "Thank you."

Minutes later and with glasses of sparkling water in front of us, Renz took the lead and asked why the families assumed that Hope and Claire were with the guys.

Mr. Usher began with what he knew and what he suspected. "For years now, Claire has had a thing for that dirtbag Gary Rhodes. Even when he was in prison, she would send him letters, and you know that teenagers don't write letters. She's been a sad sack for five years, but in the last month, it's been like she's come back to life—and in my opinion, not in a good way. She's always thought she was older and more mature than her chronological age." Adam looked at his wife. "I admit, we've created a spoiled, entitled brat, and even though we've tried, we can't backpedal out."

"Excuse me, Mr. Usher, but the easiest way to test your daughter is to cut her off—cold turkey. No credit card usage, no ATM withdrawals, and none of her bills paid for her." I paged through my notes. "Claire is twenty-one years old. She's been a legal adult for several years, yet you still support her. What college does she go to?"

He remained silent.

"Where does she work?"

Still no answer.

I looked from Diane to Mike. "And Hope? College, job, what does she do to contribute to her own life?"

Diane's attitude changed, and she sniped her response. "She's our daughter, and we love her, Agent Monroe."

"I'm sure you do. Are you going to love her as much when she's spending life behind bars? How will your neighbors react to that? Even though you've handed her everything on a silver platter, you're strangling her by not allowing her to figure out her own life, make her own mistakes, and suffer her own consequences for her actions. What you've done to shape her life may be directly related to the crimes she could be committing."

Diane stammered angrily. "You have a right to your professional opinion, but are you a mother, Agent Monroe?"

"No, I'm not."

"Then how on earth would you know what's in my daughter's best interest?"

"Because she's rebelling against you. Why do you think

she and Claire moved to Buffalo? They're trying to make their own way in life, but in doing so, they're going down a dangerous path that will lead to prison. The money you're giving her enables that."

"I don't believe for a minute that Claire went with Gary voluntarily," Adam said.

Renz took over. "You're all aware of where the credit cards have been used. What you didn't know is that we have Claire on video last week paying for snacks and diesel fuel for a white box truck off I-25 in Glenrock, Wyoming. She was at the counter by herself and didn't appear to be fearful, nor did she ask anyone to call 911." Renz turned to Mr. and Mrs. Daniels. "Hope was also spotted paying for diesel fuel but in Schaeferville, South Dakota. She didn't seem to be under duress either. The girls don't own white box trucks, do they?"

The four of them stared at the floor.

"You need to cut off their access to money immediately. Those girls are likely with Gary and Leon by choice, and even though we're early in this investigation, the signs point toward the four of them being involved in abducting minors and passing them off to be sold."

Mike slammed his fist on the coffee table. "No way! I don't believe that for a second. Hope wouldn't do that."

"Mr. Daniels, are you aware that Hope has a police record?"

"What?"

"She was arrested last year for stealing from a grocery store."

"Why? She gets plenty of money from us."

"The arresting officer asked her the same thing. Her response was that she did it for a thrill."

Diane's eyes filled with tears, and I stared at her until she looked away.

"When was the last time any of you spoke to the girls?" Renz asked.

Diane said she'd talked to Hope on the night of August 15 and not since. Claire's parents said the same thing.

"That's been just over a month now. How often have you been to their duplex?"

Diane and Laura looked at each other for a few seconds before Laura responded.

"We've gone together four times. The cars are never there, and nobody answers the door."

Mike took his turn. "Why can't you just arrest Gary and Leon and be done with it?"

"If the girls are with them, they'll be placed under arrest, too, but we aren't at that point yet. So, it's likely the girls have never returned home, but we do have eyewitness accounts of the guys being at their addresses of record. I assume they came home to be at their parole officer appointments, plan the next abduction, and leave shortly after that. Can you access Claire's and Hope's credit card and bank accounts right now?" Renz asked.

They said they could.

"We need to know what kind of transactions have gone on the credit cards during the last few weeks."

We waited as they checked the most recent use.

Diane spoke up. "Hope hasn't put anything on her card in over a week, but she has taken cash advances against it."

I nodded. "Likely to keep you from seeing what they're using the cards for. You need to cut off all access to the cards immediately, including cash advances. What about bank debit cards?"

"They have them too," Mike said.

"Freeze them. Living entirely on cash is actually harder than one would think, especially in emergency situations. Many places frown upon accepting cash transactions since it makes theft very tempting to employees."

Laura began to cry. "I need to know what Claire is doing. I'd be cutting off all ties to her."

"Believe us when we say this will end sooner than you think if they don't have unlimited access to credit use. They'll become desperate, take reckless chances, and get caught much faster. Keep in mind, unless the guys are making plenty of money on their own, they're using your daughters, which basically means they're using you to fund their criminal enterprise. Are you willing to have that go public?"

Mike raised both hands as a gesture of defeat. "I'm not going to risk my reputation or career. Hope is cut off as of now. Diane, give me all the bank and credit card information so I can make the calls."

Adam jumped on board too and reached out to Laura. "We don't have a choice anymore. If Claire is going down, it's our fault, but I'm not about to let her take us with her."

We'd finally gotten through to them, and both families

swore if their daughters reached out to them for anything, they would let us know.

I gave them my business card after we stood to leave. "Remember, tough love goes a lot farther than being an enabler. No matter what, if they call and plead for money, don't cave in. This will end a lot faster if you leave everything in our hands."

Chapter 12

"I would have thanked God that we finally made it to your apartment, Leon, but it's just as bad as this damn car. I'm surprised we didn't break down between Cheyenne and Rapid City."

"Shut up, Hope. Can't you ever say anything nice? You're nothing but a spoiled rich bitch."

She huffed then went silent. Seconds later, she spoke up again. "That's it. I'm taking my car and going to Buffalo. At least my duplex is nice."

"You aren't going anywhere. I'm sure your folks have reported you missing by now, and the cops are probably watching your place. If they are, that means they're looking for your car too. We'll use the car after I spray-paint it and swap out the plates."

Hope grumbled as she followed Leon into his apartment.

"Come on. I have beer in the fridge, and you can watch TV while I go over our plans for next week. Tomorrow, we'll go to the store and buy paint for the car."

"Where are you going to paint it? You can't do it in the parking lot."

"I'll do it in the storage garage where the truck and your car are hidden."

Hope settled in front of the TV with a beer in hand while Leon studied the map that was supposed to be his and Hope's route for the next round of abductions. He looked at her from the kitchen table and cursed under his breath. Even though they were considered a couple, Leon had reached his limit with her. He'd never been that keen on reconnecting with her after prison. It was all Gary's idea, and his ideas could bring in big money or big problems. In Leon's opinion, they would do better without the girls. He and Gary were strong and fully capable of abducting three to five girls a week easily, plus they wouldn't have to share the cash with Hope and Claire.

But if we kick them out, they'll more than likely go running to their parents and tell them we forced them to come along, and the law will be hot on our asses.

Leon cracked open his second beer, smoothed out the paper map on the table, and highlighted the route he would take south after picking up the truck from the storage garage in Schaeferville. They would go south through Rapid City and connect with State Highway 79, where they would pass through a dozen small towns, find abduction opportunities, and meet up with Gary and Claire in Glendo, Wyoming. After that, they would continue south until they reached the Denver area, where they would make the drop. Leon had a few days to think things over, and he would be in touch with Gary during that time. If there was a way to change Gary's mind, Leon would do his best to make that happen.

Hope had made herself a bowl of popcorn and began watching a reality show. Leon had no interest in joining her, and after polishing off a can of chicken noodle soup and putting the bowl in the sink, he looked from the TV to Hope. "I'm not watching that shit."

She shrugged. "Suit yourself, but I'm not changing the channel."

"I guess I'm going to bed, then." Leon disappeared down the hall and into the bedroom, where he closed the door at his back.

Sometime later in the night, Leon woke because he had to piss. Likely the two beers he'd drank earlier was why. He rolled over and felt Hope's side of the bed, but the spot was empty, and the sheets were cool to the touch. It was obvious that she hadn't been to bed at all. He sat up, clicked on the nightstand lamp, and looked around. He listened for the sound of the TV but heard nothing.

What the hell? Maybe she decided to sleep on the couch.

After throwing back the blankets, Leon stumbled out of bed, down the hallway, and into the bathroom. Seconds later, he turned the corner and peered into the living room. Hope wasn't on the couch.

"What the hell?"

Leon flipped on the lights, looked into the kitchen, and scratched his head. The apartment was small, and there was nowhere else she could be.

"You stupid bitch. You better not have done what I think you did!"

Leon spun and looked for keys on the board of hooks

mounted to the wall. One of the two keys for the storage garage, along with Hope's car keys, were missing. He slammed his fist on the counter and swore. He looked at the clock then remembered what time he went to bed.

She could have an hour's head start on me. At least she didn't take the beater, so that means she called a rideshare to take her to the storage garage. I've got to tell Gary.

Since it was after midnight, Leon assumed Gary would be sleeping, and being woken out of a dead sleep would definitely piss him off. Hearing what Hope did would send him into a tailspin. Leon steeled himself when Gary answered the phone.

"This better be good. I was sound asleep, bro."

"Hope is gone."

"What the hell does that mean?"

Leon heard the anger in Gary's voice, but he had no other choice—he had to tell him. "Hope sneaked off while I was sleeping. One of the two garage keys is missing, and so are her car keys. She hinted that she wanted to take her car and go back to her duplex, where it's nice. I told her there was no way that was happening since there's a good chance a BOLO is out on her car and her duplex is probably being watched by police. The bitch took off anyway."

"I need to go outside so Claire doesn't hear this conversation."

From his side of the call, Leon heard the door open and close.

Gary returned to the conversation a second later. "Okay, so how long has she been gone? Did she take the beater?"

"At most, she has an hour head start, and no, the beater's keys are still here. I'm assuming she called a rideshare."

"That's even worse. Now there's a record of her being at your apartment."

"I deserved a good night's sleep after driving nearly five hours from Cheyenne. I didn't know she was going to do something so stupid and reckless."

"Yeah, yeah. I'm closer to Buffalo and can intercept her before she gets there. That bitch is nothing but trouble, and I'm going to take care of her once and for all."

"But you can't drive Claire's car there. I'm sure a BOLO went out on that too."

"I know, so I'll take the truck. It might be slower, but I can still make it to Buffalo before Hope does."

Leon paced the small apartment. "Should I come too or hang back?"

"I'll need your help since I'm going to make Claire stay here. She doesn't need to get in our way or see what we're going to do."

"So, what are we going to do?"

"I'm not sure, but I have an hour-and-a-half drive to come up with an idea, so head out now. I'll let you know when I find her."

Chapter 13

"Who was that, and what are you doing?" Claire stared at Gary after he walked back inside.

"Don't worry about it."

"I thought we were partners. Why are you keeping me in the dark?"

"Because this isn't your problem. I'll be back soon."

Claire watched as Gary grabbed his clothes. "When is soon?"

"I'm not sure. Just stay put, and stay off the phone unless you're calling me, and everything will be fine."

It took another ten minutes before Gary was dressed and out the door with his phone and all the keys. He spun the combination lock on the bicycle he used for short trips around town, pulled it off the enclosed porch, and headed out. The storage garage was only eight blocks away.

Good thing the decals are still on the truck. That'll save me time by not having to camouflage it.

Once he arrived at the storage garage, Gary entered his four-digit code and waited for the gate to open. He rode down two lanes to his garage space, got off the bike, and unlocked the padlock from the roller door. The oversized garage had enough room inside for the truck and Claire's car. Once inside, he placed the bicycle against the wall next to the car, climbed into the truck, and pulled out. With the door rolled back down and locked behind him, Gary headed out. A mile down the road, he merge onto I-25 and made his way north. The only way to take Hope by surprise was to be waiting at her duplex when she got there. Luckily, Gary had grabbed Claire's keys before he'd left.

After filling the truck with fuel and buying a large coffee, he was on his way at twelve forty-five. He estimated he would arrive at the duplex around two thirty. If his math was correct, he would get to Buffalo about a half hour before Hope. He would park the truck on a side street, unlock the duplex door, and wait in the dark for her to show up.

Panic nearly overtook Gary when he thought about Hope's route. She would have to pass through Gillette on her way to Buffalo.

What if she goes to her mom and dad's house instead or stops there on her way to the apartment?

Gary had to trust in the fact that Hope was heading to the duplex and nowhere else. According to Leon, that was what she'd said she wanted to do before he'd shut her down. What her motivation was, other than being a spoiled brat, Gary couldn't figure out. She had to know that pulling a stunt like that was reckless and wouldn't be well received by the rest of them.

Unless she doesn't care and intends to turn us in. Maybe Leon slapping her face yesterday was enough to change her mind about being a part of our money-making venture. No matter what, if and when she shows up here, she's going to meet my bad side.

Gary arrived in Buffalo just after two thirty. Being a small town of five thousand people, it didn't take long to reach the neighborhood where Hope and Claire's duplex was located. Gary parked two blocks away in the back of an apartment complex then cautiously walked to the duplex. He remained in the shadows, and before he got too close, he scanned the street for suspicious vehicles that may have cops sitting inside. When he didn't see anything out of the ordinary, he scurried to the front door, quickly unlocked it, and slipped inside. He would wait in the dark for Hope to arrive.

After an hour of waiting, Gary was getting nervous. He counted his own steps as he paced the living room.

Twenty, twenty-one, twenty-two steps. Come on, Hope. What's taking you so long?

Gary grabbed his phone and called Leon. "Where the hell are you?"

"I'm driving to Buffalo just like I'm supposed to be, why?"

"I'm getting nervous. Hope should have been here already. Have you passed Gillette yet?"

"No, I'm five miles east of there."

"Then drive by Hope's parents' house and see if her car is parked outside."

Leon groaned into the phone. "Do you really think she'd do that?"

"Didn't you tell her not to go anywhere, but after you went to bed she sneaked out?"

"Yeah, good point. I'll call you back in ten minutes."

Gary pulled open the refrigerator door and looked inside. He needed a drink to calm his nerves. He didn't want to be there, but he didn't want to go back to prison either. One way or another, Hope would be a thing of the past at some point that night.

The only thing in the refrigerator was a carton of milk. He opened it, sniffed, and gagged. He poured it down the drain and started going through the cabinets.

"Bingo!"

He found a bottle of whiskey, and that would do just fine. He poured two fingers into a glass, gulped it, and poured some more. Seconds later, his phone rang. It was Leon calling back, and Gary knew as soon as he answered, their life would change forever or remain the same. Apprehension took over, but he had to pick up.

"What's the word?"

"Her car wasn't there."

Gary let out a relieved breath. "Thank God. So where the hell is she?"

"I don't know, but I'm taking the same route that she would. Hope doesn't drive back roads. She's afraid to in case she ever broke down. I'll watch for her car, but I still have an hour drive ahead of me. Keep your eyes peeled, bro. She could show up at any minute."

"Yeah, I intend to. Just get here as soon as you can, and park down the street, not in front of the duplex."

"You got it. See you soon."

Gary pulled a chair to the window, sat down, and turned the wand on the blinds just far enough to see out. With the lights off, Hope would have no idea he was inside, and that was the plan.

His head bobbed several times. Gary rubbed his eyes, stretched, and checked the time. He'd only been staring out into the dark night for twenty minutes, and he was already dozing off. He stood and paced some more.

Damn her, where is she? Maybe she stopped for food or gas. Maybe she got tired and pulled over at a wayside to sleep for an hour.

Just then, Gary saw headlights coming down the street. At that time of night, it couldn't be anyone else. It had to be Hope. He watched out the window until the car pulled up to the curb in front of the duplex. It was definitely her.

Now you're going to get what you deserve.

Gary stood behind the door and waited. He heard her reach the porch and slide the key into the doorknob. She gave it a jiggle, then the door swung open. Gary pounced and slammed her to the floor. Hope tried to get her feet under her, but he knocked her down again. Her keys and cell phone slid across the tile.

"You make one sound, and I'll beat the crap out of you. Do you understand me?"

"Gary?"

In the dark, he knew she couldn't see who he was. "Yeah. Did my voice give me away? I can be your worst nightmare if you force me to. Why did you come here when Leon told you not to?"

She stammered out her response. "His car is a piece of shit, and so is his apartment. I'm not used to that type of filth."

Gary laughed. "Well, get used to it, because wherever you're going probably won't be much better."

Hope began to cry. "What does that mean?"

Gary snickered. "You'll find out soon enough. We don't need troublemakers in our little organization."

Hope scrambled to her feet and bolted for the bathroom, but Gary was on her in a second. He slammed her head against the bathroom door, and she dropped to her knees, out cold.

"That'll teach you who runs the show."

Gary tore through her bedroom drawers and found what he needed. Several belts would do the trick. He bound Hope's hands behind her back then belted her feet together. A roll of tape sat next to him in case it was needed, but after seeing how one of their girls choked on her own vomit and died because her mouth was taped closed, he decided to hold off unless it was absolutely necessary.

With Hope secure, Gary took a seat on the hallway floor and called Leon. "Hey, dude, she showed up and won't be a problem. Just get here as soon as you can."

"She won't be a problem? What the hell did you do, Gary—kill her?"

"No, I didn't kill the bitch, but her fate is on you. You're the one who couldn't control her."

"Meaning?"

"You'll find out when you get here."

Chapter 14

Eventually, Gary had to put tape over Hope's mouth. Once she came around, the screaming began, and the last thing Gary needed was the upstairs neighbor calling the cops or pounding on the door to inquire about the noise.

"I told you what would happen if you tried anything. Now your mouth is taped closed. Remember that image of the dead girl who choked on her own puke—granted, you and Claire probably overdosed her—but I'd suggest staying calm anyway."

It took another half hour before Leon showed up. He gave the door a light rap to announce his presence, and Gary let him in.

"Where is that bitch?"

Gary jerked his head toward the hallway. "Down there by the bathroom door." He followed Leon back.

Leon marched down the hall and knelt at Hope's side. "What did I say when we got to Rapid City?" He ripped the tape from Hope's mouth. "What did I say?"

"That I couldn't go home."

"Yet you decided to break away from our group

consensus of sticking together and keeping our mouths shut to take a risk like that because the beater and my apartment weren't up to your standards. What makes you better than the rest of us?" Leon's face turned red, and his anger was almost palpable. He slapped her across the face for the second time in as many days. "Why did it take you so long to get here? Where did you go?"

"I stopped for food."

"Is that the only place you went?" He squeezed her chin and forced her face up. "Look at me."

"Yes, I swear."

Gary motioned for Leon to go back to the living room with him. "You dropped the ball on her, so you have to choose."

"Choose what?"

"Whether she lives or dies." Gary pulled a quarter from his pocket. "Heads she dies. Tails she gets sold."

"You can't be serious."

Gary's eyes remained fixed on Leon. "Don't push your luck." He handed the quarter to Leon. "Here, flip the coin."

Leon's face went white, but he flipped the coin anyway. He looked down at the floor and heaved a sigh of relief. The quarter landed on tails.

"Okay, her fate is set. It's only a five-hour drive to Denver, so let's go. We're getting rid of her tonight." Gary tossed the truck keys to Leon. "Go around the block to the Belmont Arms apartment complex. You'll find the box truck parked in their lot. Back it up to the driveway, and I'll get Hope ready."

Leon froze in place as if his feet were glued to the floor.

"Move it, now!"

Leon walked to the front door and looked back before stepping out. "You sure you want to do this? We'll never see her again after we drop her off."

"You'd never see her again if we did the alternative either. Now go."

After Leon disappeared down the block, Gary returned his attention to Hope. "We can do this the easy way or the hard way." He cocked his head and smiled. "Which do you prefer?"

After stretching tape over Hope's mouth again, Gary disappeared into the bedroom. Seconds later, he returned with a large suitcase. He placed it on the floor next to Hope. "You'll only be in there for the time it takes to put you in the back of the truck. After that, we'll let you out. Understand?"

She nodded as tears ran down her cheeks. Gary pulled her to the suitcase and lifted her over the edge.

"Get comfortable. I won't zip it up until we're ready to leave." After returning to the window, Gary peered out and saw the truck approaching. "It's go time."

He watched as Leon made several attempts to back the truck as close to the rear door as possible. Finally when the truck was in place, Leon climbed out and entered the duplex through the utility room.

"Hope is ready. Help me carry her out."

"What?"

Gary spun around. "Don't question everything I say. Just do what you're told."

Leon followed Gary down the hall and watched as Gary zipped the suitcase.

"Don't worry about her. I said we'd let her out once we're on the road. Now, help me pick her up."

Between both men, they carried the suitcase to the back of the truck and slid it in.

Gary slapped his hands together after locking the truck's rear doors. "Okay, we've got to hurry and tidy up inside. I want to be on the road in fifteen minutes."

Gary washed, dried, and put away the glass he'd drank whiskey out of, then placed the chair back against the wall. He called out to Leon, who had disappeared into the bathroom. "Check the hallway, and make sure everything looks normal." Gary did a final walk-through of the kitchen, put the milk carton in the trash, then made sure nothing was out of place in the entryway, where he'd knocked Hope to the ground. The duplex looked good. "Turn off the lights back there, and let's go."

Leon followed him out, and Gary locked the door at their backs.

"Here's Hope's car keys. We'll leave the beater wherever it is you parked it, and you can follow me in Hope's car. We'll park that in the storage garage in Casper for now."

"Yeah, okay." Leon began to walk away but stopped and looked back at Gary. "You'll let her out of the suitcase, right?"

Gary swatted the air. "Yeah, yeah, I'll let her out of the suitcase."

Chapter 15

After breakfast in the hotel's dining room, I set up my computer in the business center and we updated Tommy and Fay via video chat. We ran through yesterday's meeting we'd had with Hope's and Claire's parents with them.

"It was quite the experience." Renz rolled his eyes. "They're clueless in parenting one-oh-one. Spoiling those girls right out of the womb led to twenty-one years of entitlement, where with a snap of their fingers, Hope and Claire got whatever they wanted. They ran the show, but they wanted to do it without any parental interference."

Fay sighed. "And now they could be mixed up in human trafficking. If we get the evidence we need, there's a good chance all four of them are looking at several decades behind bars."

Tommy went over the plate-reader information with us that they'd received from the interstate locations around Cheyenne. Since we didn't know the plate numbers of either truck, there was no possibility of getting a hit, and Tommy was told that dozens of white cube vans, box trucks, and semis had passed those readers. The police report said the disturbance call came in at two seventeen a.m., and a broken taillight would show up on plate-reader cameras at night as vehicles passed them, but none had.

I groaned my disappointment. "They mustn't have driven any farther that night, or at least not on the interstate, and which way they were going and how far, is an unknown."

None of that information helped, and without license plate numbers, we were dead in the water.

Tommy said he had set up a meeting with the chief of police in Buffalo for one thirty that day. I watched as he thumbed through his paperwork.

"Here we go. That's right, the chief's name is Roger Worth. He's accumulated all the police reports from the other crime scenes and the statements from the parents and friends."

"We already have all that, and we've spoken with everyone who needs to be talked to," Renz said.

Tommy shrugged. "The man is doing what he can to help."

I let out a sigh. "What would help is an eyewitness. The closest thing we have is that bump and run in Cheyenne, yet the homeowner never actually saw anything."

"We need to have the guys followed—plain and simple. It'll put an end to this cat-and-mouse game pretty quickly," Fay said.

I chuckled. "Taft already said no to that. We want the big fish so we can shut down the whole organization, at least this regional one, and the chances of two halfwit ex-cons being given information from the higher-ups is unlikely."

"Right, but they can be followed to the drop-off location. We've already discussed that."

"Push Taft on it, then," Renz said. "Agents would have to be sitting on the duplex in Buffalo and both apartments twenty-four seven."

Tommy nodded. "I'll see what she and the local FBI field officers want to do. If you don't hear back from us before this afternoon, we'll see you at one thirty."

I added one more thing before I ended the video chat. "Fay, I need that list of dates Gary had and will have with his parole officer. We have a few hours to kill, so I'm going to start comparing those dates with the dates every girl went missing."

"I must have gotten sidetracked. I'll email it to you right away."

I ended the video chat, and Renz walked away to grab us coffee while I waited for the email to come in. My phone rang just as he returned and sat down.

I did a doubletake when I saw the name on the screen. "That's weird. It's Hope's mom." I tapped the green phone icon and answered. "Agent Monroe speaking."

"Agent Monroe, it's Mrs. Daniels."

"What can I do for you, ma'am?"

"Something is wrong."

I gave Renz a concerned frown and made sure the business center was still empty. "I'm putting you on speakerphone, Mrs. Daniels, so my partner can listen in."

"Yes, please."

"Now go ahead. Tell us what's wrong."

"I noticed an alert on my phone this morning from our home's security system. Nobody tried to break in, but it recorded movement at the front of the house last night."

"Okay."

"It was Hope. She came up to the front door, paced back and forth outside for nearly a half hour, then disappeared. She has her own house key, Agent Monroe, but for some reason, she chose not to come in."

"That is odd," Renz said. "Was the time recorded?"

"Yes, it was around two a.m."

"And was anyone with her?"

"Honestly, I couldn't tell, but her body language told me she was upset."

I wrinkled my brow as I glanced at Renz. "She was upset enough to show up but not enough to come in?"

Renz took over. "Or maybe she was afraid of the consequences if she did."

"I don't know. Either way, I'm sure she's in trouble."

I packed up my gear while Renz continued the conversation.

"We'll need to review that footage, Mrs. Daniels. Agent Monroe and I are on our way to your house right now."

"Thank you, Agent DeLeon."

Luckily, we hadn't left for Buffalo yet, and from the hotel, the Danielses' home was only a five-mile drive. We reached their house at ten o'clock, where we found Mrs. Daniels standing at the door, waiting for us.

"Please, Agents, come in. My husband is in the office,

and I've transferred the security footage to my computer. It'll be easier to view everything on the larger screen."

"Great idea, thank you," I said as we followed her to the second-floor office.

The room was as enormous as I'd envisioned, with two oversized desks. A computer sat on each one. Decorative chairs faced each desk, and the walls were lined with bookcases. Beautiful pottery sat among the hundreds of books on the shelves, and I didn't see empty space anywhere.

Mr. Daniels stood, shook our hands, and thanked us for coming by so quickly. "Please, over here at Diane's desk. She has the footage set up and ready to go."

Diane turned the monitor toward us, then she and Mike stood at our backs. "Are you ready?"

"Yes, go ahead," I said.

She excused herself, pressed play, then moved aside so Renz and I had the full screen in front of us. She narrated what we were watching as the footage played.

"Notice the glow off to the left? That must have been when she pulled into the driveway because, only seconds later, she appeared on the sidewalk and headed for the front door. It looked like she was going to come in—I mean the keys are in her hand." Diane sniffled and continued. "She started to pace as if undecided about what to do."

I added my two cents. "If Hope wasn't guilty of anything, she would have no reason to hesitate. She's pacing because she's weighing out the odds."

"Odds of what?" Mike asked.

"Odds of giving up her friends, essentially becoming a

snitch, odds of not giving them up, but giving up you two instead, and odds of what the charges would be against her when all of this is said and done."

"You mean she could go to jail even if she changes her mind, comes home, and tells the police what's going on and where to find the others?" Diane asked.

I had to wonder how long Diane and Mike had been living in their bubble. "Of course. If she's been part of the abduction process, which the videos at the gas stations would support, then she is as guilty as the others. Getting a conscience or growing tired of life on the run doesn't change what she's already been a party to. The only way she'd get a reduced charge or sentence against her would be by giving up everything she knows."

"Okay, good. I'm sure Hope will do that," Diane said.

I cocked my head. "You're sure she'll do that? Then, why isn't she here?"

Diane and Mike both went silent, and I returned my attention to the footage.

"She has to be alone. She isn't looking back at the car. I don't see shadows of movement along the driveway, and her mouth isn't moving, meaning she isn't talking to anyone. I will admit, she does look distraught, but that could be one of two reasons. She regrets bailing on the others and possibly forgot that the camera caught her image by the front door until it was too late—"

"Or?" Mike asked.

"Or she's more afraid of them than she is of the law."

Chapter 16

"Excuse me. I have to make a call." Renz stepped out of the Danielses' home office while I reviewed the footage one more time.

"Where do you think she went from here?" I looked from Mike to Diane and waited for an answer.

"Maybe to her apartment since she'd be passing here on the way," Diane said.

I gave that some thought. If Hope had been with Leon in Rapid City and left, she would be heading northwest then due west on I-90, passing through Gillette on her way to Buffalo. Maybe she just wanted to see her parents before continuing on but changed her mind because of the time of night.

Renz rejoined us in the office. "I was checking on the BOLO for Hope's car. Nothing has come in as of yet."

"There's a good chance it's at her duplex, and don't forget, this footage is seven hours old." I turned to Diane. "Does Hope have a garage there?"

"She does."

"Okay, then, it looks like we're heading to Buffalo now

instead of later. I'll call the local police department and have them do a welfare check at the duplex." I made the call and was told we would hear back within a half hour.

"We're going along," Mike said.

Renz held up his hands. "Mr. Daniels, this is an FBI investigation and we can't have you and your wife getting in the middle of that. We'll keep you posted, and I'll call you the second we hear about the welfare check, but right now, we have to go. Before we leave, do you have a key to the duplex?"

Mike shook his head. "No, but you have our permission to enter if you feel the need."

We rushed back to the hotel, packed our go bags, and checked out. Buffalo was an hour away, but because it was such a small town, I was certain we would hear back about the welfare check relatively soon.

I gave Renz a glance once he'd merged onto the interstate. "So, just between you and me, what do you think is going on?"

Renz shrugged. "Not sure, Jade, but either Hope is planning something with Leon and Gary, and stopping at her folks house was just some kind of distraction, or she's going against the guys, which could put her in a very dangerous position."

My phone rang fifteen minutes into our drive. The screen showed that Buffalo Police Chief Roger Worth was calling. I tapped the speakerphone icon and answered. "Agent Monroe speaking."

"Agent Monroe, it's Chief Worth calling about the welfare check."

"Sure thing, Chief. What did your officers find?"

"They rang the bell a number of times, but nobody answered, so they left."

"Okay, we'll be there in about forty-five minutes. The parents gave us permission to enter if we felt it was necessary. We'll keep you updated." I ended the call, sat back, and pulled in a deep breath. We couldn't do anything until we got there, and I had the feeling we would be entering that duplex anyway, locked or not.

It was after eleven when we finally reached the duplex. Renz parked at the curb. I grabbed gloves from my go bag and jammed them into my pocket, then we got out.

"Apparently, Hope and Claire live in the lower unit." I craned my neck around the house to the end of the driveway. Two single-car garages sat in the back, and an extra concrete parking slab was off to the side. "I guess one car gets the garage, and the other parks outside."

Renz followed my eyes. "Which one is their garage?"

"I don't know, but we can ask the upstairs neighbors. Let's see if we can rattle anyone's cage downstairs first."

We walked to the porch, where there were two doors, one for the lower apartment and one for the upper. I pressed the bell for the lower, waited, and pressed it again. Nobody answered.

I spun my index finger. "Let's do a walk around. Maybe we'll get lucky enough to see in some windows."

We walked the driveway along the side of the house but found only one first-floor window, and it was too high to see into. Near the rear of the house were two numbered doors—one and two. Renz turned the knob on door number one. It was locked.

"Which do you think is the easiest to get into, the front door or this one?"

"This one for sure." He grinned. "But I forgot my lock-picking tools." He gave the door a hard kick and broke it from the hinges. "Why don't you run around to the front, ring the bell for the upstairs tenants, and let them know we aren't burglars. Ask about the garages too."

"On it." I headed to the front porch and rang the bell twice before the tenant came down.

"What was that noise? Can I help you?"

"Yes." I pulled out my badge and showed the very-pregnant lady my ID. "Sorry about that crashing sound, but my partner had to get inside the lower unit. Have you seen anyone here in the last eight hours?"

"No, but of course I was asleep until two hours ago."

"Right. So nothing woke you in the middle of the night?"

"No."

"Have you seen Hope or Claire lately?"

"No, neither of them."

"Okay, thanks. Which garage belongs to the lower unit?"

"The one on the left."

"Great. Thank you."

The woman closed the door just as Renz opened the door to Hope's unit.

I crossed the threshold and joined him inside. "Is anyone in here?" I yelled.

"I've already called out her name but didn't get a response. Let's search the rooms to see if anything would lead us to believe Hope was here last night."

Renz and I gloved up and began in the kitchen. We would clear the duplex side by side since we didn't want to miss anything that could be considered a clue of their plans, their whereabouts, or if Hope had actually been there at all.

I opened the cabinet door under the sink and pulled out the trash can. Garbage cans were usually the first thing I checked as far as kitchen items, and often times, they held valuable evidence. "That's weird. The only thing in here is an empty milk carton." I pulled the carton from the can to take a closer look. I opened it and turned it upside down over the sink. A half teaspoon or so of curdled milk dripped out. I looked at the expiration date—two weeks prior. "If Hope or Claire tossed this carton before they disappeared, there sure as hell wouldn't be any liquid left in it. It would have dried up or evaporated by now."

Renz took a peek at the spot of curdled milk in the sink. "Good point." He walked to the refrigerator and opened it. "Nothing left inside, so obviously nobody has been here for any length of time. That's if either of them actually came back."

I shrugged. "Well, somebody put the carton in the trash, and I think we should have it printed." I opened other cabinets until I found saved plastic grocery bags. I dropped the milk carton in one, and we continued our search. Nothing else appeared suspicious or questionable in the kitchen. We moved on to the living room, lifted the sofa cushions, looked under the couch and in the coat closet, and opened the TV cabinet doors and drawers—nothing. I turned on the hall light and continued on. It looked like a linen closet, the bathroom, and two bedrooms were the only rooms down that way. Renz passed me and entered the bathroom as I opened the linen closet. I felt between the towels and sheets but didn't find anything hidden there.

"How's it look in the bathroom?" I continued on.

"So far it's just the usual hair products, toothpaste, and shower supplies."

I stopped in my tracks when I glanced at the open door. "Renz?"

"Yep."

"I think this is blood."

He spun and looked at what I was pointing to. Renz came closer. "There isn't much, and it actually looks like a smear, but I think you're right."

"Like somebody tried to wipe it off with a tissue or something?"

"I'd say so." Renz checked the garbage can. "Nothing in the trash, so whatever was used to wipe it off probably got flushed."

"We need to know if that's Hope's blood, and it'll tell us plenty if it is."

"I agree. What county are we in?"

I shook my head. "Hell if I know. Let me check on my phone." I typed the question into the search bar, and Johnson County came up, but it showed that they didn't have their own forensic lab. My next question was where the state crime lab was located, and the results showed Cheyenne, a four-hour drive away. "Damn it. The state crime lab is in Cheyenne. How are we going to do this?"

Renz rubbed his forehead. "First, we'd need a sample of Hope's DNA, then we'd have to collect some of that blood."

I looked around. "Okay, we *are* in her bathroom. If any of Hope's DNA is in this house, it should be in here." I pulled open drawers and found hair clips, brushes, and curling irons, all with strands of dark hair tangled in them. "These have to belong to Hope since Claire is a blonde."

"Then bag all of that stuff. Now we have to get blood samples off that door."

"Swabs would work, right?"

"Yeah, but the blood is dry. Maybe a tiny bit of water on them? I'm not sure what'll work, Jade, I'm kind of going in blind."

"Let's call Taft. She can have someone at our crime lab walk us through collecting the sample."

Renz made the call and was told a dry sample was more viable than a wet one. That was good news for us, but we still didn't know how well our efforts would work. I found a box of sandwich bags in the kitchen, pulled one out, and after Renz used swabs to rub all the blood off the door and onto the cotton-tipped end, he dropped them into the bag and sealed it.

I let out a long breath. "That's the best we can do. Now we have to arrange a quick way to transport these samples to the crime lab. What we need is a helicopter."

"I'll call the Buffalo police chief and see what he suggests," Renz said.

Meanwhile, I walked through the house to the back door and checked the damages. The door was cracked at the hinges with no way to secure it to the framework.

Shit. We can't leave the door like this.

I called Hope's mom, told her that nobody was at the duplex, and asked who owned the building. Diane put me on hold while she looked for the rental agreement. Minutes later, she was back on the phone with a name and a phone number. I grabbed a napkin off the counter and a pen from the kitchen's junk drawer and wrote down what she said.

"Agent Monroe, are you going to find Hope?"

"Mrs. Daniels, we aren't sure Hope was even here, but I promise to keep you posted with any relevant news." I thanked her, hung up, and made the call to the property owner. The man who owned the duplex said he would be there in ten minutes. I apologized for our intrusion and explained that we had a life-or-death reason for seeing if anyone was inside. I hung up and returned to the bathroom, where Renz was still talking on the phone. He lifted his index finger as if to say he was almost done.

I gave him a nod then entered the bedroom on the right. I wasn't sure whose room it was, so I began by looking in the nightstand drawer. I saw a spiral notebook inside, essentially a journal, although not a secure one. The pages were filled with daily entries going back a year. By scanning the first few pages, it was obvious that I was in Claire's room. She spoke of Gary and how she couldn't wait until his release date. They could make plans to be together without interference from her parents anymore. She was an adult and had the legal ability to call her own shots. I flipped to the last entry, which only said it was the day Gary was being released from prison. He had big ideas to share that would get her permanently out from under her parents' control. I closed the notebook with plans to take it along. I would read it later in its entirety. I continued on to the last bedroom when I heard a man's voice call out. It had to be the homeowner.

Renz stopped me in the hallway. "Who's here?"

"Probably the man who owns the duplex. I called him."

"Okay, I'll take care of it. Go ahead and finish that last bedroom, and I'll update you after I straighten things out with the homeowner about the door."

I walked Hope's bedroom, checked her dresser drawers, then opened her closet. I frowned as I stared at several pieces of luggage scattered across the closet floor. They were meant to fit into each other like Russian nesting dolls, yet the largest and likely most used piece was missing.

Hmm… maybe that's the one she took with her.

I didn't find anything of value to our investigation in her room and walked out. Renz and the homeowner were just ending their conversation, with Renz handing him his business card. "Get a quote from your insurance company, and the FBI will take care of the replacement cost. My email address is on the card, so send me the quote, and we'll make it right."

The owner said he would get some plywood to

temporarily secure the door, then he left.

"So, now what? We wait for him to come back?" I asked.

Renz sighed. "I guess. I'm waiting on the chief to call back with news of a helicopter that might be available for us. He said the sheriff's office has plenty of connections."

I took a seat on the couch and opened Claire's journal.

"What's that?"

"A daily journal I found in Claire's room. It ends on the day Gary got out of prison, so unless I read the entire thing, we won't know if plans were made before his release date."

"Go ahead and see what you can glean from it. I'm going to call Maureen. She has to arrange for local FBI units to be put on both apartments. This investigation is dragging on too long, and I feel like our hands are tied to a degree. If that blood sample is confirmed to be Hope's, then she may be in trouble too." Renz walked out the front door and made the call while I began paging through Claire's diary.

Chapter 17

Hours earlier, Leon had pulled Hope's car into the storage garage in Casper. It would stay there for the time being along with Claire's car. After being wiped down, just in case, the beater had been abandoned a few blocks from the duplex. The local police would never connect that car to Leon since it was a piece of junk, likely uninsured, and had been stolen a month earlier.

They had already arrived in Central City and were waiting on Charlie to give them the okay to drop off Hope. She'd been sitting in the back of the box truck for hours, tied, taped up, and awaiting her fate for being disloyal to the group by going off on her own. Her car could have been spotted, and she was damn lucky it hadn't, but Gary wasn't about to change his mind. They were getting rid of Hope—she was a loose cannon who he wasn't about to let ruin their enterprise.

Leon looked back at Hope, who sat against the wall. "Doing okay?"

She grunted something inaudible through the tape.

Gary spoke up. "Ignore her. She had her chance, and she

screwed it up. If Claire pulls any shit, she'll be sold too." Gary jerked his chin toward the Gold Nugget Café. It stood several buildings in front of them and across the street. "Go pick us up some food. Get Hope a sandwich and a bottle of water. It'll hold her over until Charlie takes her off our hands."

Leon climbed out of the truck and walked away.

Gary looked out the windows at the street and sidewalks surrounding the parked truck, and everything appeared normal. He climbed into the back and sat against the opposite wall facing Hope. "Regret your stupidity yet?"

She stared at the floor.

"Humph… nothing to say? Well, that's too bad. You're nothing but a spoiled brat and a liability anyway. You wondering what Charlie's going to do with you? You aren't worth nearly as much as a sixteen-year-old." Gary's one-sided conversation was interrupted by Leon's return.

Leon opened the passenger-side door and set the bag on the seat along with the bottles of water while he climbed in.

Gary entered the truck's cab through the opening and sat behind the wheel. "Hope you got something good. I'm starving."

Leon passed two sandwiches and an order of chips to Gary, then climbed into the back.

"Where the hell are you going?"

"To give Hope her food."

"Get back up here and eat. You can give it to her after you're done. What if she starts yelling the second you pull the tape off her mouth? I'm going to be back there to make sure that doesn't happen but not before I enjoy my lunch. Now sit down."

Leon did as he was told, and seconds later, Gary's phone rang.

"Damn it. I hope Charlie doesn't intend to screw up my meal." He answered and set his phone to Speaker as he took a bite of the first turkey club. "Gary speaking."

"It's Charlie. Meet me at that abandoned subdivision behind my property. Be there in a half hour." The phone went dead. Gary checked the time then nodded to Leon. "Go ahead and give her some food. Who knows when she'll eat again." Gary jerked his head toward the back. "Feed her, but don't untie her. I'll start heading to Charlie's place."

Gary heard Leon giving Hope instructions only four feet from his back.

"I'm going to pull the tape off your mouth so you can eat. Please don't do anything stupid, Hope."

That few seconds of silence turned into an ear piercing shitstorm of noise. With the tape off her mouth, Hope screamed, pleaded, and spewed out hatred for Gary. "Help me, Leon. Don't let that son of a bitch sell me, please! Who knows what'll happen—I could die. Protect me. Help me!"

Gary slammed on the brakes and jammed the shifter into Park. "That's it. You're right, Hope. You can die!" He jumped through the opening, grabbed her by the throat, and began to squeeze.

Leon punched Gary in the head over and over. "Let go of her. Leave her alone!"

Gary spun and slammed Leon into the opposite wall of

the truck. He cocked back his fist and nailed Leon in the face. Blood squirted from Leon's nose as Gary pummeled him. "Don't you ever do that again. These damn bitches are coming between us, and I'm not about to let that happen. Now get in the front, and sit your ass down!" Gary stretched a new piece of tape across Hope's mouth. "Consider yourself lucky I didn't kill you. Make another wrong move, and I will." Gary hopped into the driver's seat and took off again. He looked across the console at Leon and glared. "We keep showing up late for our meetings with Charlie, and you and I will both be out of work. You want to get a job as a bagboy at a grocery store?"

"Hell no." Leon wiped up the blood with his sleeve.

"Then knock off the bullshit, and prove you have a brain." Gary pressed the gas pedal to the floor and took off.

Twenty minutes later, they arrived at the subdivision with only seconds to spare. The last thing Gary wanted was to anger Charlie, who he was sure had connections with scary people. Anything they did to piss off Charlie could lead to Gary and Leon disappearing without a trace, and that wasn't something he was willing to risk. Gary drove to the back of the dead-end road at the defunct subdivision that was never completed. The builder had gone belly-up, and the project was nothing but abandoned half-built houses that had never been occupied.

"There he is." Leon pointed out the windshield. He held a wad of tissues against his nose as he spoke.

"Stay in the truck, and clean your damn face. I don't want Charlie to get suspicious and start asking questions."

Gary parked the truck and climbed out. He nodded at the man standing ten feet away with his hands on his hips. "Charlie."

Charlie walked closer. "Why is there blood on your head?"

Gary reached up, touched the spot where Leon had pounded him, then looked at his hand. "Let's just say the merchandise is resisting."

"Let me take a look. You said she's twenty-one?"

Gary led Charlie to the back of the truck. "You've seen her before. She helped unload the girls, but yeah, she's twenty-one and a handful."

"We have ways of calming the girls down. There is a market for women over eighteen, but it's smaller."

"Understood, but she makes up for her age by being pretty." Gary pulled open the double doors and stepped up on the bumper. "Come in and take a look."

Charlie climbed up and inside. "Ah, yeah, I remember seeing her before." He knelt at Hope's side and grinned. "I heard you've been misbehaving."

Hope squirmed and tried to kick him.

"Okay, I'll take her, but I'm only giving you seven hundred bucks. You should be happy I'm taking her off your hands."

"Done deal, and thanks. Give me a second to get her out of the truck." Gary stepped through the opening and pulled his knife from the console.

"You're really doing this?" Leon asked.

Gary frowned. "Do you think I drove five hours then sat

around for another three for nothing? Of course I'm doing this. The sooner we're rid of Hope, the sooner our operation can continue without her drama." Gary shook his head. "Wake up, man. I thought it would work out with them, but obviously I was wrong." He walked to Hope's side and cut the zip ties from the truck restraints, lifted her to her feet, and pushed her to the back doors.

She jerked away from him.

"Try anything, and I'll stab you right here, right now. Step down to the ground."

Screaming through the tape and swatting at Gary, Hope resisted as he handed her off to Charlie in exchange for seven hundred dollars.

"Good luck, dude. You've got your hands full. She's like a wild horse, for God's sake."

Charlie shrugged as he grabbed Hope by the arm. "I can tame her, but some guys like bucking broncos."

Gary thanked Charlie, said he would see him in a week, and climbed back into the truck. With a slap to Leon's shoulder, Gary grinned then turned the key in the ignition. "I feel lighter already, now that we have one less problem to deal with."

"You're a real jerk, Gary."

"Maybe so, but I'll be a jerk with a lot of money."

Chapter 18

Renz walked back into the house. "Good news."

I raised my brows. "Yeah? I'm all ears for good news."

"Maureen is going to talk with the local FBI agencies nearest Casper and Rapid City to see if they can post agents at Gary's and Leon's apartments. It's time to haul them in for questioning."

"That *is* good news. Is there more?"

"Yeah, as soon as Mr. Kline comes back with the plywood, we can leave. The Johnson County Sheriff's Office said they'll get us on one of their fastest choppers, and the regional airport is only a few miles north of Buffalo."

"Thank God. We need to let the crime lab in Cheyenne know we'll be on our way soon. How long will it take to get there?"

"According to the helicopter pilot, less than an hour and a half."

I nodded. "Okay, I guess that's better than a four-hour drive."

"It sure is. Looks like it's time to go. Mr. Kline is back. Got that milk carton and the journal?"

I headed to the kitchen, where the milk carton sat in the bag on the table. "I do. You got the baggie of swabs, hairbrushes, and curling iron?"

"Yep, let's head out."

Renz had a few parting words with Mr. Kline and offered his apologies again, and we left. The airport was less than five minutes away.

"I've already updated Tommy and Fay on our findings and told them we wouldn't be joining them at the meeting with Chief Worth. They were fine with going over the details with us later."

At the airport, we were met by a deputy who introduced himself as Ralph Zimmer. He led us to the hangar used by the sheriff's office. Waiting just outside the hangar was the helicopter we would be on and the pilot who would take us to Cheyenne.

The deputy showed us to the counter and explained what we needed to do. "You have to sign a few documents, Agents, then you can be on your way."

It was a few minutes after one o'clock when we climbed into the helicopter, buckled up, and lifted off. We would be on the ground at Cheyenne's airport in less than two hours, where somebody from the crime lab would be waiting to pick us up.

While in flight, I paged through more of Claire's diary, but so far I hadn't found anything of evidentiary value. I put it away for the time being, then Renz and I outlined what we had up to that point.

It was two twenty-five when the pilot said we were

making our final approach. We would be on the ground in five minutes. Once we'd landed and it was safe to disembark, we saw a woman dressed in business attire standing near a private hangar. She held a placard with her name and status on it. She was from the crime lab, and her name was Jennifer Shoff. We headed toward her, introduced ourselves, and walked with her to the waiting car.

"The crime lab is a short ten minutes away, Agents. Our forensic techs have everything ready to go as far as making the DNA comparison on the items you've brought."

"That's great news. Thank you. How long will it take to get a confirmation?" I asked.

"I'm an administrative assistant, not a lab employee, so I really couldn't tell you with any accuracy. Do you intend to stay in Cheyenne overnight?"

I looked at Renz and shrugged. "I guess we didn't plan that far ahead yet. I imagine it depends on how long it takes to get the results."

"Understood, and the team can explain all that to you when we get there. You'll be meeting with Carrie Kerwood and Brian Cole. They're two of our top forensic technicians."

Renz thanked her, and we settled in for the short drive.

Jen turned into the parking lot of a tan concrete building several minutes later. She circled around to the back, where we passed a sign showing that employee parking was in the rear.

I chuckled to myself when I noticed the front lot was nearly empty. "Does anyone ever use the front parking lot?"

She smiled at me through the rearview mirror. "We don't get many guests. It's mostly the police, deliveries, mail, and the like. Our employee entrance is a secured door in the back anyway, and we have ID badges that we have to swipe."

"Sounds typical and very familiar," Renz said.

"Yes, sir. Here we are."

She waited as we gathered our bags and the evidence we needed tested. We followed Jen as she passed through the security door, and after walking down two left-turning hallways, we came to a large room where the wall facing us was glass. Jen pressed the buzzer, opening to a vestibule of sorts that separated us from the actual lab. We waited there for someone from the other side to allow us into the lab. She pointed at the woman who was approaching us.

"That's Carrie, and Brian is the man working at the far left station."

I nodded. "Got it."

Carrie waved, opened the door, and allowed us in. Jen made the introductions, then Carrie escorted us to a separate room.

"Give me just a minute to get Brian. Go ahead and make yourselves comfortable, Agents."

Jen excused herself and left, then Renz and I sat down. We'd only been waiting for a few minutes when the doorknob turned, and Carrie and Brian entered the room. We exchanged handshakes, then as we sat around the table, Renz explained what we had forensically up to that point.

"We noticed a blood smear on the bathroom door as if somebody had tried to wipe it off. The amount we have was rubbed onto several dry swabs and sealed in a plastic zipper bag. We also have hairbrushes, clips, and a curling iron that contain strands of hair. We're pretty certain the hair belongs to the girl in question since her roommate is a blonde."

"And you believe the blood belongs to the girl who showed up that night at her parents' house?"

"Yes, that's our belief, although we have nothing to prove the blood smear happened then. Our intent is to confirm whether the blood is a match to the hair samples—meaning it's from Hope Daniels."

"Sure thing. A simple DNA comparison won't take long at all. We should have the results within a few hours."

"Good to know. We also have a milk carton we need printed," I said.

"Not a problem. That won't take long either."

Renz asked about nearby restaurants. "We don't have a vehicle, so is there a restaurant within walking distance of the lab? We can hang out there for a bit and grab a bite to eat."

"There sure is," Carrie said. "Two blocks to the east is a busy retail street with a variety of restaurants. We could have a driver take you there."

Renz lifted his hand. "No thanks. It's a beautiful day, and we've been sitting plenty. A nice walk will do us good. We'll be back by four o'clock."

"Good enough. Just come in through the front entrance, and somebody will bring you back here."

We thanked Brian and Carrie, and she showed us out. I would make a phone call to Tommy as we walked. Hopefully, they would have something else to update us on.

Chapter 19

"Hey, Tommy, it's Jade."

"Jade, we've been trying to reach you guys."

"Sorry. We probably couldn't get a signal while we were in the chopper." I gave Renz a frown. "Hang on a minute, Tommy. We're walking to a restaurant while we wait for the DNA results to come in. I'm putting you on Speaker so Renz can hear what you have to say."

"Hey, buddy, what's up?" Renz asked.

I pointed to a bench outside an ice cream shop, and we took a seat while Tommy went over their latest news.

"Our meeting with Chief Worth had just begun when my phone rang," Tommy said. "I excused myself and took the call. It was Taft."

I raised my right eyebrow. "And?"

"And a female body was discovered late yesterday afternoon in Colorado west of Denver. Two bow hunters came across it at the bottom of a ravine. An emergency response team was called, retrieved the body, and took it to the nearest hospital, where law enforcement officials positively identified her just a few hours ago. Her name is Jacquie Carver. She's fifteen. She disappeared last Thursday and was listed with the local police on Friday as a missing person, so she was in the database. She's from Kaycee, Wyoming, and we literally interviewed her parents two days ago."

"Good God. That changes everything. Who are we dealing with—kidnappers or killers?"

"That's a good question, Jade."

Renz spoke up. "Has there been an autopsy, and has the medical examiner given a cause of death yet?"

"No to both. The parents have to be informed, and because she was a minor, they have to give their permission to let the medical examiner go forward with the autopsy. We're on our way to Kaycee right now to meet with them. Chances are, we'll head down to Denver to try to find out what the hell is going on."

"Okay," Renz said. "By the time you reach Cheyenne, we'll know if that blood is Hope's. I think we should team up and work this case together. We aren't only dealing with trafficking teenagers now, we're also dealing with murder. I'm sure we'll need all hands on deck and I'll clear it with Taft."

"You got it, pal. Let us know where to meet you in Cheyenne, and we'll go from there. We aren't going to arrive until sevenish though."

"That's fine. Just text me when you're close," Renz said.

We continued to the restaurant, even though my mind wasn't on food at that moment. The hostess seated us, poured coffee, and gave us time to look over the menu.

"Renz, have we been on the wrong track all along? Are

Gary and Leon even involved in this at all? It seems like a push to go from having consensual sex with a teenager to kidnapping and murdering them."

Renz held up his hand. "Let's not speculate. We have to wait for the autopsy to find out the cause of death and how long Jacquie has been deceased."

Renz was right. We couldn't act before we had all the facts. We would wait to hear more, wait for Tommy and Fay to arrive, and wait for the DNA results.

"How far is Denver from here?"

Renz tapped his phone and checked. "The drive is just over a hundred miles, easily doable after Tommy and Fay arrive."

"Okay, then should I reserve hotel rooms in Denver for the night?"

"Let's find out exactly where the body was located first. We need to take a look at that area tomorrow during daylight hours, speak to those hunters, and talk to the first responders who took the body to the hospital. We have to meet with the medical examiner, too, and get the autopsy report. We also need to dig in and find out if there are kidnapping and human trafficking organizations in that area. The Denver FBI unit can help us with that."

"It sounds like we'll be in Colorado for a few days."

"Probably. I'll give Taft a call and find out if she's heard about any movement at Gary's and Leon's apartments."

"Let's place our order first so we aren't interrupted. When you're on the phone with Taft, ask her exactly where the body was located."

We both chose the dinner special of roast beef, vegetables, mashed potatoes with gravy, and a side salad with a roll. Renz called Taft after the waitress took our order and walked away.

He jotted down notes on a napkin as he listened to Maureen. Minutes later, when Renz hung up, he repeated what Taft had told him. "Apparently, Jacquie was found near Evergreen, Colorado, about forty minutes west of Denver off I-70. Also, there hasn't been movement at either apartment."

"That's weird. Whether Leon and Gary are involved or not, where the hell did they go?"

Renz huffed. "That's the million-dollar question."

Chapter 20

"So how are we doing this going forward?" Leon asked.

Gary waited at the stop light for it to turn green. "I talked to Claire while you were filling the truck with fuel. She said there's a black sedan parked three houses down that's been there for some time and two men are sitting inside."

"So how do we go back to Casper?"

"We don't. I told Claire to wait until dark, slip out the back of the building, jump the fence, and get out of town. I said she needed to find a way to Cheyenne, get a bus ticket or something like that, and we'll pick her up as soon as she gets there. We'll relocate after that."

"What about the other truck in the storage garage in Schaeferville?"

"Who gives a shit? The truck rental and storage lease are in Hope's name, and she paid the garage lease in cash. Nobody will connect it to us, plus we never leave anything behind in the trucks. We can't risk going back for it."

"I guess."

"No reckless chances if we want this gig to last awhile.

Three girls a week is plenty of money. That's twelve grand a month. We'll look for border towns and make sure the girls are from different states. That'll slow down law enforcement connecting the dots." Gary gave Leon a hearty shoulder slap. "Don't worry, man. It's all good."

"What if Claire gets caught?"

Gary shrugged. "So what? She won't know where we went, and as long as Charlie doesn't get busted, our jobs are secure."

"What happens when we decide we've had enough? You know, quit while we're ahead? Charlie isn't going to let us walk away that easily."

Gary swatted the air. "Nah. You worry too much. We'll head off to somewhere else, Florida maybe. Nobody will ever track us down. We'll change our names and be fine with a lot of cash to live on."

"So, what do we do until Claire gets ahold of you?"

Gary continued down the road after the light turned green. He would merge onto Highway 85 north in a matter of minutes.

"Where are you going?"

"I'm playing it smart. We're taking Highway 85 instead of the interstate. Better safe than sorry, right?"

"Yeah, then what?"

"Then we go to Cheyenne, hunker down in a cheap motel, and wait. We should hear back from Claire by morning."

The sun was low in the sky by the time Gary pulled into the parking lot at Vista Lodge, a motel just south of Cheyenne that sat on a frontage road next to the highway. From the looks of the façade, the lodge had seen better days. Gary parked, went inside, and paid the fifty bucks for a room with two double beds. He was given the key to room ten, the last room at the end of the building. He was instructed to park just outside the door. A gas station and Quick Mart stood a hundred feet away. Before they got comfortable, Gary and Leon walked across the adjoining lots, went inside, and bought chips, sandwiches, and a six-pack of beer.

After returning to the motel and settling in, Gary popped the tab on the beer can, tore open the sandwich wrapper, and turned on the TV. The local news broadcast showed emergency crews carrying a bagged body out to an ambulance. The anchor announced that a young female was discovered by two hunters just west of Evergreen, Colorado. Denver law officials were handling the case, and the next of kin had been notified. An autopsy was scheduled for the following day to see if the girl had met her untimely death by slipping over the edge because of loose rocks or if foul play was involved.

"What the hell?" Gary squeezed the can so hard that beer squirted out the top. "How is that even possible? She was at the bottom of a ravine and hidden by thick brush. That's just our damn luck!"

Leon snickered. "What happened to your 'it's all good' motto? You change your attitude like I change my underwear—every other day."

Gary cursed Leon. "Yeah, you're a laugh a minute, asshole."

"What's the problem? They don't have anything to connect her to us. Dead girls don't talk, remember?"

"Yeah, yeah. You checked her pockets, right?"

"Yep."

"And you can't get fingerprints off clothing or skin, can you?"

Leon shrugged. "I don't know. Look it up."

Gary did then cursed. "Damn it. The post says it isn't hard to get fingerprints off clothing, but it's nearly impossible to get it off skin." He rubbed his forehead as he thought.

"What's going on in your head?"

"I'm trying to replay when we tossed her over the edge. Were we only touching her skin or her clothing too? And what about before that? Hope and Claire probably touched her or her clothes multiple times."

"Now who's the worrier? We grabbed her arms and ankles and swung her over the edge."

"That's right, but you emptied her pockets."

"True, but she's been out in the elements for two days. Who knows how many animals have licked or sniffed her body and clothes. I wouldn't worry about it."

"Maybe you're right."

Leon huffed. "Wow, I finally get some credit."

Gary chugged the beer and popped open another can. He busied himself with a map on his phone. "The sooner we get out of the area, the better. If we don't hear from Claire by morning, we're heading west. The borders of Wyoming, Utah, and Idaho all meet. We'll make our next abductions in that corridor. There aren't a lot of towns in that area, but we'll make do, and I-80 is nearly a straight shot from Cheyenne to where we need to go. The drive from that area to Central City is around six hours—not the worst—and maybe if we're lucky, we can snag someone else along the way."

"How are we going to keep up-to-date on that girl we tossed?" Leon asked.

"We'll have to use our phone data as we drive. Reception might be spotty in some areas, but we'll figure it out." Gary chowed down on his sandwiches and chips as he kept his eyes glued to the TV. "There might be a news update in the morning, and we'll check before we head out."

Chapter 21

We returned to the crime lab at four o'clock and waited for Brian or Carrie to walk in with the DNA results. I made a quick call to Fay while I had the time.

"What's the latest, Fay?" I asked when she picked up.

"We just finished the second interview with Jacquie's parents. They're beside themselves with sadness."

"I'm sure they are. So far, Jacquie is the only girl found dead, but that easily could have been missed if not for those hunters. We'll have to reevaluate our profile of Leon and Gary to see if we truly believe they're involved."

"Right, but if they aren't, it doesn't explain why Claire and Hope suddenly vanished when the guys got out of prison, or why they were caught on video paying for fuel for those box trucks."

I sighed into the phone. "I know. We have a lot of brainstorming to do, and meanwhile, there's still no sightings of Leon or Gary at their apartments."

Fay continued. "Mr. and Mrs. Carver are heading to Denver tonight and will meet with the medical examiner sometime tomorrow. He'll explain his findings to them and us as well, plus we'll get a copy of the official report. From our interview with the Carvers on Monday, Jacquie up and vanished as she was walking to a friend's house. She never made it there, and of course, nobody knew anything was amiss until Jacquie was expected home at eight o'clock and didn't show up. For those few hours, her parents thought she was at the friend's house, and the friend thought she'd changed her mind about coming over. That gave the kidnappers plenty of time to get back on the interstate and out of the area."

"What's the population of Kaycee?" I asked.

"Would you believe less than three hundred people? The town is just a blip along the interstate."

"That's crazy, but maybe we'll get some clarity tomorrow. Are you on your way here?"

"Yep, we literally left the Carver house ten minutes ago. We should get to Cheyenne around seven, like we thought."

"Okay, talk to you later." I ended the call right as Brian and Carrie walked in.

Renz spoke up first. "What did you find out?"

"The DNA is a match," Carrie said. "The blood smear came from the same person whose dark hair was in the brushes and curling iron."

"Were you able to tell how old the blood was?"

Brian took over. "That type of testing is only seventy percent accurate."

"I'll take seventy percent over zero," Renz said. "So how old is it?"

"Forty eight hours old at most, according to the system we use."

I groaned. "So there's a good chance that Hope *is* in trouble and wasn't alone at her apartment."

"What about the milk carton?" Renz asked.

"We were able to pull several viable prints off it, and we got a match through IAFIS." Brian looked at the report. "Does the name Gary Lee Rhodes mean anything to you?"

I slapped the table. "Does it ever, and it's about damn time we got a real lead. That piece of crap just put the first nail in his own coffin. Can we have copies of the reports?"

"I've already printed them out for you."

We stood, thanked them for their quick turnover of the testing, and left.

"Now what?" I asked. "We don't have a car or anywhere to wait for Tommy and Fay." I tipped my wrist. "And we still have two and a half hours until they get here."

Renz scratched his chin. "I do remember passing a coffee shop on our way to the restaurant. There was a sign on the door showing they had Wi-Fi."

"Okay, let's go there."

Once seated at a large table with enough room to use as a work station, Renz and I settled in with coffee and my laptop in front of us. I opened a map of South Dakota, Wyoming, and Colorado. We would have to talk quietly since the coffee shop was near capacity, but it was a good place to work while we waited for our colleagues. Renz scooted in closer as I pointed out different areas on the map.

"It's more than likely that Hope came from Leon's apartment. Why it's empty now can only mean he's with her or he took off on his own for somewhere else."

Renz nodded. "I doubt he went with her. Why would he allow her to stop at her parents' house?"

I grimaced. "Either he knew something bad was about to take place, and he let her show herself on camera one last time, or he wasn't with her. She went there alone but, for some reason, changed her mind and didn't go inside."

"I'm leaning toward her being by herself. Leon wouldn't risk letting her go to the door alone, even if he took her house key away from her. She could have easily banged on the door or rang the bell to wake her parents."

I had to agree. "Okay, so if she sneaked out of Leon's apartment and took off on her own, how did Gary get involved?"

Renz tapped his pen against the sheet of notes in front of him. "Let me think about that for a second. Casper is how far from Buffalo?"

I asked my phone. "Ninety minutes, give or take."

"And Rapid City to Buffalo?"

I checked. "Three hours."

"Then Leon must have alerted Gary, and because Gary was closer, he got there ahead of Hope and lay in wait for her to show up. What I'm wondering is if Leon joined him, and now all four of them are together again with Hope more of a hostage than a coconspirator."

"That sounds probable. I think those agents should breach both apartments to make sure nobody's inside."

"I agree, and I'll alert Taft to our findings. She'll have to be the one who makes that call. We also have to make sure there's a nationwide APB out for all four of them. Even if

Hope is on their bad side now, she was an accomplice before that." Renz tipped his head toward the door. "I'll make the call outside. I don't need people eavesdropping on my conversation to Taft."

I ordered two more coffees and brought them to the table while I waited for Renz to return. We needed to speak to the Denver FBI. Jacquie was found in that particular area for a reason, and my gut said it had to be on Gary and Leon's route to the buyer. Gillette, where both sets of parents lived, was on a direct route from Rapid City to Buffalo, where Claire and Hope lived. From there, Casper was a direct line south, passing Kaycee on the way. Continuing south, they would pass through Glenrock, where they were spotted getting fuel a week prior. They would hit Cheyenne, and only another hour and a half south of that was the Denver metro area where all kinds of illegal activities could take place. I jabbed Denver on the map—it was my ah-ha moment.

The drop-off location has to be within fifty miles of Denver, and I'd venture to say it's even closer to Evergreen, where Jacquie was dumped like yesterday's trash.

Renz pulled open the door and returned to our table. "Taft said she'd give the okay to breach the apartments. Even if the guys aren't there, one would think there has to be a wealth of information inside. She also put out a nationwide APB on all four of them, but of course, unless they're out in public, nobody is going to recognize them."

"It's a start. We've got another hour before Tommy and Fay arrive. I've been searching online for human trafficking cells in the Denver area, but all I can find are articles that are years old. I think we need to speak directly with someone in the FBI's Denver office."

"I'll take care of that right now." Renz wrote down the phone number and made the call.

The coffee shop had mostly cleared out, and only a handful of patrons sat across the room next to the fireplace. After Renz reached the right department, I listened to his side of the conversation and took notes. My hopes were dashed when Renz learned that the nearest human trafficking cell to Denver on record had been infiltrated last year, and it was in Albuquerque. They weren't aware of a cell popping up in the area and hadn't heard any chatter of one.

Renz thanked them and hung up. "Damn it. That didn't help. It looks like it's up to us to figure out what's going on, what they're doing with the girls, and where those punks have gone."

My phone vibrated on the table—a text had come in. I tapped the screen and read it. "It's a message from Taft. She says the agents entered both apartments, searched them, and found nobody inside and nothing that would help our investigation."

Renz shook his head. "How is it possible that two punk ex-cons can outsmart the FBI? They left nothing behind?"

I shrugged. "I'm just reading what she wrote." I rattled my fingertips on the table, and Renz noticed.

He pointed at my fingers. "Does that mean something is bubbling up in your mind?"

"Maybe. Neither guy has a registered vehicle that we could find, but we saw two box trucks on video on the same day and hundreds of miles apart."

Renz looked intrigued. "Right."

"So how did Leon get anywhere last night if Hope took her own car?"

"It had to be the truck," he said.

"One would think, yet it was never spotted at the apartment." I began tapping my computer keys in search of storage garages around Rapid City within a few miles of Leon's apartment.

"What are you looking for?"

"Storage garages. Chances are either Hope or Claire paid for one, or maybe both. Who knows?"

"Hmm… that makes sense. Leon lives on the north side of Rapid City, right?"

I nodded while I stared at the screen.

"Try Schaeferville," Renz said.

"Why?"

"Because that's where they fueled up the truck."

I grinned. "You're brilliant, Agent DeLeon." I changed my search and found one storage facility in Schaeferville that had garages for large vehicles. "Bingo. That has to be it."

I dialed the number on the screen and waited. A man answered on the third ring, and I gestured a thumbs-up to Renz. I introduced myself to the attendant and asked if they had a Hope Daniels listed as a lessee for a garage space.

He hesitated briefly then responded. "Give me a second

to check." He was back on the phone in less than a minute. "A Hope Daniels rented a double unit four weeks ago."

"What exactly is a double unit?"

"Well, you can fit three cars in it because it's deep, or a car and a large truck."

"How about a twenty-foot box truck?"

"Yeah, that would fit."

"Is somebody at the site all night long?"

"No, but everyone who comes through has to have a code to open the gate."

I groaned. "How long will you be there?"

"I work until eight o'clock, ma'am, then after that, the facility is locked up. The only people who can get in from that point are the lessees who have the code."

"Great. Expect an FBI unit to visit you within the next hour." I hung up, and I was sure by the look on my face that Renz could tell I was ecstatic. "We might get lucky, partner. I need to tell Taft to have those agents stop at the storage garage before the attendant leaves."

I made the call and passed on the information, and Taft said she would get on it right away.

I looked over my shoulder when the door opened. Tommy and Fay had finally arrived. They saw us and headed our way.

Chapter 22

Tommy and Fay scooted the two empty chairs at the table closer to us.

"What do we know since our last conversation?" Tommy asked.

"Plenty," I said. "The blood DNA found at Hope's apartment is a positive match to the hair in her brushes. Hope may have been injured while at her apartment. We also know Gary was there with her. A milk carton in the trash had his fingerprints on it."

"Wow! That absolutely incriminates him. So, is Hope in danger now?"

"It's very possible," I said. "The agents breached both Leon's and Gary's apartments, but nobody was around."

"How about information written down? Did the agents find anything?" Fay asked.

I huffed. "I have to give Gary and Leon credit. Those bastards are smart. They left nothing behind at either place."

Tommy palmed his temples. "Okay, now where do we go?"

"We did get a lead of sorts. The agents who were at Leon's apartment are going to a storage garage in Schaeferville, a few miles north of Rapid City."

Fay leaned in. "Yeah, what's going on there?"

Renz let out a low chuckle. "Would you believe Hope rented an oversized garage space there?"

"Way to go, Agents. So, what will that tell us?" Tommy asked.

"It depends. If the garage is empty, that means Leon is driving the truck, and the state patrol, county deputies, and local law enforcement have to be even more diligent in stopping every white box truck they see. The plate readers are ineffective without a plate number to track."

"How about doing the same thing with rental companies? You know, making calls and asking if either Hope or Claire rented a truck. The company would have the vehicle plate number," Fay said.

I nodded. "That's true, but it's also a huge time suck. Rental agencies can be anywhere and in every city and state. They could have rented a truck somewhere along their route."

"Speaking of route," Renz said, "we think because of where Jacquie Carver's body was found, the drop-off location is somewhere west of Denver. Why else go into Colorado at all when all the girls so far have been kidnapped from South Dakota and Wyoming?"

"Another good point," Tommy said. "So are we heading to Denver?"

I frowned. "We are, but there's a problem."

"Uh-huh?"

"Denver FBI says they have no knowledge of a human trafficking cell currently operating in Colorado. The closest one, in Albuquerque, was shut down a year ago."

"So we're flying blind?" Fay asked.

I indicated a tiny space with my fingers. "We're this close to the answers we need. We know they use white box trucks, and it's likely they're making the drop somewhere west of Denver. Also, it looks like they'll be living primarily on cash—which isn't always easy. Hope's and Claire's parents have cut off their credit card and debit card use." I shook my head. "Damn it, we still have to update Hope's mom and dad on the DNA results. Beyond that, we don't know anything about Hope's physical condition or where she is."

"Sounds like we have a lot of irons in the fire," Tommy said.

Renz agreed. "And that's why it's going to take all four of us to bring them to justice. Let's saddle up. We need to get to Denver tonight."

We loaded our belongings into the SUV Tommy and Fay had rented. I was thankful we had a roomy vehicle to share for the next few days.

As Tommy drove, I made the call to Hope's parents. After Mike put me on speakerphone and I explained what was discovered at the apartment, and the fact that Gary Rhodes had been there, too, I heard Diane crying in the background. They wanted to know where Hope was and how close we were to an apprehension.

"I'm sorry, Mr. and Mrs. Daniels, but I don't have those answers yet. As soon as we find them, all that information should come to light. The FBI, state, and all local levels of law enforcement are looking for them, plus we have APBs out for Gary, Leon, Claire, and Hope. All I can say right now is that we're doing everything we can to track them down." I thanked them for their patience and ended the call with the promise of keeping them in the loop.

Fay took her turn. "Jacquie's parents suggested we meet up tonight. They said they'd already reserved a room at the Range Line Inn on the west side of Denver. We could do the same, go to the medical examiner's office with them tomorrow, then head out to where Jacquie was found."

"Not a bad idea," Renz said. "Do we have the names and addresses of those bow hunters?"

Fay continued. "We do, and they live within twenty miles of where they were hunting."

"Okay, we'll arrange to meet with them tomorrow too."

My phone rang minutes later. "It's Taft."

"She probably heard something about the storage unit."

I picked up. "Jade here." I set my phone to Speaker so everyone could join the call. "I have you on speakerphone, ma'am."

"Hello, Agents. I'm glad you're all together, and don't hesitate to ask for help if you need more feet on the ground. It turns out the white box truck is sitting in the storage garage. At least we now have the plate and VIN and can find out where it was rented from. If luck is on our side, the other truck could have been rented from the same company, and if that's the case, we'll find out the license tag number, and the interstate plate readers will be effective."

"If they're driving the interstates," Renz said.

"That's correct, Lorenzo."

I took my turn. "So, if the truck is in the garage, then what is Leon driving? Also, Hope's car was nowhere to be found around the duplex, and there hasn't been a hit on the BOLO either."

"Good questions, Jade. Leon must be using a car that isn't registered to him."

"It could even be stolen with multiple plate swaps."

"That's true, Tommy. Keep me posted. I imagine you're on your way to Denver?"

"Yes," Fay said, "and we're going to check in at the same hotel as the Carvers. It's called the Range Line Inn on the west side of Denver."

"Good enough. Let's touch base in the morning."

"Night, boss," I said.

"Good night, Jade."

I clicked off the call.

Chapter 23

Gary woke to a ringing phone. He swatted the nightstand until he found it, picked it up, and squinted at the screen. Nobody other than Leon, Charlie, and Claire knew his number, and Leon was sleeping in the bed six feet away. Still, it didn't hurt to make sure before answering. Claire's number showed on the screen. Gary sat up, cleared his throat, and answered.

"What's up, and where are you?"

"I'm on a bus heading to Cheyenne."

"And you got out clean? Nobody saw you or followed you from my apartment?"

"Nope."

"You sure?"

"I said no. Geez, Gary, get a grip. I spent the damn night in a bathroom stall at the bus station. What the hell do you want from me?"

"All right already. Just watch your mouth. When does the bus arrive in Cheyenne?"

"Nine o'clock. I took the one that makes stops just in case something goes to hell and I have to get off."

"So you're expecting something to go to hell?"

"No. Just planning ahead for the what-ifs."

"Right. What street is the bus station on?"

"West College."

"Okay, we'll find it. Stay invisible, and keep your head down."

"Are Hope and Leon asleep?"

"Yeah. We'll talk more later. I've gotta go." Gary hung up, grabbed the TV remote, and pressed the On button. He flipped through the channel lineup but didn't see any updates on Jacquie. Leaving the TV on so he would hear when the news began, Gary filled the coffeemaker with water and coffee grounds and started a pot.

"What's going on?" Leon rolled over in bed and grabbed his phone. "Damn, it's too early to be awake."

"Get up anyway. We have to pick up Claire at nine o'clock, and I want to eat something first."

Leon grunted and climbed out of bed. "I'm taking a shower. Anything on the TV about the chick we dumped?"

"Not yet, but I'll keep watching." Gary heard the shower running as he poured his first cup of coffee. He took a seat at the foot of the bed and flipped the channels again.

There has to be an update somewhere on one of these channels.

Jacquie wasn't mentioned on any of the news stations, not even the briefest update or a recap of last night's segment.

Leon exited the bathroom, passed the TV, and filled a cup with coffee. "Anything?"

"Nope."

"Humph. Then I guess that's good. She was just another runaway, on that lonely road for whatever reason, and slipped down the hill."

"Maybe, unless the law is connecting the dots between all the missing girls. That's why we need to go farther west—out of this area—and work the three-state corridor." Gary headed to the bathroom. "I'm going to shower, then we're out of here. Keep your eyes focused on the news."

The motel they'd been staying in was fifteen minutes from the bus station. Several restaurants were in that general vicinity, but Gary chose the one with the most crowded parking lot.

"Why'd you pick this place when the restaurant across the street has five cars parked in the lot instead of twenty?"

"For several reasons, Leon, and that you had to ask proves to me that you lack the common sense I may have given you credit for. Just remember, it'll be your fault if we ever get caught, because you're missing a good number of brain cells."

"Yeah, you're a laugh a minute, jerk. So go ahead and enlighten me."

"I intend to, but you need to pay attention. In time, you might learn something."

Leon shot up his middle finger. "You know what you can do with this, right?"

"Stick it up my ass? I thought you wanted an education."

Leon remained silent.

"Good, maybe now you're ready to listen. I chose the

busy restaurant for several reasons."

"You already said that."

Gary ignored Leon's snarky remark. "One, the lot is crowded, meaning there are a lot of people inside who are far too busy or preoccupied to give us a second glance. Two, for that same reason, nobody will remember what we look like. Three, the restaurant is packed, so that means the food must be good. It's simple and something that would come naturally to a person with—"

"Yeah, yeah, to someone with common sense."

"Quit pouting, and let's go inside." Gary climbed out of the truck and waited for Leon to get out before locking the doors. "We've got an hour before Claire shows up, so we have plenty of time to enjoy a nice breakfast."

Inside the restaurant, people lined the entryway and filled the benches while waiting their turn for a table or booth.

"This is bullshit," Leon said. "We'll never get served."

Gary looked at the people waiting. They were mostly husbands and wives or couples out for an enjoyable breakfast. He looked across to the counter, where only three men sat—likely truck drivers. Gary walked to the hostess stand. "How long is the wait for counter seating?"

"No wait, honey. Go ahead and seat yourself."

Gary jerked his head at Leon. "Come on. There's no wait at the counter."

They took the two barstools at the end of the counter. A waitress, who looked to be eighteen to twenty, strolled over, winked at Leon, and asked if they wanted coffee.

Leon grinned back and started to flirt, but a hard kick to the leg shut him up quickly.

Gary responded that two coffees were fine. He leaned closer to Leon, cupped his hand to Leon's ear, and told him to keep his mouth shut. "You're just dangerous enough to have somebody remember us if they were questioned. Be invisible, damn it." He glared at Leon. "I'm not kidding either." Gary jerked the menu out of the holder and held it up to his face. He decided on the four-pancake stack, an order of bacon, hash browns, and toast.

Leon ordered scrambled eggs, a waffle, sausage links, and a glass of orange juice.

Two state patrol officers walked in minutes later and took seats at the counter only five feet from Gary's left side.

Gary inconspicuously nudged Leon and leaned in. "Eat your food. Don't talk. Don't fart around, then let's get the hell out of here."

Leon responded with a subtle nod.

They ate, paid the check, and left without incident. Gary cursed as they walked to the truck, but he was thankful the decals camouflaged the vehicle enough that it went unnoticed to the troopers. Gary wasn't sure anyone was actually looking for them, but knowing Claire's and Hope's parents, and how they were like dogs with bones, his gut told him that he and Leon would be accused of Hope and Claire's disappearance. They had to maintain a low profile, and from that point forward, they would pick up food from grocery stores as they traveled. The likelihood of police walking in or TVs blasting their images across the screens in grocery stores were next to zero.

"Come on. We're going to wait in the bus station parking lot. I'll call Claire and tell her to come out when she gets here. I'm done taking needless chances."

"You're going off the deep end, dude. Nobody's even looking for us."

"Keep telling yourself that, Leon, but trouble might be closer than you think."

Chapter 24

Gary called Claire's phone as soon as a bus slowed to a stop in front of the terminal. It was likely the one she was on. Claire answered just as Gary was about to hang up.

"What took you so long?"

"Damn it, Gary, I had to grab my stuff, and my phone was jammed in my backpack. What's the problem now?"

"No problem. We're waiting in the parking lot. I'm not coming inside."

"Whatever. I'm going into the terminal to use the bathroom, then I'll come find you."

"Hurry up." Gary looked at his phone and saw that Claire had already hung up. "Prissy little bitch thinks she's hot shit. I swear, she's going to be the next one sold if she doesn't shape up."

"Yeah, rich girls suck. Just wait until she sees that Hope isn't with us. She'll totally lose her shit."

Gary pointed with his chin. "Here she comes."

Leon climbed out of the truck so Claire could get in.

She stepped up, squeezed around the passenger seat, kissed Gary, then climbed through the opening. Claire

143

looked deeper into the back then spun around. "Where the hell is Hope? Did she go inside to use the bathroom?"

Gary turned the key in the ignition and pulled out of the lot just in time. Claire's yelling would definitely attract attention.

"What are you doing? You can't leave without her!" Claire punched Gary in the shoulder and slapped his head.

The truck swerved left and right as Gary tried to swat her away. He yelled at Leon, "Control that bitch. I'm trying to drive, damn it!"

Leon unbuckled his belt, leapt at Claire, and pushed her into the back. "Settle your ass down, Claire, or you'll be next."

"I'll be next for what?"

Gary looked over his shoulder and sneered at her. "To be sold. Now shut the hell up and sit down."

"You didn't! Tell me you're kidding. Where's Hope?"

"She's gone, and you will be, too, if you don't be quiet."

Claire's sobbing grated on Gary's nerves. He sucked in a deep breath and tried to tune her out.

"Stop the truck. I'm getting out! I'm done with you two. You aren't any fun. What we're doing is getting too dangerous, and I don't care anymore if my parents control my life. They give me plenty of money, and it's legal money. I'm not going to let you sink me deeper into this mess, which will eventually land you behind bars."

Gary raised his fist. "I'm not stopping the truck, and you aren't going anywhere except where we go. Did you forget that you've already participated in kidnapping and trafficking minors? You don't get a pass for that, Claire. If we go down, you'll go down too."

"Where are we going? What do you intend to do?"

"The same as we've been doing, and you don't need to know where we're going. We're making good money, and if you stay calm and help out, we'll be fine. Maybe in a year, we can move to Florida and live the easy life, but you have to relax and do what I say."

Claire wouldn't let up and demanded answers. "Why did you sell Hope? What did she do that pissed you off so much?" She jerked her head toward Leon. "And you just let it happen? I thought Hope was your girlfriend."

Leon stared out the window. "I never told her she was my girlfriend, and if she assumed that, it was her problem."

Gary piped in. "Here's some advice, Claire—don't assume anything, past or present. Now sit down and shut up. We're going to be driving for hours, and I don't want to hear your screeching." He tapped Leon's shoulder. "Take away her phone. I don't trust her."

Claire screamed out when Leon climbed through the opening. "Don't touch me. I'm not giving you my phone!"

"Take it!" Gary yelled. "Just do it, right now." He heard a scuffle in the back, then Leon returned with Claire's burner phone and handed it to Gary. After smashing it against the dash until the screen shattered, Gary rolled down the window and tossed it into the ditch along the road. "There, done deal. Nothing to worry about anymore."

Chapter 25

We'd just sat down to a continental breakfast in the hotel's dining room. After talking briefly with Jacquie's parents, they headed out to meet with the medical examiner. He would sit down with them, explain his findings, and allow them to ID their daughter. I wouldn't want to be in their position, and my heart broke for them. Many times, for emotional support, I would join family members as they identified their loved ones, and it was never an easy process.

Our appointment with the medical examiner was set for ten o'clock. We would view Jacquie's body while he explained her injuries to us. We would get a copy of the autopsy report and be on our way. Her body wouldn't be released to her parents for several weeks—it was standard procedure in suspicious cases. After our meeting with the medical examiner, we would head to the scene where Jacquie was found. We couldn't call it a crime scene yet. That information would be revealed on the autopsy report and be listed as an accident, a homicide, or undetermined. The plans were in place to meet with the two bow hunters after lunch to get their statements.

The police and EMT reports had already been emailed to me. I'd printed them out, and we'd reviewed them last night in the hotel's business center.

I checked the time. We needed to finish breakfast and be on our way. Our appointment with the medical examiner was in a half hour.

"Time to chow down, guys. We've got to check out and be on the road in fifteen minutes."

We went to our individual rooms, packed up our belongings, and agreed to meet at the registration counter at nine forty-five. The medical examiner's office was only eight blocks away.

Once we were checked out, we crossed the lot to the SUV. Fay and I climbed into the back seat and buckled up. Tommy was behind the wheel, and Renz sat shotgun.

"I need directions," Tommy said.

I passed my phone to Renz since I already had the map of the building's location on the screen. I leaned forward and pointed. "Just press Start, and the phone will guide you to the medical examiner's office."

"Got it."

We arrived on time, and after clicking the right-hand blinker, Tommy turned into their parking lot. Just as Tommy pulled into a parking spot, we saw Mr. and Mrs. Carver exit the building and head to their car.

"Should we say something?" I asked. "They look devastated."

Renz shook his head. "We spoke with them last night and this morning. They have our contact cards too. If we approach them now, as heartbroken as they probably are, we'll be late for our meeting. We're going to find out the same information they just did, so I think it's better if we go inside."

I had to agree, but it felt like we lacked sympathy, which was the farthest thing from the truth. I would reach out to the Carvers again later in the day, after they'd had time to process whatever it was we were about to find out.

We entered the building and approached the counter. The woman—a pretty middle-aged-looking lady with a wide smile—greeted us. "You must be the FBI agents. Dr. Simpson is expecting you." She stood and came around the counter. "Please, right this way."

We followed her to a large office connected to the autopsy room and morgue. Dr. Simpson stood when we entered and extended his hand to each of us while Renz made the introductions.

"We saw the Carvers walking out," I said.

The doctor let out a long sigh. "It's always an emotional task for family to identify a body, then having to explain my findings is even harder." He pointed at the two guest chairs that faced his desk. Two more sat along the wall. "Please, have a seat, Agents, and we'll go over the autopsy report before I show you the body."

He rounded the desk, and his chair squeaked under his weight when he sat. Dr. Simpson had five sheets of paper in front of himself. He looked up at us, nodded, and began. "Jacquie Carver was a fifteen-year-old Caucasian girl, five foot two, and one hundred and five pounds. She appeared to be in good physical condition and, according to her parents, was very healthy and participated in sports at school. Her body had no visible scars or tattoos. From my findings, I'd say she's been deceased since Monday." He waited for comments before continuing.

"So, she went missing a week ago today, died sometime on Monday, and was discovered on Tuesday." I rubbed my chin. "I wonder what the guys were doing between last Thursday and Monday."

"Picking up more girls, I'd assume," Tommy said. He looked at Dr. Simpson. "I guess we shouldn't get ahead of you. Sorry, bad habit. We often think out loud."

"Not a problem, and yes, I have her death listed as a homicide, and here's why. Her parents insisted Jacquie was abducted. She was a good kid, they said, and wouldn't run away. I haven't been to the site myself, but I've heard the rocks and gravel there are lose and easy to slip on, especially if you're near an edge—"

Fay spoke up. "I hear a *but* coming."

"You're right, Agent Geddes, there is a *but* coming. Jacquie had residue of duct tape across her mouth, and her wrists and ankles had cuts and scuffs that appeared to be from zip ties. She had vomit in her throat and lungs. Her tox screen showed an alarming amount of alcohol and antihistamines in her system. I'd say that toxic amount made her throw up, but because her mouth was taped closed, she literally suffocated. Homicidal asphyxiation, I'd call it."

The images of a death that horrible swirled in my mind. Jacquie died in their custody because she was drugged, likely to keep her quiet, then the guys tossed her into that ravine to dispose of her like trash with the hopes that she would never be found. I wondered how many other girls could meet that same fate during the transport to the buyer.

I was beside myself with anger. "We've got to stop them now. Gary and Leon have gotten far too dangerous, and we still don't know what happened to Hope. Girls are being sold to who knows who, and when they put up a fight, they're drugged. If they die, they're tossed over a mountainside like garbage. Jacquie may not be the only one—more dead girls could be out there that'll never be found."

Dr. Simpson stood. "I'll show you the body before I put her in cold storage."

We followed the doctor into the autopsy room, and I shivered at the drastic change of temperature. As we surrounded Jacquie lying on that stainless steel table, covered from her chest to her thighs with a white sheet, Dr. Simpson went over her injuries with us.

I don't think any of us were prepared for what we saw. I'd never wondered what a body looked like after being thrown over a cliff, but now I knew the extent of the injuries. From her head to her toes, Jacquie's skin was scraped and torn open with wide gashes. Broken bones had punctured through her muscle and skin and were exposed. Animals had also taken their turn. The sight was horrific, and I was sure all of us were doing our best to keep the tears at bay.

The medical examiner pointed out that many of the open wounds had pieces of bark and shards of rock imbedded in them. "From the evidence I've removed from her body, it's apparent that she hit plenty of rocks and trees as she fell. Her internal organs were deeply injured too. Even if she had been alive when she went over the edge, the fall definitely would have killed her."

Renz shook his head. "Well, if there's any saving grace, it's the fact that she was already dead when they did it."

We thanked Dr. Simpson, took our copies of the autopsy report, and left. I was happy to get outside. I needed fresh air, and I imagined my colleagues did too. We climbed back into the SUV and headed out. The Evergreen area where Jacquie was found was the next stop on our list.

"I need to call Taft and update her," Renz said. "Maybe by now they've found out where the truck was rented from."

I huffed. "And if we're really lucky, the second truck was rented from the same company."

Tommy blew out a loud breath. "Don't count on it. If we were that lucky, those two punks would already be back in prison."

Renz updated Taft, telling her just how dangerous Gary and Leon were and what the autopsy report revealed. After a ten-minute conversation, Renz hung up. "Taft said they found out where the truck was rented from, but only one vehicle was on the lease contract. Maureen was also told that none of their vehicles had tracking devices. Something about violating the customers' privacy."

My phone alerted us to make a right-hand turn a quarter mile ahead. We were getting close. Tommy turned onto Evergreen Road, continued for a mile, then made a left on

Rushing Brook Canyon Road. According to my phone, we were to go another quarter mile, and we would be at the spot.

"This has to be it," Tommy said when we saw the disturbance in the dirt and gravel.

It looked like a number of vehicles had been there, and evidence of shredded yellow police tape was caught in tree limbs. Tommy slowed to a stop, and we got out. We cautiously walked to the side of the road but stayed several feet back. The edges sloped downward just enough that the loose gravel could cause a person to slip and fall to their death.

Renz pointed to a large, flat rock that jutted out from the edge of the road. He walked over, stood on it, and looked back to where we were gathered. He cupped his hands around his mouth and called out to us, "I can see where she went over just below you. Pieces of torn material are snagged in the brush. Lots of sharp pine limbs and rock edges too."

"How far down does it go?"

"To the bottom of the ravine, I'd say it's two hundred feet."

I couldn't imagine how those hunters had ever found her, but I thanked God that they did. "Is there any way to get to the bottom from here?"

Renz looked around. "I don't see any. One would probably have to hike in from a lower elevation. That's likely what those hunters did."

I shielded my eyes and scanned the area. "Why here? It's

off the beaten path, a very narrow road, and not on the way to anywhere as far as the map showed."

"That's exactly why," Fay said. "You can't dump a body in a public place. Out here, the coyotes, bears, wolves, foxes, mountain lions, hawks, and all sorts of wildlife could make short work of a carcass. I doubt they're particular. Food is food."

I cringed at Fay's analysis, but she was right. I was sure that reason and the fact that nobody would be around to witness the deed was why Gary and Leon chose that spot.

"Have you guys seen enough? There's no way to get any closer to where Jacquie was found from here."

Renz rubbed his forehead and looked at Tommy. "Are we done?"

"Yeah, let's go meet with those hunters. Where are they from?"

"An old mining town called Central City about a half hour west of here. We're meeting them at the Gold Nugget Café. I guess it's the best diner in town," Tommy said.

I tipped my chin toward the SUV. "Then we better get going. I'm sure the guys have a lot to tell us."

Chapter 26

"How are we going to recognize the hunters?" Fay asked.

Renz chuckled as he looked over his shoulder. "Have you lived in the city your entire life?"

"Well, yeah, why?"

"I guess I assumed most people could spot a hunter—fit, rugged, jeans and a sweatshirt, or maybe a denim jacket over a flannel shirt, sturdy shoes, possibly a ballcap."

Fay waved Renz off. "You're full of it."

He shrugged. "We'll see."

I grinned as I envisioned Jack, my partner when I worked at the sheriff's office in North Bend. He was still a hot, rugged, fit guy, and one of my dearest friends.

We arrived at the Gold Nugget Café right on time. Tommy found an open parking spot on the street and killed the engine. We got out. I grabbed my notepad, and we headed for the door.

Renz walked in first then looked back over his shoulder at Fay. He whispered, "I told you so," to her as we followed him inside.

Sitting at the far end of the café in an oversized booth

were two men who looked to be in their late thirties. One raised his hand to get our attention, and both were dressed exactly as Renz said they would be. I laughed under my breath.

We crossed the restaurant, and Tommy made the introductions when we reached them. They said their names were Ted Case and Pete Jackson, but we already knew that from reading the police report. Ted offered us seats, and seconds later, the waitress brought a carafe of coffee to the table.

I looked around. "Is this place always this busy?"

"Yep, it's the best diner in Central City. We're lifelong residents and know the good places to eat. I come here every morning for coffee and a doughnut and every evening for coffee and pie," Pete said.

I grinned. "And your wife doesn't join you?"

"Nope—happily unmarried. I work from home and hunt when I'm not working."

Renz piped in. "Sounds like a nice life."

"It is, and I wouldn't trade it for the world." His expression changed. "But I could do without ever again coming across what we saw on Tuesday."

"I bet. Sights like that are hard to erase from your mind." I glanced to our left and right and was glad the crowd was thinning out. We would have a better opportunity to speak freely with the men. After our cups were full and the waitress walked away, we began by asking when they'd arrived at the scene on Tuesday, how they'd ended up at that location, and how they'd gotten there.

Ted took the lead by saying they'd been bow hunting for deer late Tuesday afternoon. They'd hunted that area many times and knew it well. He'd driven his truck along a well-worn trail on the valley floor, then they'd gone in on foot, like they always did. They knew the areas where deer frequented and oftentimes saw them grazing out in a nearby meadow. Ted had taken a shot from one of their tree stands after a buck had passed through. He'd hit it, and they'd been tracking it deep in the brush when they'd stumbled upon Jacquie's body.

Pete shook his head. "I have to admit, I nearly lost my lunch. I've never seen a dead person before except in a coffin, and I've never seen anyone in that condition." He glanced at Ted. "I'm sure we were both in shock. There was no cell service in that ravine, so Ted ran back to the truck, drove out to higher elevation, and made the 911 call."

"Do you remember what time it was when you found her, and did you touch the body at all?"

"God no," Pete said. "I had a hard enough time being twenty feet from her. Every time I close my eyes, I see that poor girl."

I understood exactly what he meant, and horrible images seemed to have a way of lingering in people's minds forever.

"And the time was?" Tommy asked.

"Sorry. I just saw her again in my mind." Pete shook his head, as if to clear Jacquie's image from his thoughts. "What was it, Ted, around four o'clock?"

Ted nodded. "I think so. Deer start to settle in when the shadows take over the valley. We saw four does grazing, and that's when the buck wandered close enough for me to take aim. We tracked the blood trail for a half hour before we spotted him in the brush. We were closing in to finish him off when we saw the girl wedged between trees and rock outcroppings. I really couldn't believe my eyes."

"And how long did it take before you were able to call 911?" Renz asked.

Ted scratched his cheek. "I ran like hell back to the truck, shot up to the main road, and made the call—so fifteen minutes max."

"And the first responders showed up when?" I asked.

"A few minutes after five. Several vehicles came in where we were parked, and a few others went up to Rushing Brook Canyon Road. I imagine they wanted to see how she managed to fall."

I kept quiet as I glanced at my colleagues. "How was she taken out?"

"It wasn't easy. They couldn't get a backboard through the brush, so they had to take in a body bag, put her in it, and carry it out through the tangle of trees and boulders."

"So the emergency vehicles parked by you took her out?"

"That's right, then we were interviewed for about a half hour. There was still enough light to get our deer out before we were let go, so I'd say we took off around six thirty. What a hell of a day."

"I bet it was," Renz said. "Has anyone talked to you about it since?"

Pete shook his head. "Nope. Since we don't live around Evergreen, we weren't bombarded with questions from the locals. I did see a segment on yesterday's news. The authorities are thinking foul play may be involved?"

"It's too early to speculate," Tommy said. "Did you guys come across anyone else out there while you were hunting?"

"Nope, dead quiet," Ted said. "Sorry, that was a stupid thing to say."

I raised my hand. "Words slip out. Don't worry about it."

"I do have a question though," Pete said.

Renz tipped his chin. "Sure, go ahead."

With a frown he looked from one of us to the next. "Why is the FBI handling this?"

Tommy fielded that question. "We don't have all the facts, and it's an ongoing investigation, so we can't say much, but Jacquie could have been a victim of a kidnapping ring."

"Around here?"

"We don't know where they're based, but we're doing our best to find out." Jokingly, I made the next comment. "So if you ever see a white box truck that isn't local to the area, give me a call." I handed each of them my card, shook their hands, thanked them for their time, and we walked out.

"So, we have the police report, the autopsy report, and the firsthand account from Pete and Ted. Do you think it's redundant to go talk to the first responders too?" Fay asked.

"We're passing Evergreen on our way back to Denver anyway. Maybe a quick visit wouldn't hurt if they're on duty today," Tommy said.

I pulled my phone from my blazer pocket and the police report from my briefcase. I made the call to the Evergreen Police Department and asked if Officers Chip Orr and Dan Kemp were working that day. I was told they both were. I thanked the officer that had answered the call and said we would be there in thirty minutes. We had questions to ask them.

Chapter 27

Gary was a bundle of nerves, and that made him a danger to his partners. In his opinion, Claire was becoming more of a liability than she was worth, and as long as he and Leon didn't butt heads too often, Gary was sure they could pull off the abductions without Claire's help. She was living on borrowed time.

Driving US Highway 40 was far slower than the interstate, but in the mindset Gary was in, he wasn't going to take any unnecessary chances. They would get to the area he wanted to work without the risk of seeing state troopers and county deputies or going through tollways. They would be off everyone's radar, which was exactly where he wanted to be. As they passed through small towns, they would search every street. Nobody would be the wiser since small towns were considered safe and people trusted each other. Residents wouldn't have their guards up—at least he was counting on that.

Once they reach Vernal, they would stock up on supplies before continuing north. The town was a decent size and would likely have a big box store where they could buy more zip ties, duct tape, booze, and over-the-counter sleep medication. The liquid cocktail, along with the plastic restraints, would subdue and silence their captives and keep them from becoming a problem.

It was three o'clock by the time Gary pulled into the store's parking lot. After leaving Vernal, they would head north on Highway 191 until they hit Interstate 80. Wanting to avoid those large highways, Gary planned to keep the amount of time on it short. He would drive it for twenty minutes before exiting onto Highway 30 and weaving northwest for the duration. His plan was to scout out the area between Cokeville, Wyoming, Montpelier, Idaho, and Laketown, Utah. If that proved successful, he would expand the locations farther out on the next trip. Gary ran the numbers, and even a fifteen-hundred-mile week was doable and would still net them plenty of money, especially if Claire was out of the picture, but he would give her one more chance to prove herself useful and trustworthy in order to stay in his good graces.

"Stay in the truck, and don't make a peep." Leon looked back at Claire.

"Hell no. She's getting bound and gagged. Your problem, Leon, is your inability to see the worst in people." Gary jerked his head at Claire. "And she is already showing us that she can't be trusted."

"You can't make me stay in here. I have to go to the bathroom!"

Gary snickered. "Piss your pants. You're the one who'll have to sit in it."

"I have to take a shit. Do you want to smell that for the entire drive?"

Gary balled his hand. "I swear, if you do anything in that store to piss me off, you'll be the next girl tossed over a cliff. Do you understand?"

"Yes, I understand."

They exchanged glares until Claire lowered her eyes and looked at the floor.

"I'm warning you, Claire. Don't make me hurt you." Gary turned to Leon. "You get the supplies. I'm going to stand outside the bathroom doors."

"I don't need a babysitter, Gary!" Claire shot him the middle finger.

"Actually, you do, and you get five minutes in the bathroom. If you aren't out by then, I'm coming in to get you."

Claire stood, smoothed her hair, and climbed through the opening. "You're a real prick, Gary."

"And you're a real bitch. Now go."

They entered the store. Leon pulled a cart from the rack, and they headed to the hardware section.

Gary whispered instructions to Leon. "Keep your head down, and don't look at any cameras. Grab the duct tape, zip ties, booze, and the sleep medication, then head to the bathroom area. We'll take turns in the bathroom after Claire comes out. After that, we'll be on our way then stop for the night when we get to Cokeville."

They parted ways at the back of the store. Gary and Claire headed to the bathrooms, and Leon disappeared down the hardware aisle.

"Make it fast." Gary clenched Claire's arm.

She jerked out of his grip and went inside. Gary paced just beyond the hallway that led to the bathrooms but still within sight of the ladies' room door. He'd seen the Employees Only entrance at the end of the hall that likely went to the offices and lunchroom, and he wasn't about to let Claire sneak away.

Obeying the warning Gary gave her, Claire was out in less than five minutes. They lingered until Leon showed up with the items in the cart.

Gary nodded at Leon. "Hit the bathroom, then I will. We need to get the heck out of here and back on the road."

Several minutes later, the three of them walked to the checkout lanes. Gary whispered to Leon that he was taking Claire out to the truck and that he would buy the next round of supplies. Leon got in line, and Gary walked out with a tight grip on Claire's hand.

"Sit in the back," he ordered when Claire climbed into the truck.

"Why are you so mean to me?"

"Why were you punching me and slapping me in the head earlier? We could have crashed."

"Sorry."

Gary huffed. "You'll definitely be sorry if you ever do that again."

Gary kept a watchful eye on the store's exit. Leon should be out any minute. Through the windshield, flashing lights caught Gary's attention. Two squad cars had just pulled up to the building. He turned the key in the ignition, drove out the side exit, and parked on a residential street.

"Did you do something, Claire?" Gary leapt from the seat and raised his fist.

She cowered and covered her head. "I didn't do anything. How could I? You took my phone and pitched it out the window. Maybe somebody got caught shoplifting."

Gary yanked his phone from his pocket and called Leon. "Leave the building now. Go through the garden center exit and make it fast. I'm parked on Lilac Street just around the corner."

Minutes later, Leon reached the truck, tossed the bags inside, and climbed in. "What the hell were the cops there for?"

"I don't know, but I wasn't about to stick around to find out."

Leon tipped his head toward the back. "You think she had something to do with it?"

"She says no, and she better not be lying."

"I'm not lying!" Claire yelled. "Somebody probably got caught shoplifting."

Leon shot daggers at her with his eyes. "You better hope so."

Chapter 28

We'd spent the last fifteen minutes going over the first responder's report with the officers at the Evergreen Police Department. They gave us their accounts of Tuesday afternoon when the 911 call came in, and it mirrored what Ted and Pete had told us.

Two more officers entered the room we were in and joined our conversation. They were the first officers who arrived at Rushing Brook Canyon Road, where Jacquie went over the edge. Other than tire tracks that may or may not have been from the vehicle she was in, they said they hadn't seen anything in the area that didn't belong in nature. No cigarette butts, paper scraps, or any other kind of waste was present.

"Did either of you take pictures of the tire tracks?" I asked.

They both shook their heads, citing the fact that people drove that road on occasion because two locals owned cabins back in the woods.

Tommy took his turn. "Did anyone question them?"

Officer Denning spoke up. "I went to both cabins, but

nobody was at either one. The cabins are more of vacation homes rather than permanent residences. The owners don't live there year-round, and they come and go whenever they feel like hanging out there."

"You can't blame them. This is beautiful country," I said. "Do you happen to know the owners' names?"

"Sure. Bruce Rand owns the cabin on the east side of the road, and farther in is the cabin owned by Darryl Woods—both longtime Evergreen residents."

"Remembering back to the tire tracks you saw, would you say the impressions were wider than car tracks?"

"For sure, but then again, both Bruce and Darryl own trucks. Damn near everyone in mountain country owns some type of four-wheeler because of the volume of snow we get in the winter."

"And both men live in town?"

Denning continued. "Yep, they're retired old geezers and are usually home. I'll get their addresses for you."

Renz nodded. "We'd appreciate it."

I checked the time. "Another hour or so here, then we can head back to Denver or get rooms in the area if we plan to scout around more tomorrow."

"Let's see if either man has anything of value to tell us first," Tommy said. "We'll decide after that if it's worth sticking around or not. In my opinion, Gary and Leon are probably long gone."

With the men's home addresses in hand, we thanked the officers and left the police station. It didn't take long to find Bruce Rand's home. Getting from one end of Evergreen to the other was an easy drive, considering the population was under ten thousand people.

Tommy parked, and we walked up Mr. Rand's sidewalk. He answered the door immediately, and I assumed it was because the curtains facing the street were open. He must have seen us coming.

"If you're trying to preach or sell something, you might as well keep walking," he said after opening the door.

"Mr. Rand?" Tommy asked.

"That's me, but how would you know my name?"

"We're from the FBI, sir, and have a few questions for you." Tommy pulled out his badge and passed it to Bruce.

"Is this real?"

"Yes, sir, and we each have one if you'd like to see them all."

Mr. Rand shook his head. "Nah, I believe you. What can I help you with?"

Bruce invited us in, and Renz took the lead. He asked Mr. Rand when he'd last been at his cabin on Rushing Brook Canyon Road.

Bruce scratched his chin. "Over the weekend. I guess I came home Monday. Why?"

"Did you happen to see anyone between your cabin and the main road as you were driving out?"

We waited as he gave that some thought.

"It's very important, sir," I said. "Any vehicle at all?"

"Sorry, but I don't recall seeing anyone."

My shoulders slumped. There was no reason to stick around. If he didn't see anything or anyone out of the ordinary, then that was the way it was. We thanked him, continued on to the house belonging to Mr. Woods, and got the same response. Neither man saw a single person or vehicle on Rushing Brook Canyon Road.

We returned to the SUV with the consensus that we would drive back to Denver, grab supper, then figure out what our next move would be. I was disappointed that nothing had come of our talks in Evergreen or Central City. I was sure we were on the right track and the buyer had to be near the area where Jacquie was tossed over the mountainside, but maybe I was wrong.

We were on the outskirts of Evergreen, heading toward Denver, when Renz's phone rang. He looked at the screen and commented that it was a blocked number.

"Answer it," I said. "You know police departments usually block their numbers."

Renz picked up and put the call on Speaker. "Agent DeLeon here."

"Agent DeLeon, it's Chief Worth in Buffalo. Are you still in the area?"

"We're a half hour west of Denver following up on a lead, so not really. Why? What's going on?"

"We got a hit on our nationwide APB for Claire Usher."

"You've got to be kidding me! How did that come about, and where is she?"

"A call came into the Vernal, Utah, PD about an hour ago. It just alerted on my phone, and I called Vernal and got the information directly from them. A girl who claimed to be Claire used a borrowed phone from someone in the ladies' room of a big box store and called the local police. They were told that she feared for her life. Her burner phone had been taken away from her, and she, Leon Brady, and Gary Rhodes were in the store buying supplies. She said Hope Daniels had been sold, and she had been threatened with the same fate if she didn't toe the line. She only had enough time to say they were heading to the area where Utah, Idaho, and Wyoming met. The police said the call abruptly ended after that. They told me two units rushed to the store, but she, the guys, and the truck were nowhere to be found."

"I guess it's asking too much to assume she gave them a plate number?"

"That would be asking too much, so no, she didn't offer a plate number."

"Damn it. We don't actually know if that was a crank call or a legitimate one, then."

"I doubt it was a crank call, Agent DeLeon. She had information that hasn't been released on any news broadcasts."

"Okay, thanks for the heads-up. We'll get roadblocks in place and hopefully catch those lunatics before they snatch more girls. I appreciate your call." Renz hung up. "Jesus! They sold Hope!"

I squeezed my temples. "I'm not surprised. She obviously sneaked out and ended up paying the price for doing that. Why she didn't go into her parents' house is beyond me, but in hindsight, wherever she is now, I'm sure she regrets that decision. The question is, do we call Mr.

and Mrs. Daniels and tell them what we've heard or wait until it's absolutely one hundred percent confirmed that Hope is gone?"

"We have to wait," Renz said. "It would be reckless to tell them something that devastating on hearsay."

"I have to agree," Tommy said.

I blew out a sigh but knew they were right. "We've got to find out where the drop-off location is. Once those girls are sold, the chances of ever finding them again is about as close to zero as you can get."

Fay spoke up. "I'll try to locate the company where they rented the truck they're using. We have to be proactive, and getting a plate number is imperative. If they're traveling on any interstate and pass a tollbooth or plate reader, the state patrol would be right there to apprehend them."

"You're right," Tommy said, "but so far they've proven smarter than that."

Chapter 29

They still had a two-hour drive ahead of them before they would reach Cokeville, Wyoming, where they would stay overnight. Gary pulled off the road to get a coffee and fill the fuel tank. He ordered Claire to remain in the truck and keep quiet.

Leon exited the passenger side and joined Gary at the pump. He stared at the ground with his hands buried deep in his pockets.

Gary's forehead wrinkled. "Something on your mind?"

Leon pointed a thumb at the truck's box area, where Claire sat only feet away. "What are we going to do with her?"

"Get rid of her, what else? There's no love lost on my end. Hell, I've never even considered the thing she and I had as love. I rolled in the sheets with her once in a while, and she helped out—sort of—but now she's nothing but a pain in the ass."

Leon sighed. "Just like Hope became."

Gary swatted the air. "Don't worry about her. We're just lucky she never stopped at her parents' house after she sneaked out. Nobody other than us will ever know that less than seven hours after she made that stupid decision, she was in Colorado and sold to Charlie, and what he does—or did—with her isn't our concern."

"I know, but damn, that's brutal."

"You going soft on me and growing a conscience?" Gary stared at Leon, waiting for a response.

"No, just stating a fact."

"Here's a tip you might want to remember. Keep your facts to yourself." Gary put forty dollars of diesel fuel in the truck and returned the hose to the holder. He pulled his wallet from his pocket, grabbed two twenties, told Leon to go inside and pay for the gas, then to grab a coffee for each of them. Gary climbed back into the truck and focused on Leon through the gas station's wall of glass.

"What are you going to do with me?" Claire asked from behind him.

"That depends on you. You turn on us, and things will go sideways fast."

"What does that mean?"

"I'll leave that to your imagination. We've got two more hours before we're there. I'd suggest you shut up and relax."

"Where is *there*?"

"Cokeville."

"Cokeville, Colorado?"

"No, idiot, Cokeville, Wyoming."

Leon climbed back into the truck with the coffees, and Gary was on his way. They would stop once more to pick up food when they got to Cokeville.

Gary jerked his head toward Leon. "Check for cheap motels in that area. Look for something off the beaten path that will probably accept cash."

Claire spoke up. "I have my credit card."

Gary snickered. "Trying to offer a peace treaty? I know damn well your mom monitors the use on that card, and you better not be doing anything with it behind my back."

"I'm not. I just thought I'd offer."

"Thanks, but no thanks. We'll pay with greenbacks."

"I think I found something. It's a shithole called Hideaway Rentals, but they have openings and take cash. You can rent rooms by the day or by the week for a ten percent discount."

Gary's grumble said he wasn't happy. "A fitting name, but you'd think with the money we're making we could stay in swanky places."

"We could if we weren't doing something illegal, and swanky means credit cards, not cash."

"Yeah, yeah. How much is it?"

"Two double beds are fifty-nine bucks a night or three hundred seventy-one bucks for a week."

"Plus tax, right?"

"Yeah, plus tax."

"Nah, we've got to keep moving. We'll stay one night, pick up three girls over the next two days, then head back to Central City." Gary cleared his throat to get Leon's attention.

Leon looked over and saw Gary indicate with four

fingers then point over his shoulder. They would deliver four girls to Charlie in a few days, and one of them would definitely be Claire.

Chapter 30

We didn't know if Taft had been updated yet with the information about the ABP hit on Claire. I needed to call her, even though she had probably gone home already.

"Should I go ahead and call Maureen's cell phone, or aren't we allowed?"

"She won't mind," Fay said. "It's an emergency, and if she already knew about Claire's 911 call, she would have contacted us."

"Good point." I dialed our boss and waited as her phone rang. "She isn't picking up."

Renz looked over his shoulder at me. "Leave her a message anyway and try again in fifteen minutes. She could be taking a shower, for all we know."

I watched as Fay searched rental companies within fifty miles of Casper, Wyoming, on her phone.

"I can help speed up the process by taking on some of those companies."

Fay shook her head. "I'm not getting anywhere. It seems like most have already closed their offices for the day."

"Damn it. Let's see exactly how many there are then pick

it up again first thing in the morning."

Fay began counting while I asked my phone what the distance was from Evergreen to Vernal, Utah. It was a daunting five and a half hours. We needed to know if we should continue in the opposite direction, toward Denver, or turn around and head northwest instead.

"Try Taft again," Tommy said.

I pressed the recent calls tab and tapped her number. That time I got lucky. Taft answered right away.

"Maureen, it's Jade. I tried you fifteen minutes ago but didn't get an answer."

"Sorry, that must have been when I took out the trash. Do you have an update for me?"

"So you haven't heard?"

"I guess not. What's going on?"

"The police chief in Buffalo was notified that the APB was hit on Claire. She called from a borrowed phone in a big box store in Vernal, Utah, saying something about heading to the tristate corridor of Utah, Wyoming, and Idaho. We're making our way back to Denver, but that's taking us in the opposite direction. Should we turn around, get state troopers in force out on the interstates, put up roadblocks at off-ramps, or what?"

"All of the above, and I'll arrange it. What's the closest interstate that heads in that direction?"

I looked at Fay, and she already had a map up on her phone.

"Going due north out of Vernal, you'd take Highway 191, which would land you on I-80 between Rock Springs and

Green River. They left Vernal about an hour ago, to the best of our knowledge. Troopers could intercept them as soon as they reach the interstate since it's two hours between Vernal and Green River, where they'd start heading west."

"That's all speculation, of course. We don't know if they're taking that route at all."

"You're right," I said, "but it's the best idea I can come up with at the moment. According to the map we're looking at, the tristate area falls pretty close to Cokeville, Wyoming. The interstate starts leaning south about twenty miles west of Green River, but State Highway 30 would take them northwest, and that's exactly where they want to go."

"Okay, we'll cover that off-ramp too. I'll call you back when everything is in place. Until then, head to Vernal."

I hung up and looked at Fay's map. "Keep going toward Denver, Tommy. We'll jump on I-25 north, and that'll take us to I-80, where we'll head west. Going backward would be much slower since we'd hit every small town along those state highways."

Tommy knew the route since we'd come from that direction through Cheyenne, Wyoming. We would reach I-80 in two hours, then it would be another four before we would get to that Highway 30 off-ramp. We had a long night ahead of us, and as soon as we got near Denver, Tommy suggested gas, coffee, and bathroom breaks.

"I'll take over the driving after that so you can get some rest," Renz said. "Hopefully, the state patrol intercepts them somewhere on I-80 so we can end this nightmare once and for all."

My phone rang twenty minutes later. Maureen called back to say the roadblocks were in place and that the state patrol driving I-80 would be on the lookout for a white box truck going west. Having the plate number would have been a valuable tool, but we had to make do with what we had, and at that point, all we had was what we'd seen on the truck stop video from last week—Claire climbing into the passenger side of a white box truck.

Chapter 31

At the last minute, Gary swerved left so hard that Leon's head hit the passenger-side window.

Leon yelped and rubbed his ear. "What the hell are you doing?"

"Playing it safe. I still don't trust her." He shot his thumb over his shoulder.

Claire whined. "Thanks. I just crashed against the wall, psycho. I've already told you it must have been a coincidence that the cops pulled up to that store when we were there. Geez, Gary, people shoplift and get caught all the time. You need to get a grip."

"Don't care, and don't tell me what to do. My gut says to take a different route. The idea of being on the interstate was already rubbing me wrong."

Leon groaned. "So we're taking the slowass state highways instead?"

Gary's head snapped to the right. "You have a better idea, or would you rather be sitting your happy ass in a prison cell?" Gary sneered when he noticed Leon's shrug to Claire. "So now you two are going to tag team me?"

"No, I just want to get a good night's sleep in a real bed."

"Well, too bad. Maybe you should drive for a while since I've been behind this wheel for eight hours."

"Yeah, okay. Pull over, and I'll drive. What road is this?"

"State Highway 44. You'll stay on it until we get to Manila. By then we'll probably need fuel, a bathroom break, and coffee. After that, we go west on 43."

"I have to pee."

"Shut up, Claire. You can wait until we get to Manila. It's less than an hour away, but for now, I'm going to catch some sleep, so zip it. We have under three hours to go before we're in Cokeville. Tonight we'll all be sleeping soundly in real beds." Gary closed his eyes, leaned against the window, and drifted off.

The violent thrust snapped his head forward and into the dashboard. Gary was knocked out cold, and when he woke, he had no idea what had happened or how much time had passed. He was completely disoriented, and his head was pounding. The door on his side was open, and the truck was in a ditch facing the woods. The only thing he could see out the windshield was the ground and trees in front of him. Looking to his left, Gary saw blood pooling in Leon's right ear and running down his neck. Gary reached across the console and swatted Leon's shoulder, but he didn't move. He called back to Claire—no response. After pressing the seatbelt's snap, Gary fell forward. "What the hell happened? Leon, Claire?" Groaning, Gary braced himself against the dash and stood. He crawled through the back to see if Claire was okay. "Claire?" Gary patted his pocket and pulled out his phone, then pressed the flashlight icon and scanned the back. Claire had vanished, and the box of the truck was empty. Gary turned back and stared at the open door, then the realization hit him like a ton of bricks. Claire had fled while he was unconscious. She'd found the opportunity and had taken full advantage of it.

Where the hell would she go? It's nearly dark out here— wherever here is—and she's afraid of the dark, not to mention wild animals. There isn't a car or a house for as far as I can see.

Gary returned his focus to Leon. "Dude, come on. Wake up. You stupid ass, you probably fell asleep while you were driving." Gary shook Leon then slapped him across the face. "Wake up, you son of a bitch! I need you to help me find Claire!" Gary knew he couldn't get far on foot, and he had no idea which direction Claire went or how long she'd been gone.

Why does everyone let me down? Why couldn't they just go with the plan and not screw up? This can't be happening!

Gary unbelted Leon and pulled him from the seat. He placed him on the floor in the back and felt for a pulse. "No, no, no! You aren't dead. Please, Leon, don't be dead. I can't do this alone, damn you!" Gary felt again, but there was still no pulse. He kicked Leon in the ribs, but Leon didn't move. Gary spun toward the front. Leon's phone had been in the cup holder, but it was gone.

Did it fall on the floor?

Getting down on his hands and knees, Gary searched with his phone's flashlight. He checked in the back, in Leon's pockets, and between the seats. "That bitch grabbed his phone before she ran off." Gary jumped into the driver's seat and shifted into reverse. He slammed the gas pedal to the floor and heard the tires spin.

Okay, okay, slower this time.

He tried again and turned the steering wheel left and right. The truck moved ever so slightly.

"Come on, come on. Get some traction." He pressed the gas again but not as hard.

Ease up a little and turn the wheel harder.

He was making progress. The truck moved back a foot that time. "Little by little, inch by inch." He felt the back tires grab, then they hit asphalt. "Yes! Keep it up." He pressed the gas harder, and the truck lurched back onto the road. Gary let out a relieved sigh, buried his face in his hands, and cursed. Claire was out there somewhere but which way was the question.

Wait a minute. If she had half a brain, she'd go in the same direction we were heading. She heard me say that Manila was only an hour away. Damn it, why did I fall asleep? I don't know how far Leon went before he dozed off and veered into the ditch.

Gary looked back at his friend.

Falling asleep and rolling into the ditch wouldn't kill him, so what did?

He put the truck in Park, returned to the back, and lifted Leon's head. Gary saw that a blood pool had formed beneath it.

What the hell? Did Claire do this? Did she crack him in the head with something?

Gary crossed to the built-in toolbox at the far end of the truck, yanked it open, and saw that the largest wrench was missing. "I guess you got what you deserved, Leon. Trusting Hope was a big mistake, but trusting Claire cost you your life." Gary climbed out and rounded the truck. He looked both ways and didn't see headlights approaching from either direction, then he unlocked the padlock that secured the rear doors. He opened the doors wide, emptied Leon's pockets, and carried him down into the ditch. "Sorry, dude, but you're no help to me anymore, and I can't have a dead body in there stinking up the truck. The animals will take care of your sorry ass soon enough." Gary locked the doors again and climbed back in. Turning the wheel, he pointed the truck toward Manila and floored the gas pedal. He had no idea if the distance was near or far, but if he didn't find Claire fast, everything would blow up in his face.

Chapter 32

We had just passed Laramie, Wyoming, without hearing a word from anyone.

"What the hell is the holdup? You'd think the state patrol would have spotted them on I-80 already."

"One would think," Renz said.

"We still have three and a half hours before we reach the Highway 30 exit ramp to Granger." I saw Renz's grin in the rearview mirror. "What's so funny?"

"Nothing, but you do realize that you're going to lose consciousness soon."

I huffed. "Meaning?"

"You'll suffocate before long with all the jabbering you're doing."

"Is that your gentle way of telling me to shut up?"

Fay and Tommy started laughing too.

"We can't do anything more short of getting a speeding ticket for driving a hundred miles an hour. Sit back. Chill out, and wait for the call from Taft. I'm sure we'll be the first ones she contacts when they're in custody."

"Yeah, easier said than done."

"How about napping?" Tommy suggested.

"Nah, my mind is too active. I guess I can play solitaire on my phone."

The SUV went silent for a few minutes.

"Ahh, peace and quiet," Renz joked.

"I wonder why they aren't in custody yet. This is killing me."

Renz kept up the ribbing. "And you're killing me. Go to sleep, Jade. I'm sure you'll hear your phone if it rings."

I closed my eyes and tried to relax. I jumped to the sound of my phone ringing and hadn't realized that an hour had passed. I actually had drifted off. I looked at the screen. "It's Taft."

"Put it on speakerphone so you don't have to repeat everything to us," Tommy said.

I cleared my throat and answered. "Agent Monroe here. Yes, ma'am. I'm putting you on Speaker so we can all talk."

"Hello, Agents. It sounds like the state troopers are coming up empty. Nobody has spotted a white box truck heading west on I-80. They've gone in both directions, and even went south for ten miles on Highway 191. They haven't seen any white trucks at all except a pickup or two."

"But that's the only route north out of Vernal," Fay said.

"Unless it was a ploy to throw us off their real route."

"So a setup from Claire? Why bother? We didn't know where they were to begin with."

Taft continued. "That's true, but maybe they wanted to get through a congested city without being spotted. If everyone had their eyes on western Colorado, Utah, and

Wyoming, they could have driven through downtown Denver without so much as a passing glance in their direction." Her sigh was audible through my phone. "I'm afraid they've slipped away, and we don't know to where."

"But if the call went through the Vernal PD, then they were really there."

"I suppose so, but instead of going where Claire said they were, they went somewhere else."

I gritted my teeth. "How in the hell is it so tough to locate a big white box truck?" A thought buzzed in my head for a second. "Unless—"

"Unless what, Jade?"

"Unless it isn't white anymore."

"But it's a rental. They can't alter that," Tommy said.

I rubbed my chin as I thought. "Maybe not permanently, but it is possible."

Taft told us to pack it up for the night. "Find a decent restaurant, have dinner, then get a good night's sleep. We'll regroup in the morning and figure out what the next move should be."

We signed off, and I ended the call. I noticed the road sign showing Elk Mountain was twenty-five more miles. I checked my phone for the population. "Okay, we're at the halfway point between Laramie and Elk Mountain. The population of Elk Mountain is under two hundred people, so it's doubtful that we'd find a hotel or a decent restaurant there. Laramie has plenty of hotels and restaurants and a regional airport in case we need it. I'm for heading back."

"Same here," Fay said.

Renz turned off at the next exit. "You don't have to ask me twice. As long as you're on your phone, find a nice restaurant and a clean hotel—and preferably close to that airport."

"You bet. I'm ready to call it a night."

Chapter 33

The road sign showed Manila was four miles ahead. Gary had to find Claire before she was close enough to town to get phone reception. The winding road, thick tree cover, and mountainous area made reliable cell service nearly impossible. Gary was sure most people didn't care since he hadn't passed a single house. Up ahead, a flash of movement caught in the headlights, and the last time he'd checked, deer didn't wear clothing. It was Claire, and he had to snatch her up before she got any farther. She had walked about a mile from where Leon had gone into the ditch, and Gary was sure she would disappear into the trees the minute she realized it was him.

He saw her stick out her thumb in a hitchhiking gesture. "Careless idiot. You deserve to get picked up by a serial killer and cut into bite-sized pieces."

Gary clicked on the brights, since the darkness had taken over, with the hopes of blinding her so she couldn't tell it was the box truck approaching. He slowed to a stop and leapt out just as she realized it was him. Claire dove into the woods with Gary closing in. He was only inches behind her, and he extended his arm to grab her. Gary got tangled in the bushes, and she bolted ahead. Swearing, he picked up his pace and pushed through.

"I'm going to catch you, Claire. You'll run out of energy soon enough, and it's going to be me or a wild animal that'll grab you."

He stopped and listened. Twigs snapped on his left, and they sounded close. He turned in that direction and continued on.

If only I'd grabbed my phone from the cupholder, I would have a flashlight, damn it.

He stopped again then he heard it—her breathing. Gary knew he was within feet of her, yet he couldn't see a thing, but to his benefit, she probably couldn't either. One more step was all it took. Claire charged ahead then screamed. Gary pounced when he heard a thud. In her panicked state, Claire had tripped over a log and landed face down on the ground. Gary had her, and that time she wasn't getting away.

He grabbed her by the hair and yanked her up. "You stupid bitch. What the hell is wrong with you? For some reason you thought it was a good idea to murder Leon?"

Claire flailed wildly and swung. She caught Gary in the shoulder with that same wrench she'd killed Leon with.

"Yeah, I don't think so." Gary fisted his hand, cocked it back, and punched Claire in the temple. She went limp. "Now, we're going to do things my way, like we were supposed to all along. You three idiots are the ones who screwed everything up." Claire moaned as he dragged her through the brush and back to the truck.

Inside the box area, he took away Leon's phone, zip tied her hands and feet together, then zip tied those restraints to the truck's interior supports. Claire wasn't going anywhere.

She groaned out his name. "Gary?"

"What?"

"I'm bleeding everywhere."

"Tough shit. Deal with it. You had plenty of chances to be a normal person, but instead you decided to be a spoiled rich bitch who can't take any discomfort. Between you and Hope, you've killed two people. Leon and me? We didn't kill anyone. Sit on that thought for a while. If we get caught, you're going to serve more time behind bars than I will. Now, shut up. I don't want to hear your annoying voice again." Gary got behind the wheel but then changed his mind. He still didn't trust Claire and was sure she would do whatever she could to attract attention every time he stopped. After lifting the lid of the console, Gary pulled out the duct tape, ripped off a six-inch strip, and returned to Claire's side. He knelt next to her. "Just in case you think you can outsmart me. If you try to bite me or scream, I'll knock you out cold."

Claire glared her hatred for Gary but remained still as he stretched the tape across her mouth.

He pushed off his knee and stood, then made sure she was one hundred percent secure. She'd dropped the wrench somewhere in the woods, but there were more items in the toolbox that she could use as weapons, and Gary had no intention of being her next victim. He climbed back in behind the wheel and drove away with over two hours yet to go. Snatching up girls on his own seemed daunting and something Gary had never considered doing, but the thought of keeping all that money for himself was enough to motivate him.

Chapter 34

I'd reserved four rooms at the Terre Vista Suites, a nice-looking hotel only three miles from the airport, and there were plenty of restaurants off West Curtis Street, which was only two blocks away.

"Looks like we have a good selection of restaurants near the hotel. Want to stick with the typical American fare—steaks, chicken, that sort of thing?" I asked.

"Sounds good to me," Renz said. "I'm starving."

I laughed. "You're always starving. The Lone Pine Restaurant has a nice menu and great reviews."

"Then the Lone Pine it is," Tommy said.

We checked into the hotel twenty minutes later, agreed to meet back in the lobby in ten minutes, and we each went to our rooms to freshen up a bit. It had been a long day, and I was ready for supper, a hot shower, and a good night's sleep. Tomorrow would bring what it would bring, and unless we figured out how Gary and Leon had slipped between the FBI's and the state troopers' fingers, we were back to having no idea where they went. Cokeville still weighed on my mind. It was in the general area Claire had described in her 911 call, but it was a long way to drive on just a hunch. I would discuss it with the group over dinner.

We arrived at the restaurant right on time. They were taking the last orders for the night. We put in our orders with the waitress, asked for a bottle of Cab, and were set for the time being. A nice glass of wine and a delicious meal sounded like heaven at that moment.

The restaurant was large but cozy, and I'd noticed that no other customers were seated within earshot. We could discuss the case as much or as little as we wanted without being overheard. I brought up Cokeville to my colleagues.

"Do you guys think they slipped past the troopers or decided on another route? Or do you think the call could have been a setup, like Taft thought, and they never planned to go to the three-state corridor at all?"

Renz shook his head. "I don't buy that. I think Claire's call was legit. Either they did something to change the appearance of the truck, like you suggested, Jade, or they took another route and wanted to stay off the interstate, like Tommy had said earlier. Let's wait until Taft calls us in the morning, go over our options and opinions with her, then decide. If they did actually go to Cokeville or some small town in that general area, then they're likely going to be there for a day or two before heading to the drop-off location with a truckful of girls."

I grumbled. "You mean the drop-off location that eludes us? That invisible one?"

"Yeah, that's the one I mean."

Minutes later, the waitress arrived with our food. She

carried a platter filled with steaks, baked potatoes, sides, salads, and dinner rolls. Everything looked delicious, and since we were all starving, I figured it was time to shelf the discussion about the case and enjoy our meal. Tomorrow was another day, and we would continue that conversation in the morning.

After supper, we returned to the hotel at ten o'clock. I was exhausted but hadn't spoken with Amber or Kate since I'd left for Rapid City on Monday. They'd received a few texts from me, but that was it. On that Thursday night, I was almost too tired to call. A hot shower might wake me up temporarily, but I still planned to keep the conversation short. All I wanted to do was lay my head on the pillow and fall asleep. After my shower, and dressed in my pajamas, I tapped Amber's name on my contact list and waited as the phone rang.

"Hey, Sis," I said when she answered.

"Thanks for not calling all week."

I grinned and knew full well she would scold me. It was Amber's thing. "Sorry, kind of been busy or just never alone. It's all about the timing, you know."

"Yeah, yeah. When are you coming home?"

"Who the hell knows?"

"So in code, that means you haven't found the bad guys yet."

"That would be correct, and I'm tired of always being a half day behind them. We're kind of in a holding pattern right now, but hopefully something will break tomorrow. How's everything at home?"

"Good. Kate and I went out for pizza last night with the whole gang. Always a good time, but I drank too much beer and woke to a killer headache this morning."

"That, little sister, is actually called a hangover."

She laughed. "Yeah, I guess that's true. You sound tired, Jade, so I'm going to let you go. I'll tell everyone hi for you."

"Thanks, Sis. Good night."

I clicked off the call, set the alarm for seven a.m., and put my phone on the charger. I knew I would be asleep as soon as my head hit the pillow.

Chapter 35

It was late by the time Gary pulled into Hideaway Rentals. Leon had made the reservation over the phone earlier. All Gary had to do was check in, pay in advance, and get Claire inside the room without any mishaps or attention. He would have to make her understand his threats were real before cutting the zip ties that bound her. He killed the engine and parked just beyond the office, and after locking the doors, he went inside to confirm the reservation and get the room key.

A disheveled man who looked like he'd been asleep in the room behind the counter that led to who knew where came out when the front door opened and the buzzer rang. He addressed Gary with a head nod and asked if he would like a room.

"I called in earlier and asked for a double. I was told there was availability." Gary saw clearly by the single car at the far end of the lot that there were plenty of empty rooms.

"For one night?"

Gary pulled out his wallet. "Yep, one night."

"That'll be sixty-five dollars with tax."

Gary unfolded three twenties and a five and placed them on the peeled linoleum counter.

The man pulled the key to room six off the hook and slid it to Gary. "You're halfway down the building."

"I appreciate it." Gary walked out and was thankful that he would be at the center of the building, even though he would prefer the end. The car he'd seen was parked four units to the right, and there were five units to his left. If Claire happened to make any noise at all, it was unlikely anyone would hear it, and Gary would silence her immediately anyway.

He backed as close to room six as he could. He needed three feet of space to swing open the rear truck doors and pull Claire out. The thought of leaving her in there crossed his mind, but having her in his sights was the smartest way to go. Tomorrow, she would be tied and gagged in the truck while Gary scouted the area for someone to snatch. As soon as he had three girls—one from each state—he would make his way back to Central City, get rid of them all, including Claire, and look for a new area to hit.

After jiggling the key in the slot, Gary turned the knob and pushed the door open. He cursed the musty stench that hit him in the face, and the lighting was dim from the lack of working light bulbs. The TV had rabbit-ear antennas, something he thought wasn't even an option anymore. The room wore dark paneling that was likely from the seventies and the bedspreads were probably as old. It reminded him of an abandoned hunting cabin, and the thought of lying on that bed made him question if the sixty-five dollars he'd just handed Mr. Unkempt was worth it at all.

Gary groaned and vowed to do better going forward. He would work alone, stay under the radar, and make good money. As soon as he got back to Central City, he would ask Charlie about getting in touch with somebody who would provide him with a new ID. It was the safest and smartest way for Gary to continue the lucrative enterprise without constantly looking over his shoulder.

After unlocking the padlock at the back of the truck, Gary climbed into the front and locked the cab's doors behind him. With his phone's flashlight, he located the knife he'd placed in the door pocket then crossed through to the truck's box. As he shined the light into Claire's eyes, he told her what he was about to do.

"I'm going to cut the zip ties from the wall supports then from your feet so you can walk. We're exiting the back of the truck and going straight into the motel room. One wrong move, and this knife will be twisted into your spine right up to the handle, understand?"

She nodded.

"Whether you live or die in the next five minutes is up to you." Gary cut the plastic restraints from the supports then from Claire's ankles. He pulled her to her feet, grabbed the bag of supplies, and pushed her to the truck's rear doors with the knife's tip poking her back. "Go directly into the room."

After she entered the room, he motioned for her to sit on the bed while he padlocked the truck doors. With the doors secure, Gary walked into the motel room and locked the door at his back. The relieved breath he exhaled was audible.

"Now, what to do with you?" He walked into the bathroom before deciding and lifted the toilet lid. "Go take a piss so that's out of the way. I don't want you bugging me after I tie you up again."

The glare she gave him spoke for her. Claire walked into the bathroom and tried to kick the door closed.

Gary kicked it back toward her. "Nope, it's staying open, so take care of your business, and get back out here." She remained standing and bugged her eyes at him. "Jesus." He unsnapped her pants, yanked them down to her knees, then jerked his head toward the bathroom. "Go on. Get busy."

Claire returned to the room a minute later, and he pulled her pants up with a few choice curse words in the process.

"Lie down on the bed."

Claire did as she was instructed. Gary proceeded to entwine zip ties to each other to make lengths long enough to reach the bed frame at all four corners. He zipped them to Claire's wrists and ankles, then pulled on each to make sure they were secure.

"You hungry?"

She nodded.

"Me too. I'll order takeout. Fries and a burger?"

She nodded again.

"Good enough." Gary searched his phone for a fast-food restaurant in the area that offered delivery service. "Damn it. I can't do it without a credit card. Stay put." He chuckled at his own words as he looked back at her. "Like you're going anywhere. I'll go see if the guy in the office has any suggestions." Gary made sure the tape on Claire's mouth was snug then walked out and locked the door behind him. He headed to the office again, where he would likely wake up the man for the second time. As soon as he passed through the door, the buzzer sounded, and the man came back out.

"Forget something?" The man scratched his stringy gray hair.

"No, just wondering if there's a fast-food place in the neighborhood or even a vending machine." The man's laugh infuriated Gary. "Why was that funny?" Gary cocked his head and stared at him.

The old geezer swiped the air. "There isn't a single store in this neck of the woods, let alone a restaurant. Hell, I only make a meager living because I added onto my house and rent out a few rooms a week. I'll tell you what. I have an unopened bag of potato chips inside that I'll sell you for five bucks if you're that hungry."

Gary rubbed his chin. "Five bucks, huh?"

"Yep. One Abe Lincoln, and they're all yours. It's a big bag too."

Gary nodded. "Okay, go ahead and get it. I'll decide once I take a look."

"Sure. I'll be right back."

The man disappeared through the same door he'd come out of. Gary wondered what else was back there and what the man had socked away, as far as food and cash. It was time to find out. Gary stood along the wall next to the door and kept his eyes on the doorknob. He heard footsteps then saw the knob turn.

As soon as the man crossed over the threshold Gary jammed the knife into his gut and twisted it deep until it wouldn't go any farther. He pushed the man back into the room so blood wouldn't spill out onto the floor. The bag of chips clenched in the man's hand fell to the ground as he stumbled backward.

Gary shoved him onto the recliner and took a seat on the threadbare couch. "I'll go ahead and wait until you croak, old man, before I tear your house apart. Showing my respect, you know."

Blood sprayed from the man's mouth as he tried to speak. He stared at Gary with questioning eyes.

"Want to know why I killed you? It's because I'm hungry, man, and you mocked me. Now, I'll be taking all your food and whatever money and valuables I can find. Hell, you aren't going to need them anymore, and why waste a good thing? I bet you have some booze or beer back here too. You want to die on the chair, or should I drag your ass to bed and cover you up?" Gary waited but didn't get a response. "I'll take that as you being comfortable right where you are."

He stood and crossed the room to the man. Gary leaned over, stared into his fixed eyes, then put two fingers against his neck. "Guess you've passed on already, so tell Leon hi for me if you see him." Gary turned the man onto his side and removed his wallet and phone from his pockets. He opened the wallet, removed his own sixty-five bucks and another two twenties. "Hmm... I wonder if your debit card will do me some good. I'll be taking it along just in case."

Gary walked around the house, checked drawers and cabinets for hidden money, and found a hundred-dollar bill tucked inside a bible on the book shelf. The only thing in the refrigerator Gary cared about were the four cans of beer, the sliced cheese and turkey, a half loaf of bread, and the two Granny Smith apples. Gary emptied the kitchen cupboards of food, placed everything in a clothes basket he'd dumped out, then carried the items back to the front desk area. He snatched up the bag of potato chips before closing the door behind him. After checking the drawers at the counter for more money, Gary carried the basket of food out and down to room six. He and Claire would eat, catch a few hours of sleep, and be on their way before daylight. Later, he would find another two-bit motel or converted home to stay in and distance himself from Hideaway Rentals.

Chapter 36

The annoying sound coming from my phone woke me. I hit the screen a half dozen times trying to shut off the alarm before I realized the phone was actually ringing. It wasn't the alarm at all. I put on my glasses lying on the nightstand and took a look. It was Renz, and it was six forty in the morning. I sat up in bed, pissed that I could have slept for another twenty minutes.

I groaned when I answered. "I'm a responsible adult, Renz, and my alarm was set for seven o'clock. Where's the fire?"

"You need to get up. We're meeting in the lobby in fifteen minutes."

I dove off the bed and crossed to the bathroom, where I turned on the faucet to warm the water. "Okay, why are we leaving in fifteen minutes, and where are we going?"

"To Manila."

"The capital of the Philippines?" I asked trying to lighten the moment.

He chuckled. "Good one. I'll explain everything in the car. Just hurry and pack up your stuff. I doubt we're coming back. It's an hour-long flight to Vernal then an hour drive to Manila from there. Vernal is the closest airport, but it's still better than driving three hours to Manila."

"But we'll only save an hour and won't have a car when we get there."

"It's still faster, and the airport in Vernal has a car set aside for us. Hurry up and get ready. We're wasting time on the phone."

I bagged my pajamas, used my toothbrush, and pulled my hair back into a ponytail. I was glad that last night I'd set out my clothes for the day. I didn't have to think. I dressed, grabbed my phone and charger, gave the room a quick scan, and headed out.

I was in the lobby with two minutes to spare. Tommy was already at the registration desk checking us out. I took advantage of that time to pour four cups of black coffee from the complimentary self-serve coffee station. Everyone could add their own cream or sugar if they wanted it. I drank mine black. Seconds later, Renz and Fay walked in.

I tipped my head toward the coffee station. "I poured coffee for you guys."

"Thanks," Fay said.

Renz nodded, headed for a cup, and poured cream into it, then joined us near the lobby door.

"You going to keep me in suspense or what?" I asked.

Fay raised her eyebrows. "I'm in the dark too. What's going on?"

Tommy walked over and joined us. "We're all checked out, and a private plane is fueling up as we speak. Let's go."

We crossed the parking lot, and Renz explained to Fay and me what the urgency was all about.

"An APB hit came in on Leon about an hour ago. A county road worker spotted a body in a ditch five miles south of Manila, Utah. Deputies arrived, and luckily they used fingerprint scanners in the field. The prints from the body came up positive for Leon Brady."

I shook my head as we climbed into the SUV. "That's because of the time he served in prison. Gary's posse is getting smaller by the minute, and it sounds like Claire has turned on him, too, if that call was the real deal. Any idea what happened?"

"Not yet. The sheriff's office has cordoned off the area but will leave the body where it is until we arrive. The nearest medical examiner has an hour drive to get there anyway."

Fay frowned. "I saw Manila on the map last night. It was just west of the route we thought they would take from Vernal to I-80."

Tommy clicked the blinker then made a right-hand turn into the regional airport's main entrance. "Exactly. So if the call from Claire was real and Gary had any inkling that she was up to something—"

I cut in. "Which he probably did if she had to borrow a phone from somebody in the ladies' room."

Renz nodded. "Right. So Gary may have decided on a different route at the last minute and headed toward Manila instead of the interstate."

Tommy parked the SUV, and we walked to the hangar

to fill out the documents for our group. We each showed our IDs before we boarded, and five minutes later, the six-passenger Cessna rushed down the runway and lifted into the sky.

"So, they were heading to the tristate area after all?" I asked.

"It would seem so since Manila is northwest of Vernal," Renz said.

Fay spoke up. "And what did Maureen say since we didn't get the chance to have a morning powwow?"

Renz continued. "She said to call her after we've seen the body and done a visual confirmation that he is indeed Leon Brady."

"So at this point, nothing has been decided on whether we continue north or not?" Tommy asked.

"Not yet."

I rubbed my chin. "We've got Gary and Claire on the run, but as far as we know, she may be an unwilling accomplice."

"That's correct," Renz said.

"Hmm…"

He jerked his head toward me. "In English please."

"We need to find out from the Vernal PD what store they were at. If that store could pull up the parking lot footage, there's a good chance we'll see the truck. There's also the chance that if anything has been altered on the truck, we'll see that as well."

"And possibly a license plate," Fay said.

Tommy nodded. "Not a bad idea, but that means we'd

be spending time in Vernal instead of heading immediately to Manila."

I agreed with Tommy but knew that stopping at the big box store could give us the lead we desperately needed. "True, but if we do get eyes on them in the store or see the truck outside, that information is enough to push the case forward quickly, especially if we see the truck's plates."

Renz gave me a thumbs-up. "You're right, and it isn't like the body is going anywhere. The weather is cool enough that it being outdoors for another hour won't make much difference."

"Good, then I'll call the Vernal PD and have them email me their report right away. We'll see what store the police were dispatched to and what time that was."

Everyone's eyes were on me as I made the call. Minutes later, with my laptop and email open, I was ready to read the police report the second it came in.

"Here it is," I said when it showed a new message had come into my FBI email address. I opened it, sucked in a deep breath, and paraphrased the report to my colleagues. "Okay, here we go. The 911 call came in yesterday at ten after three in the afternoon. Two units were dispatched and arrived at Shop n' Save at three nineteen p.m. Nobody inside claimed to be the caller, and nobody was seen making a speedy exit from the parking lot." I sighed. "In other words, they had no idea who they were looking for."

"We'll have to review the footage ourselves no matter what. The police there wouldn't immediately recognize their faces in a store full of people, and if the APB hit only came in for Claire, they wouldn't have photos of Gary or Leon anyway." Renz indicated to Fay with his chin. "Find the phone number for Shop n' Save, and tell them to expect us"—he tipped his wrist—"in an hour. I want them to have the footage from yesterday at two forty-five on, up, and ready to go. Tell them we need to see all indoor and outdoor camera views too."

"You got it."

Ten minutes later, we were set to go. All we needed to do was land in Vernal, grab our rental car, and head to the big box store, which I had already mapped out the directions to from the airport.

Renz checked the time. "We'll be landing in twenty minutes."

Chapter 37

We were on the ground before nine o'clock and heading to Shop n' Save. Once there, we approached the service counter, asked for the contact person who Fay had spoken with, and waited as the woman behind the counter paged a Mr. Ellison. Moments later, he walked toward us with his hand extended. He introduced himself, and we did the same, then followed him to the second-floor group of offices.

"Here we are." He opened the door that had a plaque with the word Security written across it.

Inside, two men were seated in front of a wall of monitors with multiple camera views of every store aisle. On the opposite wall were the outdoor cameras showing live feed of the parking lot. Mr. Ellison introduced us to Stan Lawrence and Robert Bass, the store's security personnel. They had been told in advance what we needed and had the date and time already queued up for us to watch.

"These guys should be able to help you with everything you need," Mr. Ellison said.

We thanked him, then he excused himself and walked

out. We took seats alongside the men and told them we were looking for two men and a blond-haired woman, all in their twenties, entering the building together, or possibly the woman entering alone. The call to 911 had been made shortly after three p.m., so we asked to begin watching the footage at two forty-five. If we did spot them, we would follow them through the store and out to the parking lot, where we hoped to see them climb into the truck. We'd been watching the footage for a good twenty minutes when we saw them enter the store. My eyes darted to the time located at the bottom corner of the monitor—3:07. Seeing all three of them together was exactly what we were hoping for. Leon grabbed a cart. They walked down an aisle to the rear of the store then parted ways. Leon headed left toward the hardware aisle, and Claire and Gary disappeared in the opposite direction.

"Is that where the bathrooms are?" I asked.

"Yep. Straight back then to the right and down a hallway," Stan said.

We focused on the footage that played out in front of us. Gary and Claire entered the hallway together. She jerked her arm out of the grip he had, then seconds later, Gary walked out alone.

"Did you see that?" I asked. "She doesn't look like a willing participant any longer. He's waiting for her outside the bathroom."

We watched as Gary paced just beyond the ladies' room door.

"Notice how he keeps glancing at the hallway then at his

wrist? He must have given her a certain amount of time to be in there before he yanked her out," I said.

Fay spoke up. "And that had to be her only chance to call 911, when she was out of his sight. What we've seen appears legit as far as her call for help."

Seconds later, we saw Leon approach with items in the shopping cart.

"Can anyone make out what's in there?" Tommy asked.

We shrugged in unison. The items were small, and the camera location wasn't advantageous for seeing inside the cart.

"We can back up the footage and follow Leon through the store," Fay said.

"Yeah, maybe, but let's play this out and see if we can identify those items at the checkout lane instead," Renz said. "It'll be faster."

We watched as Claire reappeared. The men took turns using the restroom, then the three of them headed to the front of the store.

"They must be ready to leave." I pointed when I saw Gary whispering something to Leon as he got in line to check out.

A second later, Gary grasped Claire by the hand and walked out.

"Seems like Gary wants to get Claire out of the building as fast as he can. If she'd yelled for help or made some kind of distress signal, security would have been notified immediately."

We kept our eyes on the items Leon put on the belt. He

took a bottle of booze, zip ties, a box of something we couldn't identify, although it looked like medication, and a roll of duct tape out of the cart.

"Those items are definitely meant for abducting people. We're going to need a copy of this footage," Renz said.

Tommy pointed at the screen. "Let's see what happens next."

We continued watching as Leon paid cash for the items, took a call, and then bolted to the right instead of leaving through the main exit directly in front of him.

"Wait a minute," I said, "what the hell was that?"

Seconds later, we saw flashing lights outside the glass doors, then two officers rushed into the building.

Renz shook his head. "We'll have to see what's in the direction Leon went when we walk out. I'm guessing there's another exit that way."

"So Gary warned him that cops were outside?"

"He must have," Fay said, "otherwise he would have walked out the front door."

"Okay, we need to see the parking lot footage." Renz asked Stan to set that up for the same time that showed on the screen.

We watched as two squad cars with lights flashing screeched to a stop just outside the building's entrance and officers leapt out.

"There!" I pointed to a man who walked out the farthest door on the left. From what we could see on the building's façade, he exited through the garden center door, made an abrupt right, and disappeared around the building. "You have to be kidding! Where the hell is the truck?"

Tommy turned to Stan. "Are there cameras farther out in the parking lot?"

"No, sir, only on the building. They face the parking lot and every door. That's it."

"How much of the parking lot do they cover?"

"Straight out. If somebody parked on the side of the building, the cameras wouldn't catch them, since that area is normally used by store employees only."

Renz fisted his hand. "Damn it. So we don't have a view of the truck at all. We see them in the building, and at that time, we know for sure Leon was alive. So they bought an abduction kit. Claire made the 911 call. They got out of the building by three thirty without being seen, and somewhere between Vernal and Manila, Leon died."

"How does any of that make sense?" Fay asked.

I shook my head, pulled out my phone, and checked the distance between the two towns again—only sixty two miles and just over an hour's drive. "All we can do now is have the store send us a copy of that footage, take off, and get to Manila. We'll know more after we find out what Leon's cause of death was. At the rate they're dropping off though, Gary's kidnapping enterprise will be a thing of the past damn soon, and we'll never find out where the drop-off spot is or who's running the show."

Tommy agreed. "That's a real possibility."

The footage was sent to my email address. We thanked the store's staff, and we headed out for Manila. I was sure by the time we got there the medical examiner would be on-site, the cause of death would be determined, and we would have something to work with. No matter what, we still didn't know where Gary and Claire had gone, if the plans had changed, and if they would disappear forever.

It was after eleven o'clock by the time we arrived on scene. Several county sheriff's cars were there with the coroner's van. We parked along the road, showed our credentials to a deputy, then made our way to the twenty-by-twenty-square-foot area that had been taped off. A portable barrier blocked Leon's body from view for anyone who might pass by on the road. We approached the medical examiner, who sat in his van filling out a report.

Renz took the lead and made the introductions. The medical examiner said his name was Timothy Sedgewick and walked us to the body. Leon lay among the weeds and tall grasses, and all we could see was that he was fully dressed. Other than his skin wearing a whitish color, he looked as if he could be sleeping. He lay prone and didn't appear injured.

Tommy wrinkled his brow. "What was the cause of death? I was expecting to see some signs of injury."

"There is. If you come around to the right side of the body, you'll see evidence of a blow to the head. Blood has pooled in his right ear, and there are several hard cracks to the back of his skull on that same side."

"So he was bludgeoned with something?" I asked.

"It appears so, although I won't be able to see the damage clearly until he's on the table and his head is shaved. I haven't seen any other blood or damage to his body, but I didn't want to alter anything or lift him off the ground until you agents had a chance to take a look."

I pulled up Leon's prison identification photo on my phone, knelt alongside his body, then looked up at my colleagues. "I'd call this a positive ID." I turned to Timothy. "Go ahead and check his pockets."

He did, removed the wallet, and opened it for me to take a look at the driver's license.

I nodded to Renz. "It's definitely Leon."

"Okay, I'll let Maureen know." Renz walked up and down the road as he spoke with Taft. He returned to our sides ten minutes later and updated us. "Taft wants us to continue north. It's only another two hours to the Cokeville area, and once we're there, we'll scout out the surrounding towns, ask about a possible sighting of a white box truck, and find out where people stay when they're in the area. We might get lucky."

I wasn't feeling hopeful, but we had to push on. "Fay and I will work on the rental locations during the two-hour drive. Maybe we'll get lucky and end up with the company the truck came from and a plate number too."

Tommy huffed. "We can only wish. So are we done here for now?"

Renz gave the medical examiner his card and said we would need the official autopsy report sent to my email address, and we headed back to the car. We would reach Cokeville by midafternoon, and that would give us plenty of time to search the area and talk to local residents.

Chapter 38

Gary found a wayside to park at early that morning. It was off the beaten path, a good ten miles from Cokeville. Nobody was around, and it would do just fine until he crossed into Idaho. He realized he'd made a mistake, but until he reached the area, he hadn't known how huge of a mistake it had been. Those small towns were so small it was as if nobody lived there. Most were unincorporated with only a few hundred residents. The chances of finding the types of girls he was looking for were slim to none. Gary had to move on to towns with at least a five- to ten-thousand-person population. That meant driving farther west then heading south. He would scout out the area along Bear Lake before moving southwest to Logan, Utah. Plenty of small towns lay between Logan and Ogden, then he would move to the Salt Lake area before circling east toward Central City. It was Friday, and he figured by Monday, he would easily have four girls to drop off, one being Claire. After that, he would consider going into southern Colorado and northern New Mexico to see who he could find.

Gary had peeled the tape off Claire's mouth earlier and

allowed her to eat. He had made two sandwiches, one for him and one for her, torn open the bag of chips and polished them off, then he'd let her drink from his bottle of water. She was set until later, and as he looked into the back of the truck, he saw that she was sleeping. Gary stared out the windshield at the empty wayside, but sitting there wasn't bringing in the money. He needed to move on. He checked the time—it was closing in on one o'clock.

Time to hit the road and find a companion for Claire.

Just as Gary was about to turn the key in the ignition, he saw a car pull in.

What the hell is this?

He would wait to see who climbed out of the unexpected vehicle before leaving. Gary kept his head down while the vehicle circled the parking lot before stopping. The car faced away from him, which was good. He didn't want anyone to spend time staring at the truck.

The driver's-side door opened. He heard conversation, then a man who looked to be around Gary's age climbed out and walked the hundred feet to the outhouses. Curiosity took over. Gary needed to know who the man was talking to. He carefully stepped out of the truck, made sure his knife was ready to go if he needed it, and crept over to the passenger side of the car. He saw that the window was open, and a young woman was engrossed in her phone. Gary inched forward and knew if he was able to catch her off guard, he may score a success. He was two feet from the car and glanced at the outhouse the man had gone into—the coast was still clear.

Gary reached the window. "Psst."

She jerked her head, and he coldcocked her in the face, knocking her senseless. Gary pulled open the door, yanked her out, pocketed her phone, and heaved her over his shoulder. He rushed back to the truck, where he tossed her inside and drove away. He would find the first road to turn onto, get as far from the wayside as possible, and make as many turns onto other roads as he could before stopping to secure her in the back with Claire.

He finally got a good look at the woman as he barreled down the road. She appeared to be in her early twenties, had thick black hair, and other than the bloodied nose he'd given her, she was a good-looking girl. He pumped his fist in the air and pulled over. He had to move fast—she was starting to come around.

Gary shifted into Park and killed the engine. He dragged her into the back and zip tied her hands and feet, then stretched tape over her mouth. Only then could he take a breath. She wasn't going anywhere. Gary let out a roaring laugh when their eyes met. By the look on her face, she knew damn well she was screwed. She flailed and bucked when he leaned in closer.

"I'll tell you one thing, sweetheart. That was the easiest snatch I've ever made. Now scoot against the wall opposite Claire. I need to secure you to the wall mounts."

She remained in place.

"Defiant, aren't you?" Gary pointed to the other side of the truck. "Either you scoot over there right now, or you'll have a couple of black eyes to go along with that bloody nose."

Claire muttered through her tape and jerked her head.

"That's right. Claire learned the rules quickly. Now get your ass over there. I'm not going to say it twice."

The girl scooted to the opposite wall as tears streamed down her cheeks.

"You'll be fine, so don't act so dramatic." Gary zip tied her hands to the vertical supports in the truck. He looked at Claire and grinned. "Two down, and two to go."

Chapter 39

Fay and I had eliminated half the list of vehicle rental companies within fifty miles of Casper that carried an inventory of box trucks. We still had twenty companies to call, and with a sigh, we pushed on.

Renz looked back at us. "Nothing yet?"

"Nope. So far, no rented trucks are in Hope's or Claire's name, and the guys don't have money or credit cards of their own. How much farther do we have to go?"

Renz looked at Tommy. "What do you think? Another half hour?"

"Yeah, about that."

"Okay, maybe we can get this done and checked off the list. Have you made contact with the Cokeville PD?" I asked.

Renz frowned. "To say what?"

I shrugged. "I don't know. Something like, 'Have you seen a big white box truck lumbering around the area?'"

Renz chuckled. "No, I haven't called or asked that question, but feel free to do it yourself if you'd like."

I shot up my middle finger. "Just trying to be proactive, Lorenzo."

Fay laughed then swatted my shoulder. "Hey, I think I have something! The guy on the phone said Hope's name sounded familiar."

"Put it on Speaker," Tommy said.

She did just as the rental agent came back to the phone. "Yeah, we rented a white box truck to a Hope Daniels three weeks ago for an extended term. It looks like this month's payment was denied though, and that's going to be a problem."

"Don't you have tracking devices on those vehicles?" Renz asked.

"Excuse me, who am I speaking with? I thought I was talking to a woman."

Fay spoke up. "You are, but you're on speakerphone with my colleagues too."

"Oh, all right. As far as tracking devices go, they aren't placed on vehicles that are leased on ongoing contracts."

"Damn it," Renz said. "Okay, give us the plate number and VIN then. It's the next best thing, I guess."

"Sure thing, Agent. Are you ready to write it down?"

I pulled out my notepad and gave Fay a nod.

"Yes," she said, "we're ready."

He read the numbers to us, and Fay repeated them back. "Yes, ma'am, that's correct."

She thanked him, hung up, and called Taft. "She'll be able to get that plate number out across the interstates a lot faster than we can." She tapped her fingers on the sheet of paper I'd given her as the phone rang on our boss's end. After Taft picked up, Fay read off the numbers. Taft said she would take care of getting it on all the plate readers immediately and ended the call.

"Finally! Something positive is happening." Fay high-fived us then sat back and relaxed for the duration of the drive with a smile on her face.

Minutes later, my phone rang. I pulled it from my pocket and frowned. "That's weird. I don't recognize that number or the area code." I swiped the screen and answered. "Agent Monroe speaking." I listened as the man on the line reminded me of who he was. "Yes, Mr. Jackson, I remember you. Do you mind if I put you on Speaker so my colleagues can join in on the conversation? We're all in a car together." I waited as he responded then tapped the Speaker icon. "Okay, thank you. You're on Speaker with all of us now. What can we do for you, Pete?"

"Well, I got to thinking after you made that comment to me when you handed me your card."

I looked from Renz to Fay and shrugged. "Yes, go ahead."

"You said if I recalled seeing a white box truck that wasn't local to the area to give you a call."

It was my turn to swat Fay's shoulder. "Okay, you have our attention. What have you seen?"

"Well, remember how I said I go to Gold Nugget Café every morning and evening?"

"I do."

"I always sit at the same table facing the window that overlooks the street. One could call me a busybody, I guess, but I just like watching people and traffic go by."

"Understandable."

"Your comment got me thinking about a box truck I'd seen parked out on the street twice in the last ten days or so. The only reason I noticed it was because of the advertising on the side."

My shoulders slumped, and I was sure what he was about to say wasn't going to be what we needed to hear. "What was the advertising?"

"A pizza joint, but it was a Wyoming address and phone number. I thought it was odd that a pizza delivery truck, one I assumed delivered to grocery stores, would be in our town and parked where it was. It was directly across the street, and there aren't any grocery stores nearby, only out by the highway."

"Maybe the driver stopped to eat," Renz said.

"Maybe, but there's plenty of places to eat out by the highway too. You'd have to come into town deliberately then park that big truck along the street in a parallel parking spot. I just thought it odd, especially since you said to call if it wasn't a local truck, which it wasn't."

"And you saw it twice?" I asked.

"Yes, ma'am. The last time it was here, I saw a man walk out of the restaurant with a bag full of food. He rounded the truck and climbed into the passenger side."

That piqued our interest.

"Can you describe that man?" Tommy asked.

"Sorry, but no. I wasn't looking at customers waiting at the counter for takeout. I only noticed him because I was staring out the window and saw him cross the street and walk to the truck."

"How about the color of his hair or his body type, then?"

"Um, let me think. Nothing really stood out about the guy, average all the way around, I'd say. Not overly tall or overweight, just a regular-looking guy from behind."

"That's unfortunate. Do you remember the name of the pizza delivery service?"

"Yes, I do remember that."

"Great," Tommy said. "What was it?"

"The side of the truck read, 'Guido's Gourmet Pizza—Our Own Slice of Italy.'"

"Hmm… clever logo," I said. "And the address was somewhere in Wyoming?"

"Yep, Cheyenne."

"Okay, we'll check into that, and we sure appreciate your call." I hung up. "What do you guys think?"

Renz grunted. "I'm not optimistic. We can't force every box truck to be the right truck just because somebody we spoke with saw one."

"Yeah, I guess you're right, but it's worth a shot to find out if that company is licensed as a business in Cheyenne, Wyoming."

Tommy took his turn and looked at us through the rearview mirror. "You girls are on a roll, so why don't you make a few more calls before we get to Cokeville?"

I looked up the phone number for the Laramie County Public Records Office and called it. After a few transfers, I was connected with the person who handled business licensing and told her who I was and what I needed. I gave her the name of the company, hoped that Pete had remembered it correctly, and was put on hold for at least a minute.

"I'm sorry, Agent Monroe, but there isn't a business in the entire county under that name or Guido's Pizza or anything with the name Guido in the company title at all."

"You're sure?"

"Yes, ma'am."

I thanked her and hung up. I wasn't so sure anymore. I thought back to several days ago, when my gut told me the drop-off location was likely somewhere west of Denver. Jacquie had been tossed over the mountainside just outside Evergreen, and Pete, who lived in Central City, saw a white box truck parked along the street with the name of a pizza company out of Cheyenne, Wyoming, that didn't exist.

My suspicion meter was moving into the red zone at a high speed. "I still think we should have a chat with the Cokeville PD."

Tommy shook his head. "Give me a good reason, and if it sounds logical, we'll stop in and introduce ourselves. Just because we're FBI agents doesn't mean we need permission to check out the area."

"You're right, we don't, but if it's a sleepy town, and the police don't have much going on, there's a chance while they're patrolling the area, they might have passed a white box truck."

"Humph." Renz looked at Tommy and chuckled. "Okay, let's go introduce ourselves, but we aren't going to hang around for long. We're conducting an investigation, and I want to check out the area before dark."

"Sure. We'll ask a few questions, let them know we'll be in the area for a day or so, then head out."

We reached the Cokeville PD five minutes later, after I located their address on my phone. We entered the brick building and, after showing our credentials, asked the older female officer behind the desk if the chief or any patrol officers were present. We had a few questions for them and promised not to take up too much of their time.

She sounded frazzled as she spoke. "I-I'm sorry, Agents, but everyone is scattered about the county right now. We've got two emergencies going on at the same time, and everyone is spread way too thin. Maybe another time."

I tipped my chin at Renz as a signal to find out what was going on.

"Ma'am, we'd certainly like to help if you'd tell us what's wrong."

She squeezed her temples. "Things like that just don't happen here. We're a tiny town, and everyone knows each other."

Tommy took over. "Ma'am? We'd be happy to assist."

The woman blew out a loud sigh. "Old Man Dobbins was found murdered an hour ago, and I can't wrap my mind around the horror of it."

"Murdered? Who is he, and where was he found?"

"At his house. Willard didn't have much money, so he rented out rooms that he'd added onto his home. He wasn't licensed, but he paid his taxes on time, so the county didn't press him. Dan Sumpter went out to Willard's place today to give him a quote on repairing the roof over some of the rooms. Several customers had complained about rain leaking through the ceiling. Well, my lord in heaven, when Dan got there, he found Willard slumped over dead on his recliner with a wound to his midsection. Doc Evans, the chief, and three officers are there right now."

"And they know it was a murder how?" Tommy asked.

"Because the chief said there wasn't any type of sharp object near Willard to assume he'd inflicted the injury on himself. Doc Evans said he was certain it was a knife wound."

"Can you tell us how to get there? I'm sure the FBI has more resources to use to locate the person who committed the crime."

She nodded and wrote the address down. We thanked her, climbed back into the car, and left.

I leaned forward before buckling my seatbelt. "What do you make of that? I mean, what are the odds that Gary possibly headed this way, then out of nowhere an old man who rents out rooms to travelers ends up murdered?"

"It's suspicious enough for us to check out." Renz punched his open hand. "Damn it."

"What?"

"We forgot to ask what the second emergency was."

Chapter 40

We reached Hideaway Rentals ten minutes later and found the driveway blocked by a squad car. The officer climbed out and walked toward us when Tommy stopped nose to nose with his vehicle.

"You can't be here, sir. The rentals are closed for business."

Tommy pulled out his ID and turned it toward the officer, whose nametag showed J. Cannon. "We're FBI agents, and this incident may be related to a case we're investigating. We need to speak to the chief and the doctor."

"Sure thing, Agent Pappas, and I'll move my car so you can pass through."

I stuck my head out the window and thanked him, then Tommy continued on down the driveway. Two police cars, a fire department ambulance, and what looked to be a civilian car, I assumed belonging to the doctor, sat in the driveway.

An officer stood alone outside the office door. After approaching and showing him our credentials, he allowed us entry.

"Everyone is back there." He pointed at the door behind the counter.

Fay and I followed at Renz's and Tommy's backs. We didn't know if the people present were being careful in preserving evidence as they walked through the crime scene, since it didn't sound like they'd ever worked a murder before. Because we didn't have gloves, we were cautious not to touch anything.

Renz pushed the door inward with his elbow, and the four of us crossed over the threshold into what looked to be the living room. Three people turned and set their focus on us.

A man stepped forward with his arms outstretched as if to corral us out the way we'd come in. "Whoa, whoa, whoa, this is a crime scene, and civilians aren't allowed in here."

"We're FBI agents." Renz showed his badge. "And we were told by your officer back at the station what happened here. We were there to talk to you about a case we're investigating that may have taken a turn into Lincoln County." Renz pointed at the dead man lying on the floor. "That man may have died at the hands of the person we're looking for, that is if his death was definitely deemed a murder. Has anyone checked on or spoken with the guests?"

The chief, Bud Cartwright, spoke up. "There's nobody here. Dan Sumpter, the roofer, arrived about ninety minutes ago and found Willard this way." Bud jerked his chin at the blood-soaked chair. "Except he was slumped over in that recliner."

I looked around. "So where is Dan now?"

"We took his statement, and he left. No need to sit here all day."

"Has anyone looked at the guest register to see who's been here lately?"

Bud continued while pointing a thumb over his shoulder at the officer behind him. "Pauly looked at it."

"And?" Renz asked.

Pauly spoke up. "And it was last filled out in 2019."

"How about a scratch pad at the counter? Anything like that?"

Bud rubbed his forehead. "Agent…?"

"DeLeon," Renz said.

"Agent DeLeon, we've only been here for an hour and haven't had a lot of time to conduct a full search of the premises."

"Sorry."

"We kind of have our hands full, and the sheriff's office isn't any better. A report of a missing woman was called in about a half hour ago."

I drew back. "Where?"

"About ten miles west of here at a wayside right on the state border but still in Wyoming. You can probably find out the exact location by calling the sheriff's office dispatch number."

Tommy spoke up. "We'll be back later. Please, don't do anything except remove the body. We may need a forensic team to come in from Cheyenne to go over everything."

"That's almost a six-hour drive," Pauly said.

Tommy nodded. "But we can get them here a lot faster

if it's necessary. We'll be back later and touch base, but until then, don't move, alter, or take out anything other than Willard's body."

Bud promised they wouldn't. He exchanged cards with Tommy, and we took off. If a woman went missing less than an hour ago, and Gary was the reason why, then we were the closest we'd been to him in the last week of chasing leads.

We barreled out of the driveway, and Renz made the call to the Lincoln County Sheriff's Office. After explaining who he was, Renz was given the name of the wayside and exactly how to get there. We were nine miles away, and the man who had made the 911 call was still on-site with the deputies.

We arrived at the wayside just before three o'clock. Two Lincoln County deputy cars were parked next to a canine unit van, and ten feet away sat a red Kia Sportage. A deputy was talking on the radio alongside his car when we pulled in. Tommy parked, and we got out.

The deputy held up his hand, but Renz was one step ahead of him. He showed his ID badge, and the deputy gave us a nod, then ended his call seconds later.

"What brings you out this way, Agents?"

"We've been on the trail of a group of kidnappers for nearly a week. We heard a woman went missing from this wayside an hour or so ago."

The deputy tipped his head at the man sitting in the Kia. "He's the caller and is inconsolable. He blames himself for her disappearance. According to his story, he pulled into the wayside to use the outhouse, and his wife, Melanie, remained in the car. He returned to the vehicle in under ten minutes and found her gone. He said he thought she went for a walk, maybe to snap some nature pictures, but he called out, searched the entire area, and couldn't find her. That's when he called 911."

"And you pulled up his name in the system to make sure he's legit?"

"We did, and he's squeaky clean. They were traveling through from Rock Springs on their way to Pocatello to visit relatives when this happened." The deputy jerked his head toward the man with the dogs several hundred feet away. "That's our canine expert, Ray Russo. He said the dogs haven't caught the scent of anything out there. They were most interested in the parking lot area."

Renz continued. "Sure. We'd like to speak with the husband, and his name is?"

The deputy looked at his notepad. "Ben Gentry, and again, his wife's name is Melanie."

"Thanks."

We approached the car where Ben sat. He got out, stood, and shook our hands as Renz made the introductions. Renz pointed to a weather-worn picnic table that sat under a pine tree. It would serve our purpose for the moment.

"How about we take a seat over there, and you can tell us everything you know?"

Ben wiped his eyes with his sleeve and joined us at the picnic table. I pulled my notepad and pen from my pocket and was ready to write.

"Just walk us through it starting with the moment when you decided to turn in at the wayside," Renz said.

"Nothing out of the ordinary, really. I turned in and said I had to use the bathroom, and Mel said she was good. She was reading a crime thriller on her phone. I got out and walked away—" He dropped his head onto his crossed arms and sobbed. "I looked everywhere. I wasted a goddamn half hour walking around thinking she'd wandered off and was taking pictures with her phone, but nothing. She wasn't here."

"Was her purse left behind?" Fay asked.

He nodded. "Mel and her phone are gone, and that's why I thought she went out to take pictures. How stupid can I be? Why would any woman leave her purse in an unlocked car that had the window down?"

"I imagine it's hard to think when you're in a state of panic, Ben. Don't be so hard on yourself," I said. "How about passing vehicles or any that pulled in or out after you turned in?"

His eyes widened. "Wait! There was a truck, or maybe it was a van, that was parked over there." He pointed to the far side of the lot. "I turned in, made a wide circle, and parked facing away from it. I didn't give it a second thought."

"Think hard," Tommy said. "We need to know everything you can recall about that vehicle or if you saw or heard anyone inside."

"Um, no. I mean, I don't know. Music was playing on the radio, and the windows were up. I guess Mel rolled hers down after I parked so it wouldn't be stuffy in the car. I didn't hear anything, and I don't think I even looked at the parked vehicle for more than a second."

"Okay, take a breath. Close your eyes, and think about it as you circled the lot. Was it shaped like a van, a pickup, or like a commercial delivery truck? Do you remember its primary color?"

Ben squeezed his temples as he tried to recall. "It wasn't a pickup. That much I remember."

"Okay, so a passenger van, a large van, or a large delivery-style truck?" Renz tried to narrow down the options without leading Ben to answer in any particular way.

"That's it! I saw writing on the side, although I didn't pay any attention to what it said. That means it was something large enough to have advertising on it, also meaning it was probably a commercial vehicle, right?"

"I'd say so. Do you recall the actual color of the vehicle minus the writing?"

"White! I know it was white."

Renz stood and excused himself. He walked over to the deputy we were speaking with moments earlier, had a brief conversation with him, then returned to the picnic table. "Did you leave the wayside at all in your car to look for her?"

"No. I ran out to the road, looked both ways, and yelled her name but never drove off."

"So your car hasn't moved since you pulled in?"

"That's correct, why?"

"The deputy over there said the dogs sniffed around

your car a lot and also the area where you said the truck was parked." Renz looked back at the ground around the Kia. "Unfortunately, the ground's surface has been trampled by people and the dogs, so we can't get a forensic idea of what took place. There could have been footprints, a sign of a struggle, or something to that effect."

"So you're saying the person who was in that truck kidnapped my wife?"

"It's looking that way, Mr. Gentry."

I visually checked the distance from the car to the outhouse. It was a hundred feet or so. "You didn't hear anything, like screams for help from your wife?"

He shook his head. "I didn't hear a damn thing."

I gave my colleagues a concerned glance. To me, that meant Gary had disabled Melanie long enough to get her into the truck and speed away. At that point, we had no idea what direction he went, but I would put my money on him crossing the border into Idaho then heading south into Utah. Luckily, being in the FBI gave us jurisdiction throughout the country. That also told me Gary probably didn't know we were involved in the hunt for him.

We needed to jog Ben's memory since we had a good description of the truck from Pete. If that actually was the vehicle we were searching for, along with knowing the plate number in case Gary took to the interstates, we should be able to track him down in short order.

I went ahead and asked, "Ben, is there any chance the advertising on the side of the truck was for a pizza delivery company? Maybe Guido's Pizza? It's really important, but if you don't know, don't feel obligated to say it was. Just be honest. Any answer is okay."

He squeezed his eyes closed and thought. "I see an image of food, even though it was only for a split second. It could have been a slice of pizza. Wait! I remember seeing the word 'slice' somewhere in the ad."

That was enough of a positive ID for us. The truck was one and the same, and Gary had Melanie—there was no doubt about it. We had to update the BOLO with a new description. I walked away, called Taft, and gave her the news.

The good thing about the region was that the area was mountainous, and that gave Gary little choices in roads to take. Most were interstates, but there were several state highways too. He had a good hour and a half on us—pushing two—so we had to move fast. A nationwide updated alert would go out for a white box truck with the delivery service logo, "Guido's Gourmet Pizza—Our Own Slice of Italy," written on the side with a picture of a slice of pizza. A truck like that should be easy to spot.

A memory buzzed through my head like a lightning bolt, and I had to share it with my colleagues. Ben was back at his car with our contact information, and we were about to head out.

"Guys," I said, "I just remembered something."

Tommy tipped his head. "Yeah, what?"

"Well, it's something Renz and I would know from the interview with Hope's and Claire's parents at the Danielses' home."

Renz furrowed his brow—it was obvious he didn't remember.

"The cat. Remember Diane shooing the cat off the couch so we could sit down?"

He shrugged.

"She called the cat by name—Guido."

Renz shook his head. "Damn it, you're right."

Chapter 41

Gary hugged the two-lane road along Bear Lake as he traveled south. He would exit onto State Route 30, which would eventually turn into US Highway 30, but he couldn't take a chance on anything larger than a state highway. Even the US highways were too exposed. Hope was gone for good. Leon was dead, and Claire was a liability who he couldn't risk hanging onto for much longer. It would be a slow, deliberate drive through mountainous backroads, but he needed to get to Central City and do it while staying off the main highways. He would travel south on State Highway 16 until it turned into State Highway 89, when he would cross back into Wyoming. That would skirt the eastern part of Utah as State Highway 150, but then it would veer west—not the direction he needed to go. Mountainous areas were preventing him from heading east.

Gary pulled off onto a dirt road and slowed to a stop. He had to check out his options, and he needed to take a leak anyway. Stopping at one of those comfortable welcome centers at state borders where there were food machines, coffee, soda, and clean bathrooms was a risk he couldn't take. State patrol units often hung out at those facilities.

After weighing his options, Gary concluded the only thing he could do was stay on those back roads. It would take several days to get to Central City, but getting there was more important than getting there fast. Driving those country roads would also make dealing with the two tied up in the back far easier.

His new arrival screamed through the tape covering her mouth, but her effort was in vain. Her voice was too muffled to be a problem. Gary climbed into the back and grinned as he moved closer to her. She writhed frantically to free herself.

"You're only going to tear up your skin by doing that. I guarantee you aren't going anywhere, so save your energy and relax. If you piss me off, you won't like the results."

He walked farther back to check the food supply he'd taken from the old man's house at Hideaway Rentals. They had enough to last the three of them another day. Gary returned to the cab, opened the driver's-side door, and climbed out. He sized up the area and checked his surroundings. No other vehicle was in sight, and given the fact that the dirt road he was on wasn't much more than an overgrown path probably used only by hikers, he wasn't worried. He returned to the truck and looked from Claire to the new woman. "I guess now is as good a time as any to give you something to eat. What you get now should hold you over until tomorrow." He ripped the tape off the new woman's mouth. "What's your name, honey?"

She spit in his face and was met with a closed fist to the

nose. Gary wiped his cheek and sneered at her. "Stupid bitch. Looks like you're going without a meal today." He turned and crossed to Claire's side of the truck.

"Wait, I have to pee."

"Tough shit. It's your body, so figure out how to hold it." He knelt at Claire's side and peeled the tape off her mouth. "Want some chips and water?"

"Yes please."

Gary looked over his shoulder at the newcomer. "See how that works? You play nice, and I'll play nice back." He fed Claire one chip at a time then gave her half a bottle of water to drink. "Here, have a piece of cheese, too, before it spoils." He folded the cheese slice in half and placed it in her mouth, ate several pieces himself, and polished off the bottle of water. "Time to hit the road." He grabbed the roll of tape, stretched a piece over the new woman's mouth, then returned to Claire.

"Please, Gary. My lips are raw from you ripping that tape off. Can't I go without it?"

"I don't trust you, Claire, and you haven't given me any reason to change now."

"I'm sorry I ran off."

Gary laughed. "You're sorry you ran off? How about being sorry that you killed my best friend so you *could* run off?"

"Please? It isn't like we're going to be around other people."

"Except when I need to stop for gas."

"You can pull over somewhere before that and put the tape on my mouth then."

He shook his head. "Don't make me regret this decision."

"I won't. I promise."

Gary grumbled as he returned to the driver's seat and backed up to the main road. He would be driving through the night—it was the safest time. Between the remote mountain roads and the dark sky, he would remain invisible. Nighttime was his friend, and he needed to take full advantage of it.

Chapter 42

With the updated BOLO in place and all law enforcement hands throughout Wyoming, Idaho, and Utah, on deck, we returned to Hideaway Rentals to look through the rooms. There was a good chance Gary had stayed in one of them to catch a few hours of sleep before heading out again. Willard's home had ten attached rooms that looked to be equivalent to two-star motel accommodations at best. They smelled horrible, as if they hadn't been aired out in years, and the furniture, as well as the bedding and towels, were old and tattered. I couldn't imagine why anyone would want to stay there.

It was late afternoon when we reached the halfway point. I'd just closed the door to room five, and so far we hadn't found anything. Tommy and Fay had already looked through everything in the office space, and we had no reason to think Gary would spend much time in Willard's living quarters other than to kill and steal from the old man. Our other two colleagues joined us in room six so we could finish up faster and move on to figuring out Gary's route.

Inside that room, we immediately noticed that one of

the beds had been pulled out from the wall.

"What's up with that?" I stepped closer to the bed to give it a thorough inspection. Down on my hands and knees, I looked under it and spotted a piece of zip tie. "Hey, take a look at this!"

The others knelt down and looked.

Renz shook his head. "Let's pull the bed out farther so we can get around it."

We discovered more zip tie fragments at the front of the bed. Gary had somebody, who we assumed was Claire, zip tied to the frame, yet there wasn't evidence of zip ties under the other bed.

"So when he cut the ties, he missed picking up everything?" Fay asked.

"That's how I read it," Tommy said. "I'll search this room from top to bottom, and you guys can go through the other rooms. We need to get the hell out of here and find that truck."

We continued on, found nothing, then gathered back in room six. Tommy had just finished his search and said he hadn't found anything more.

Renz stepped over the threshold. "I'll call Taft for an update on those plate readers."

We needed a route to follow, and hopefully Maureen had something new to pass on. As we waited for Renz to finish his call, we gathered outside and joined the one deputy who had been told to stay behind.

"So, did Willard have any family in the area?" I asked.

"No, ma'am. His wife, Alice, died nine years ago. He

gradually went downhill after her passing, and these rooms were all he had left to occupy himself."

The whole thing saddened me. A helpless man had been killed for reasons I didn't know or understand. I assumed Gary had just wanted his money, but by the looks of the rooms, I couldn't imagine that being much.

Renz ended his call and walked over. The sun was about to set, and we needed some type of direction from our boss as to what our next move should be.

"Taft said none of the plate readers in Wyoming, Idaho, or Utah have had a hit on the box truck. She also said nobody as far as city, county, or state patrols have seen him."

I was frustrated. "So a truck that size with a pizza advertisement logo on the side is invisible? That bastard has to be somewhere."

"We need to see a map large enough to show us the secondary roads," Tommy said.

The deputy tipped his wrist. "Our public library is open for another half hour. They have large maps."

"That'll work. What's the address?" I asked.

"Come on. I'll lead you there myself, and I'm sure they'll stay open as long as you need them to."

We followed behind the deputy's car into town. Inside the library, Deputy Leeson explained to the librarian what we needed and asked if they would stay open a bit longer for us. She agreed and showed us to the table that held the oversized state maps. We thanked both of them and got busy. A thought bubbled in my mind, and I excused myself to make a call.

Standing in a back hallway, I waited as the phone rang on the other end. He finally picked up.

"Pete, it's Agent Monroe."

"Agent Monroe, what can I do for you?"

"You were right on target with that pizza truck. We're at the border of Wyoming and Idaho, and a woman has been kidnapped in the area. The description of the vehicle the husband saw matched the truck you described."

"Holy shit!"

I snickered. "You can say that again. I need your help, Pete."

"Anything I can do, just name it."

"Ask around. We need to know how many times that truck has been in Central City and where it was seen. You said you've lived in the area your entire life?"

"That's correct."

"Okay, do you know of, have seen, or have heard rumors of anybody living in the area and possibly on a piece of land outside the city limits, who is into illegal activities of any kind? The person is obviously a local, maybe has more money than they can account for legally, as in with a job, or seems shady? The person could possibly be a recluse, maybe has their property fenced and alarmed? I know I'm throwing a lot at you, Pete, but I believe there's a kidnapping ring going on somewhere right in your backyard."

"Damn! Let me chew on that. I'll talk to Ted and the other lifelong residents I know in the area, especially the ones who are acquainted with people who have land. I'll get the word out, Agent Monroe, and get back to you as soon as I can."

"I really appreciate it, and there's a good chance that truck is heading back your way, so keep your eyes peeled."

"You can count on it."

I ended the call and returned to the table where my colleagues were mapping out the likeliest route Gary would take.

"Everything okay?" Renz furrowed his brow.

"Yep. I made a call to Pete and asked for his help. My gut is telling me that the drop-off spot is somewhere in the Central City area. He's a lifelong resident, and so are most of his friends. Somebody has to know or has heard of questionable characters or activities in the area. It doesn't hurt to have as many feelers as possible out there helping us. It's really no different than asking for the public's help on news broadcasts."

Renz nodded. "Great idea, Jade, and we need to get Gary's, Claire's, and Melanie's faces on every news station in that three-state corridor."

"Colorado too," Fay said. "And that's especially true if that's really where he's going."

"The truck will be noticed before the occupants," Tommy said.

"Okay, then we need to include a description of the truck and the plate number on TV along with the photos and the probable direction Gary's headed. That ought to help a lot, and it's time to get John Q. Public involved."

Chapter 43

During the night, Gary had passed through Evanston, Wyoming, and followed the route he'd taken before—through Manila and Vernal. He finally exited US Highway 40 with a relieved sigh. He would get back on the two-lane roads and take them all the way to Colorado. Gary merged onto State Highway 45 south of Naples, Utah, and continued on.

He needed sleep. His eyelids felt like boat anchors, and even with the radio blaring and the windows open, nothing seemed to help. He had to find a place to stop, catch a few hours of shuteye, then be back on the road before daylight. If everything went according to plan, he would make it to Central City by early evening that next day. With luck and a little ass-kissing, Gary might be able to convince Charlie to allow him a place to rest on his property for a day before leaving again.

Even as tired as he was, Gary's mind was in overdrive. He needed a reset, a different vehicle, and a new place to live. With that taken care of, he would be good to continue on, and even with bringing in two girls a week, he would still make plenty of money and remain under the radar.

Gary thought about the woman he'd snatched from the wayside and wondered if her husband was able to describe the truck to the authorities.

Maybe it's time to pull off those decals before going any farther. I'll take my chances with a plain white truck since it'll be less obvious than one with a huge pizza slice on the side.

He reached Bonanza, a virtual ghost town, forty-five minutes later. Gary turned off the two-lane road, parked, and exited the truck. Behind the seat was a folding step stool, which Gary yanked out. He was tired, cranky, and unsure at that point what the future had in store for him. He hoped tomorrow, and with some sleep and miles behind him, his outlook would be better. Gary set up the step stool and began pulling off the magnetic decals. With that done, he climbed back into the truck.

Only a hundred feet ahead, Gary noticed a large barn set off the road. His curiosity was piqued since no house went along with that structure. He drove closer, pointed the high beams at it, and saw that it appeared abandoned. The roof had collapsed, and it was nothing more than a building waiting to fall flat to the ground. That night, it would be the perfect structure, given its size, to park behind, hide completely out of sight, and get some sleep. Gary pulled ahead into the weed-filled driveway, rounded the barn, and killed the engine.

Finally, a safe place to get some shut-eye.

He set his phone alarm for five a.m. and, after locking the doors, climbed into the back, bunched up his jacket under his head, and closed his eyes. He knew he would be out for the count within minutes.

"Gary?"

"What?"

"Just wondering where we are."

"Near a nothing area that used to be a small town called Bonanza. Now shut up, and let me get some sleep."

"Thanks for not taping my mouth."

"You're welcome, but you're already making me regret it. Close your mouth, or I'll grab the roll of tape and close it for you."

Chapter 44

Since nobody had seen hide nor hair of the white box truck visually or by a license plate hit, we concluded that Gary was taking mountainous two-lane roads, which would slow him down substantially. We could only hope that he would run out of gas with no place to fuel up.

Taft said we should head to Colorado where the truck had been spotted on at least two separate occasions in Central City. Gary had a reason to keep returning to that area, and we were pretty sure we knew why.

Pictures of Claire, Melanie, and Gary were splashed across all channels throughout the region, along with the truck information. It would be difficult to spot them at night, but once daylight broke, there would be a four-state manhunt for them.

During our last phone call with Taft, she'd said she had directed the Gilpin County Sheriff's Office as well as the Central City Police Department to be on the lookout for that truck.

At that point, we were playing a waiting game for information that could get us one step closer to Gary. We were all tired, but we pushed ourselves to Vernal, where we would sleep for the night then head south that next morning. Gary couldn't be more than a few hours ahead of us, but on what road was the million-dollar question.

We found a decent hotel just off the highway and called it a wrap for the night. If an urgent update came in on any of our phones, we would be back on the road within minutes.

I showered and put on my pajamas, but had everything ready to go for a quick exit if necessary. Before I plugged in my phone and shut off the light, I sent off a quick text to Amber saying I was too tired to talk, we hadn't caught the kidnapper yet, and hopefully tomorrow would be a better day. I turned off the light and closed my eyes just as my phone buzzed.

"Come on, Sis, I'm too tired to do this back-and-forth text thing. Talking would be faster than tapping." I sat up with a groan, grabbed my phone off the nightstand, and was prepared to tell Amber to let me sleep. I tapped the message and was surprised to see it was from Pete. He'd spoken with a half dozen locals and had a few names of shady characters, not anyone they knew to be criminals, he'd said, but shady none the less. I returned a text thanking him and said I would check out those people in the criminal database first thing in the morning. After asking for his continued help, I said we were spending the night in Vernal, Utah, and would cross into Colorado tomorrow.

It was a five-hour drive from Vernal to Central City, which would get us there in the early afternoon unless word came back that Gary had been captured somewhere else. No matter what, if he was in custody, we would get him to tell us where the drop-off location was. He would have kidnapping, human trafficking, and murder charges brought against him, which didn't give him much leverage. Claire would have the same charges brought against her, and if she was still with him, one of them would give us what we wanted. Whoever talked first would get a sweetheart deal. The other would serve a life sentence.

I sent off a quick text to Renz saying that Pete named three people in a message. Although he said there wasn't any proof of wrongdoing against them that he was aware of, they were sketchy and shady enough to warrant checking into.

A return text only showed a thumbs-up emoji, which I was grateful for. Tomorrow was another day, and we would have plenty of time to research those names during our drive to Central City.

I clicked off the light and hoped my phone wouldn't alert me to anything else that night.

I woke at six a.m., grabbed my phone, and turned off the alarm. I checked for new messages and saw there weren't any, and no texts had come in during the night. That told me Gary was still in the wind.

How in the hell is he evading every type of law enforcement agency out there?

I started the four-cup coffeemaker and headed to the shower for a quick wake-up rinse. We would discuss our next move over breakfast and hope the daylight hours would finally expose the man who, up to that point, had remained invisible.

During breakfast, I told Fay and Tommy about the text I'd gotten from Pete the night before. The three names could be people of interest, he'd said, and worth checking into, in his opinion. A Malcomb Crane, a Rod Ramirez, and a Charles Dunn were all locals who had property outside town and were reclusive and suspicious-seeming people who had assets without logical explanations of how they'd acquired their good fortune. As far as Pete knew, none of them went to everyday jobs.

"Sounds like people who may be conducting business under the radar. We'll definitely check them out," Tommy said.

"Anybody hear from Taft yet this morning?" Renz looked from one face to the next.

We shrugged in unison.

"Okay, then let's finish eating, check out, and continue our route on those secondary roads into Colorado. I'll call Maureen in an hour to see what she knows."

We had a choice to make before setting out—take Bonanza Highway south, which was a state highway, or US Highway 40, which was also called the Dinosaur Diamond Prehistoric Highway. They would both take us where we needed to go, but US 40 was faster and busier.

"We have to think like Gary. Would he risk that exposure on a US highway, or would he prefer to stay more hidden on those slower, winding roads?" I asked.

"He'd stay under the radar. He hasn't come this far to

be caught if he could avoid it," Tommy said.

Fay nodded. "I agree."

Renz headed for the car. "So, we're all in agreement to take the Bonanza Highway?"

We said we were. He climbed in behind the wheel, and we set out on our southbound route by seven o'clock. Sooner or later, Gary would wear down and need to rest if he hadn't already. As for us, we had four able-bodied people who could take turns driving if someone needed a break.

We had been on the road for twenty minutes when two sheriff's office cars sped past us with their sirens blaring and lights flashing.

"What the hell was that?" I asked.

We had no way of knowing since the car we were in was an everyday rental and not a police vehicle with a radio on board.

Renz shook his head and continued on. "Maybe there's an accident farther down the road. Those squad cars probably came from Vernal since it's the largest city in these parts, and whatever happened, I'm sure we'll pass it."

Chapter 45

The ear-piercing shriek that came from Claire jarred Gary awake. He jumped straight up and realized it was daylight and that he'd missed his five a.m. alarm. He lunged at her and slapped her across the face. "What the hell are you screaming about, you stupid bitch?"

Gary spun at the sound of pounding against the driver's-side door then on the wall of the truck's box.

A male called out, "What's going on in there? Who's inside? I heard screaming."

Gary turned back to Claire and kicked her in the gut, then knelt next to her and yanked her head back by the hair. The other woman cowered against the wall and sobbed through her taped mouth.

"Why did I trust you to keep your mouth closed? You're nothing but a lying piece of shit!"

The man continued to pound on the truck. "Come out of there, or I'm calling 911."

Gary had his knife ready when he climbed back into the cab, unlocked the door, and stepped out. "What's up? Why are you threatening me, man?"

"I heard screaming. Who's in there?"

"Nobody. I was watching a movie trailer on my phone. Why are you being so damn nosey anyway?"

"I'm not. I saw some debris lying on the side of the road, so I pulled over to check it out. When I got out, I heard screaming from behind the barn."

Gary rubbed his brow and stared at the dirt. He thought about the decals he'd left along the road last night. It was obvious he'd forgotten to pick them up. "Like I said, it was a movie trailer on my phone."

"Then why are you parked back here like you're hiding? I'm not buying the bull you're selling." As the man grabbed the doorhandle and stepped up on the running board, Gary jammed the knife into his back and shoved him to the ground.

Gary ran to the car that was still running, pulled it behind the barn, and killed the engine. He popped the trunk then walked to the man's side. After yanking the man's wallet from his pocket, Gary stuck it in his own then returned to the truck. He stormed into the back, ripped a piece of tape off the roll, and stretched it across Claire's mouth as she tried to bite and fight him off.

"Guess what, bitch. You're staying here with that dead guy. You're nothing but trouble, and I'm so sick of you I could kill you right here, right now, but instead, I'll let you starve to death and die on your own. You aren't worth the aggravation of taking along."

Seconds later, he was across the truck and cutting the zip ties that secured the new woman to the truck supports. He pulled her to her feet as she fought him with everything she had. "You're going to make this difficult. Aren't you?" A punch to the face silenced her temporarily, then he grabbed her bound arms and dragged her to the rear of the truck. After stepping back outside, Gary rounded the truck, opened the padlock and doors, and jerked her out. She fell three feet to the ground with a thud. She fought and flailed as he dragged her to the car's trunk, threw her in, and closed the lid. "There, one down, and one to go."

Gary grabbed the man by his legs and pulled him to the back, lifted him, and rolled him in. "See ya, Claire. Hope you have a nice, slow death." He slammed the rear doors and snapped the padlock closed. "There." Gary pulled the keys from the ignition and gathered what he needed from the truck's cab, then climbed into the driver's seat of the Accord and drove away. He chuckled to himself. "Nice wheels. Now I don't have to look over my shoulder for the rest of the trip."

Gary still had a two-hour drive ahead of him before he hit I-70, but once he was on it, he could make up time. He would get a grand for the woman, maybe a little less because he'd punched her and bloodied her face, but the money would easily hold him over for a week. He would swap out the car plates with another's, move on to a different state, and find a van to steal. A large vehicle wasn't necessary anymore since he would only be snatching and delivering two girls a week going forward.

Note to self—ask Charlie about getting that new identity too.

Chapter 46

Another twenty minutes passed. I'd already spoken with Taft and said we were taking a two-lane highway through the mountainous areas in hopes that it was the same route Gary had taken. She was fine with us continuing on to Central City and that Pete had given me three local names to drop into the database.

"The Wi-Fi and phone service is spotty in the area. It comes in and out."

"Give me the names, and I'll look them up," Taft said. "I'll get back to you when I know more."

I clicked off the call, and seconds later, when we rounded the next curve, we saw the squad cars parked on an overgrown driveway, but the only building there was a broken-down barn. As we passed, we didn't see a crashed car, or any other car for that matter.

"That's weird." I frowned and looked back out the right rear window as Renz was about to round the next curve. "Stop!" I didn't mean to yell that loud, and I was sure I nearly gave Renz a heart attack, but in looking back, I saw the rear side of the barn and what was sitting behind it. The view as we approached had been blocked by the squad cars. "It's the truck."

"What are you talking about?" Tommy wrinkled his brow as he looked over his shoulder.

"The box truck, Gary's truck. It's parked behind that barn! Turn around, Renz, hurry!"

Our heads snapped forward as Renz slammed on the brakes, made a Y-turn in the middle of the road, squealed the tires, and floored the gas pedal. We braced ourselves as he made a hard left into the driveway a quarter mile back, and as soon as the car came to a stop, we all leapt out, our badges already in hand.

"What's going on here?" Tommy yelled.

"I should ask you the same thing. Why is the FBI in this neck of the woods?"

Tommy pointed. "Looking for that truck, I think. It was reported to have a pizza-company logo on the side, but now that we can see it up close, it doesn't."

"Yeah, it did. There's a bunch of magnetic decals lying alongside the road, a dead unidentified man in the back, and a young lady, who the other deputy is cutting the restraints off of, also in the back. If you know what the hell this is about, we'd appreciate hearing the story."

"Only one lady?" I asked.

"Yes, ma'am."

I ran to the back of the truck and saw that a padlock had the doors secured and also that the taillight was broken. It was definitely the right truck. I jerked my chin toward the driver's-side door, and my colleagues climbed inside. In the box of the truck, we saw Claire being cared for by the deputy and an unidentified deceased man lying on the floor.

"Claire, where's Gary?"

"I don't know, but this man was banging on the truck door, and the next thing I know, Gary opened the back, punched the other woman in the face, took her out, and rolled this guy in. He obviously thought he'd killed him, but the guy lived long enough to dial 911. I couldn't do anything because I'm zip tied to this damn truck!"

I nodded at the deputy. "Can you help my guys get her and the dead man outside and into the daylight?"

"Yes, ma'am, not a problem."

Once Claire was sitting on a patch of weeds outside, I told the deputies to call for an ambulance to remove the dead man from the scene, then I began the round of questions. Claire, although banged up, was a fugitive, and she wasn't leaving our sight.

"What was that man's name?"

She shrugged. "I don't know, and I'm not saying another word without a lawyer. I've already said too much."

"You're a criminal, Claire, and you're impeding this investigation, which won't serve you well."

"You don't have a speck of proof that I've done anything wrong. I'm a victim!"

I shook my head and felt like adding to her injuries, yet even though she was a spoiled, entitled brat, I couldn't touch her or continue asking questions.

"I'd like to use a phone now to call my parents."

"Too bad. Phone service is sketchy out here, and you're

an adult in FBI custody. No amount of coddling your parents do can erase the charges you're facing."

"What does that mean? I was held hostage!"

I raised my hand to her face, walked away, and vowed not to give her one more second of my time. I approached Renz. "That brat lawyered up. I can't ask her any more questions to learn what the guy was driving or his name, if he even mentioned it before dying."

Renz put his hand on my shoulder. "Take a breath. We'll find out everything we need to know by going through his phone. We'll get the deputies up to speed and wait here until the ambulance takes away the dead man's body."

I kicked pebbles on that dusty driveway. "But we don't even know how much of a head start Gary has. Who knows how long after Gary took off was the man able to call for help? The guy may have passed out for a while, and Gary could be an hour or two ahead of us. Claire won't tell us a damn thing."

Tommy opened the trunk and pulled a pair of cuffs from his go bag. He walked to Claire, read the Miranda rights to her, and cuffed her. "Sit in the back seat, and don't move."

While grumbling, she did as she was told.

Fay called me over to the road while Tommy and Renz discussed the case we were working with the deputies.

"Take a look at this." She pointed to the magnetic decals lying where the gravel shoulder and the ditch met.

I rolled my eyes. "What an idiot. He didn't even try to hide them."

"No kidding, right? We'll need to take those along with us as evidence. I'll get gloves from my bag, then we can put these decals in the trunk."

A half hour later, and with the man's body loaded in the ambulance, we exchanged contact info with the deputies and continued on. We'd arranged for the box truck to be flat-bedded to Salt Lake, where the nearest state crime lab evidence garage was located. The local FBI office would handle the search of that vehicle and pass on the information to us.

"That was a significant find." Fay looked at Claire, who was wedged between Fay and me, then shook her head.

We couldn't talk freely with an uncooperative suspect sitting with us. Tommy looked over his shoulder then back at Renz. "You need to pull over for a minute so I can get out, call Maureen, and update her. Like Fay said, this is significant news, and we need to end the BOLO for the truck and set up a new one as soon as we find out what kind of vehicle that man was driving."

Renz pulled off to the shoulder, and Tommy got out. He walked to an open area fifty feet away—likely to keep Claire from hearing the conversation and possibly to get better cell service.

I doubted Gary would be using an abundance of caution anymore. I was pretty sure he thought the man was dead and hadn't felt a need to scoop up his cell phone and take it with him. That would be a costly mistake on Gary's part as soon as we found out who the man was and what kind of car he owned.

Renz grabbed the phone from the bag he'd put it in and

opened the car door. "Jade, come with me and bring your notepad and a pen. There's no time like the present to get this taken care of."

"You bet." I gave Fay a look. "You okay alone with her?"

Fay nodded. "She's cuffed and won't be a problem."

I joined Renz along that same ridge where Tommy was talking with Taft.

"Let's see what we can do with this phone." Renz turned to block the sun's glare on the screen. He pressed the button on the side to wake up the home screen. "Shit. It's password protected. I had a feeling this wasn't going to be easy."

"Now what?"

"Now everything depends on where Gary's headed and who he's going to meet there."

I walked to Tommy's side. "Ask Taft if she's found out anything on those names. We need to know Gary's final destination."

Chapter 47

Gary had the phone set to Speaker as he talked to Charlie. "Hey, man, I should be there in about five hours. Should I come directly to the ranch?"

"How much merchandise do you have?"

"Just one girl. I left Claire behind. She was too much of a pain in my ass, and I couldn't deal with her for another second. I got rid of the truck, it was too big for my needs going forward."

"Yeah, why's that?"

Gary groaned. "Claire offed Leon."

"What the hell, dude? It sounds like your enterprise is going off the rails. I think it's time to go our separate ways."

Panic took over Gary's mind. "No, no, no. Hear me out, Charlie. This way is much better. Sure, I won't have a large delivery every week, but you have other runners besides me anyway. I can easily guarantee two girls weekly, and there won't be any bitch drama. I'll be working alone, no loose ends, and no other people who can screw things up. I'll be so under the radar that I won't even be a blip."

"You better hope so. What are you driving?"

"A newer charcoal-gray Accord."

"Fine. Call me again when you get to Central City. I'll tell you where to go then."

After ending the call, Gary sucked in a deep breath. Everything would be okay—he felt it inside. He would have a new identity before long, earn a couple grand a week, and be satisfied with that.

Don't forget what Willis said. No need to be greedy and take stupid chances. I'll find a town to settle into within a few hours of Central City, get a nice apartment with a garage, and buy myself a cool car. Soon, everything is going to be perfect. I've seen the last of the idiots from my past. No more Claire, Hope, or Leon. No more screwups, and no more prison cells in my future.

He settled back, tapped the cruise control, and set the GPS on his phone to guide the way.

Chapter 48

Renz handed the cell phone to Tommy. "Maybe Tech can track down something for us by using the brand and the serial number on this phone. It's all we have right now."

Tommy tipped his head. "It's worth a try. I'll read it off to Taft, and she can pass it on." Tommy gave Maureen the information from the phone and ended the call.

"So what has she found out about the three names Pete gave me?" I asked.

"The only one who had a prior police jacket was Charles, aka, Charlie Dunn. The other two are just run-of-the-mill weirdos, I guess."

Renz rubbed his brow. "So, what and when were his offenses?"

"Drug sales and distribution across state lines, but that was fifteen years ago. He served two years behind bars and hasn't been on anyone's radar since. Now that weed is legal in Colorado, nobody has paid any attention to him in years."

"I think it's time to see what he's been up to. We need eyes on, or a drone above, his place. Going from selling and distributing dope across state lines to doing the same with human beings isn't that much of a stretch. Do we know the size of his property?" I asked.

Tommy huffed. "Big… he has seventy acres about five miles outside Central City."

I pulled my phone from my pocket and tapped out a text.

"What was that?" Renz asked.

"Pete and Ted are hunters. I bet they can scout around Mr. Dunn's property without being seen, maybe take a few pictures of the buildings at least."

Renz let out a long groan. "We can't get civilians that involved, Jade. It's too dangerous."

I grinned. "They're just two guys scouting out hunting locations. Maybe they'll accidently see something fishy going on, or maybe they won't want to hunt"—I air quoted the word *hunt*—"at all. I'll see what Pete says when he texts me back."

Tommy looked from me to Renz. "Okay, are we ready to head back out?"

"One more question," I said.

"Yep."

"What are we supposed to do with Ms. Entitled?"

"Taft said to have the Gilpin County Sheriff's Office toss her in a jail cell for the time being so we don't have to deal with her. We'll call them when we get closer. We still have a long way to go."

We returned to the car, that time with Tommy behind the wheel, and continued on.

"I'm hungry, and I have to pee," Claire said.

"You'll have to wait until we reach Rangely. It isn't like there's a McDonald's out here. Pee alongside the car, and eat some pine needles or wait for a half hour. I imagine we'll need gas by then anyway." I wasn't about to have a twenty-one-year-old criminal tell me what to do, and it was doubtful that my colleagues would either. She would have to wait.

We exited Bonanza Highway and took Stanton Road east into Colorado then merged onto Highway 64. Minutes later, Tommy turned in at the first gas station and pulled up to a pump. As Tommy filled the tank, Fay and I escorted Claire into the building and to the ladies' room. After walking out, I bought her a premade turkey bacon sandwich, a bag of corn chips, and a soda. I grabbed sandwiches for all of us and went to the cashier to pay while Fay took Claire back to the car.

We were on the road again ten minutes later with four and a half hours still to go. I ate my sandwich then rested my head against the window. I felt myself begin to drift off, but my vibrating cell phone brought me back to consciousness. After pulling it out, I saw the text was from Pete. I was wide awake and alert as I read it. He said that he and Ted would check out the Dunn ranch from the road to see if there was any way of getting close enough to view the buildings. He didn't know if the ranch was fenced or not, but that would also factor in if it wasn't. They could claim they were hunting and had no idea where the property lines were, especially if nothing was posted.

I shot off a reply, said we would be there in four hours, and told him to be extremely careful. I didn't want anyone to be in harm's way. Before sending the message, I told him to text me back with their findings.

Since we were sitting shoulder to shoulder, Claire was watching my every move. It was unavoidable. What she couldn't see was who the text was from or how I responded to it. She had made it perfectly clear that she wasn't telling us anything without a lawyer, but if she happened to say something on her own without me asking, then that was perfectly legal. I felt it was worth a try.

I dropped my phone back in my pocket. "Humph."

Renz took the bait. "Humph, what?"

"Pete just texted me."

"Yeah, what did he say?"

"That local law enforcement and FBI agents out of Denver are moving in on a resident who lives five miles outside Central City. His name is Charlie Dunn."

Claire's body stiffened like a lightning bolt had struck her. "What?"

I looked at her and frowned. "What's wrong, Claire? Do you know Charlie Dunn, and why would you?"

She stared at her cuffed hands and didn't utter another word, but that one word she'd said spoke volumes. That was my "gotcha" moment, and I enjoyed every bit of it.

Tommy pulled off the road at his first opportunity. He shifted into Park, wagged his finger at me, and asked me to join him outside. I obliged. We stood a good thirty feet away with our backs turned toward the car.

"Let me see Pete's text."

I handed him my phone. "He and Ted are going to put eyeballs on the Dunn property. It's better not to get law enforcement involved yet since we need Gary too. I'm sure none of the kidnappers talk to Charlie until it's time to drop off the girls, for safety's sake. If Charlie was already in custody and didn't answer when Gary called, we could lose Gary for good."

"True, but we need Mr. Dunn in custody as soon as possible. We can set up a trap right at Charlie's compound, and by the way, that was a brilliant move on your part. You got Claire to confirm that Charlie is the man we're looking for just by that one simple word. Way to go, Monroe."

I grinned when Tommy patted my shoulder. "Now what? We need law enforcement to get there and take Dunn and whoever works with him by surprise and into custody before Gary arrives."

Tommy glanced at his watch. "Damn Claire. If only we knew how much of a head start Gary had."

"Let's figure two hours max. That still gives the sheriff's office time to move in on them."

Tommy rubbed his forehead. "I know, but takedowns like that usually involve planning and a good amount of reconnaissance."

I shrugged. "You're a senior agent. Get Maureen's opinion, but the longer we stand here, the closer Gary gets to Central City."

"You're right, plus Taft can get people to move in quickly with her connections. I'm sure the Denver FBI has access to choppers. They can have a dozen agents in Central City in less than a half hour. Let me call Maureen quick then alert the Gilpin County Sheriff's Office. A group effort will be our best chance to capture not only Gary but the local trafficking ring too."

"And rescue Melanie in the process," I said.

"Right."

I climbed into the back seat while Tommy made the call. He gave us a thumbs-up when he returned to the car ten minutes later. I let out a silent sigh of relief and knew the local trafficking ring, as well as Gary and Claire, would be behind bars that very day.

I fired off a text to Pete to let him know the Feds were on their way. He replied with photos of outbuildings and six animal trailers, yet not a single cow or horse was seen anywhere on the property. He said what they saw through their rifle scopes was that the only fenced area was around the perimeter of the house and outbuildings. That in itself was a lot of help. I thanked him and said they should retreat. I would find him later to thank him in person. As soon as I sent that text, I forwarded Pete's text to Maureen. The more information they had going in, the better.

All we could do was continue east and get there when we got there. We wouldn't be part of the takedown, even as much as I wished we were, but getting those criminals in custody as soon as possible was far more important. We would likely receive updates from Maureen or the FBI team on the ground as the day progressed. I couldn't wait to be eye to eye with Gary Rhodes or to deliver Claire to the local officials, which would probably be the Denver FBI.

Twenty minutes later I received a text from Maureen saying the FBI's Child Exploitation and Human Trafficking Task Force was en route and coordinating with the Gilpin County Sheriff, Cal Dorfman, and his deputies. They would have feet on the ground any second and would be at the Dunn ranch in fifteen minutes. Taft had passed the details and photos from Pete's text onto the task force, and they'd said they appreciated the up-close surveillance. Maureen said the agent in charge of the task force was a fifteen-year veteran of the FBI named Matt Weston, and he would be our contact person going forward until Charlie Dunn and his associates were all in custody.

Chapter 49

The Dunn property was surrounded, and through binos, Matt Weston and his team had eyes on several people walking back and forth between the outbuildings and the animal trailers. They watched as one man opened the sliding barn-styled door of one building while another attached a horse trailer to the hitch on a truck and backed it into the building.

"Looks like they're ready to load one trailer for sure, maybe more." Matt adjusted the right diopter ring on his binoculars to get sharp focus of the man's face who had just climbed into the truck. He glanced at the photo of Charles Dunn on his phone, and the faces were a match. "We need to get eyes inside that building to see what they're loading. Pearson and Tyler, move in closer and find out what's going on. You see one female being loaded in that trailer, and it's go time. We'll rush them, secure that building, then move in on the house. Sheriff Dorfman?"

"I'm here, Agent Weston."

"On my go, you and your men will move on that second outbuilding and secure it."

"Got it."

"Pearson, let me know what you guys see the second you reach the building."

"Roger that."

Weston watched as the two agents scurried around trees and boulders as they closed in. They finally reached the rear of the building, where Matt lost visual of them. He waited for something to come across his radio and into his earpiece. Finally, whispers of what they were witnessing came into his ear. His men had eyes on the inside, and they saw at least seven females who were cuffed and blindfolded being taken out of horse stalls and led to the trailer. That was all he needed to hear. Through the radio, Matt told the rest of his men to rush the building, secure it and the men inside, then head to the house. He called out to the sheriff to have his deputies take the second outbuilding. Matt's radio squawked seconds later.

"Boss, we have Dunn and the other guy disarmed and cuffed to the support beams in the first building. Tyler will stay behind with them. I'm ready to move in on the house."

"Stay put until we reach you. We're heading that way. We'll move on the house together, surround it, then breach every door at the same time. Give us three minutes to get to the building you're in."

"Copy that."

With hand signals, Matt alerted half his men to move to the outbuilding the deputies were clearing. They needed that barn to be completely secure as well before continuing to the house. With that done, and only finding two trucks inside, they all gathered behind the first building.

Matt addressed three of his men and two of the deputies.

"Split up at the rear and the left side of the house. The rest of us will take the front and opposite side. Stay below the windows since they may have men looking out. On my go, we'll breach the doors, with my men leading the way. Secure every person inside with cuffs. I don't care if they're men, women, or teenagers. Until we find out who everyone is, they're all going to be restrained. Any questions?"

The two teams said they were ready to go. They moved ahead until everyone was in place.

Through his radio, Matt counted down from three to one then yelled, "Go!"

They kicked in the doors, guns drawn, and ordered people to the ground. In total, they had three more men and two women in custody. The women said they were hired help, but that would be confirmed later, and if they were aware of the crimes being committed, they would be held accountable too.

Matt high-fived everyone who helped in that successful takedown. Not a single bullet had to be fired, and taking the criminals by surprise had worked like a charm. He needed to address Charlie Dunn and find out when Gary Rhodes was expected to show up.

Matt and his men entered the building where Charlie and his gopher were cuffed to the beams. Sheriff Dorfman was addressing the people in the house and had called for a bus to take them to the county jail, where they would all be interrogated. The Feds would take it from there, and the people involved would be charged with kidnapping and human trafficking.

The girls had been moved to a different building for the time being. EMTs were called in from the fire department, and every girl would be checked for injuries and dehydration.

Matt jerked his head at Tyler then walked to the horse trailer. He held his gun on Charlie the entire time. "Bring Mr. Hotshit over here. I need a word with him."

Tyler removed Charlie's cuffs just long enough to allow him to walk that thirty-foot distance to the horse trailer.

"Sit your ass down, Mr. Dunn."

Cursing under his breath, Charlie dropped to the floor of the trailer and sat.

"Cuff him again, Mike. Dirtbags like him aren't to be trusted—ever." Matt checked the time. It was pushing four o'clock. Gary Rhodes had to be close. "We need information, Charlie, and we need it now."

"Go to hell, pig."

"I'm not a pig. I'm a federal agent, and I can make life really bad for you. I have the ability to influence where you end up serving your life sentence. It can be in a normal prison, where people don't get shanked daily or in a sweet place like USP ADX Florence. Hell, that's right here in Colorado, so suggesting it will be an easy pitch to a judge. I'll definitely make sure you and your pals end up in gen pop too. One of you will likely get the crap beat out of you on day one—like a frat boy initiation, you know?" Matt smiled and waited for a response.

Charlie growled. "Fine, what do you want to know?"

"When are you expecting Gary Rhodes to show up, and what is he driving?"

Charlie shrugged. "I don't know what time it is."

"It's four o'clock."

"Then he should arrive at the usual place in the next few minutes. I'll make the call and tell him where we'll meet."

"Has he ever come directly to the ranch?"

Charlie nodded. "Yeah, once."

"Where is the usual place, and what is he driving?"

"He'll wait outside the Gold Nugget Café in town, and he said he's driving a charcoal-gray Accord."

Matt tipped his head at one of his guys. "I guess you won't mind if we take the blue truck from the other building into town so we can put eyeballs on him."

"Why don't you just pick him up there?"

"We need to catch him in the act of selling a female to you. That means you're going to accept the sale and give him the cash. You vary from your role, and you'll have hell to pay. Got it?"

Charlie glared at Matt.

"I asked if you understood the instructions."

"Yeah."

"Good. Now, where are the keys for that truck?"

Charlie tipped his head to the right. "In that cabinet. It'll be the keyring with the happy face on it."

Matt laughed out loud. "You just can't make up this shit. Pearson and Tyler, go together and call me the minute you have eyes on that vehicle."

"Roger that, Boss."

Matt took a seat across from Charlie and stared him down. "Now we wait."

Chapter 50

We were a half hour west of Central City and hadn't heard anything yet. I fidgeted with anxiety. I wanted everything to go according to plan yet my phone remained as silent as a rock. I'd checked it a half dozen times to make sure I hadn't missed a text or accidently turned it off. It was fine, but I wasn't.

Gary had to be in Central City by then, but I could be wrong.

What if my entire gut feeling of him going there was off?

Just because Pete and Ted saw animal trailers at Charlie's ranch, yet not a single animal other than a possible cat, didn't mean that was the drop-off and pick-up spot for girls bought and sold in human trafficking.

My self-doubt was increasing—then my cell buzzed.

I let out a sigh of relief, but I didn't want to get ahead of myself. I had to read the text first. I pulled the phone from my pocket, tapped the message icon, and read what was sent. It wasn't long, but it was to the point and told me exactly what I needed to know. The message came from Matt Weston, the task force leader, and he said the takedown had been a success. They found a half dozen captive girls and as many men who were holding them as merchandise for sale at the ranch. Charlie was in custody, and they were still waiting for Gary to arrive. Matt said his men were in position outside the Gold Nugget Café, where Gary was waiting in his car for instructions.

"Wow."

"Is that a good wow?" Renz asked.

"Almost. Another half hour, tops, and I'd say it'll be a super-good wow."

Claire huffed her obvious disgust for us. "Do FBI agents always talk in code?"

I gave her my best glare. "Only when we're babysitting criminals." I returned a simple thumbs-up text. I would have plenty of time to spend with the agents, the sheriff, and his deputies once we arrived at the ranch.

Chapter 51

"What's the word?" Matt asked. "Is he there or not?"

"That's affirmative, sir."

"Good. I'm going to have Charlie call him now, then you should see him pull out shortly." Matt hung up, handed Charlie his own phone, and told him to make the call. "You go off script for one second, and your life as a man's man will end as soon as you pass through the prison gates at Florence."

Charlie sneered. "What the hell is that supposed to mean?"

Matt cocked his head and smiled. "What do you think? Maybe you should let that image rattle around in your brain for a minute. Now, call Gary, and tell him to come here. That's all you need to say then hang up."

Charlie did as he was told, kept the conversation short, got to the point, then clicked off the call. Matt took the phone away from him and addressed a member of the task force. "Put this safely in an evidence bag, and don't let it out of your sight." He turned back to Charlie. "How long is the drive from that café to the ranch?"

"Ten minutes, tops."

"Okay. Pay close attention because this is what you're going to do. Curt will be standing outside with you when Gary arrives, just in case you try something stupid. There will be seven guns aimed at your center mass, again, just in case you do something stupid. That's when you're going to exchange cash for the woman. Curt will escort her back to the building. You'll tell Gary to get you more girls next week, then you'll walk away. We'll take over after that. Any questions?"

"Yeah. How'd you figure this out?"

"That's not your concern. We aren't buddies, and you don't need to know how we operate."

Matt walked away to call Pearson again for an update. Gary should have headed for the ranch as soon as Charlie ended that phone call, and Matt wanted confirmation that Tyler and Pearson were following him.

The phone rang in Matt's ear more times than it should have, and Tyler finally picked up.

"Why are you answering Pearson's phone?"

"That son of a bitch made us somehow and is barreling down dirt roads that lead to who knows where. We don't have any idea where we're going, and we can't do a pit maneuver on his car with a hostage inside."

"Damn it. You can't lose him, Tyler. Are there any road signs or markers nearby?"

"No, but it wouldn't matter anyway. We're going eighty miles an hour, and we can't keep up. He's going to crash that damn car if we stay in pursuit. These dirt roads are slick as hell."

"Stay on him. I'll get the sheriff's office involved since they know the area. It's going to be dark in an hour, then you'll lose him for sure. I want an update every five minutes." Matt yelled out orders to get everyone who was still present, including Charlie, to the Gilpin County jail. He didn't have time to focus on the ranch at the moment. They needed to capture Gary, and they needed to do it before the sun set. Matt called Jade's number. Back-and-forth texts would take too long.

She answered immediately. "Agent Weston?"

"Agent Monroe. There wasn't time to text you again. It seems Gary spotted my men, and now they're in a pursuit up and down dirt roads with no idea where they are. I need you to drop off your detainee at the sheriff's office right away—the deputies have taken most of the people from the ranch there already—then we need your crew to help us capture Mr. Rhodes. I'll text you my two task force agents' numbers so you can be in direct communication with them. We need to scoop up Gary before we lose the light."

"On it, sir. We'll get rid of Claire right now, then I'll call Agent Tyler to see if they can give us some idea of where they are."

"My agents are in a blue pickup, and Gary is driving a late-model charcoal-gray Accord."

"Got it."

Matt clicked off the call and turned to Sheriff Dorfman. "How many deputies can you spare, Cal? We need everyone on board to reel in this kidnapper, and you guys know the area best."

"I can spare six men. The rest are processing everyone we just hauled in."

"Six is better than none. Apparently, Gary realized he was being followed about a mile out of town, then he floored it. My guys are on a wild-goose chase with him on dirt roads, and they have no idea where they are."

"How about using that chopper you came in on? Your pilot is sitting here, doing nothing."

"Absolutely. Get him up and circling a five-mile area between town and the ranch. We need to stop Rhodes before that woman gets hurt."

Chapter 52

I clicked off the call. "Tommy, head for the sheriff's office now. We need to drop off Claire."

She jerked and bucked between Fay and me. "No! I want my mom and dad."

"Stop it right now! We follow the law, and you're going to sit behind jail bars until we get this situation under control. You'll get one call when the sheriff's office has time to deal with you. Right now, they're kind of busy, so you'll just have to wait your turn."

Tommy squealed to a stop in front of the sheriff's office several miles north of Blackhawk, a town just east of Central City. Fay and I took the crying Claire inside and told them to process her with the rest of the people from the raid on the Charlie Dunn ranch, that she was one of the kidnappers, needed to be locked up, and we would address her later.

We bolted from the building and dove back into the car. I called the number Matt had texted me. Agent Tyler picked up. I explained who I was and asked if they had the slightest clue where they were. The only thing he could tell me was that they had passed the Central City Cemetery on their right about ten minutes earlier. Since I didn't know north from south in that area, it didn't help me guide Tommy in the right direction. I made an urgent call to Pete.

"Pete, it's Agent Monroe. We've got a big problem, and you know this area like the back of your hand. We have agents hot on the rear bumper of a fugitive, but they don't know where they are. The last landmark one of the agents said they passed was the cemetery, and he said it was on his right."

"That means he's going north on Upper Apex Road. There's a half dozen roads that turn off that one though. How long ago did he say they passed it?"

"Ten minutes ago."

"Damn, it's tough to say which way they're going now. I live two miles north of the cemetery though, and I can be in that area within minutes. What are we looking for?"

"A dark-gray Accord being chased by a blue pickup." I saw a text alert come in and read it while Pete was talking. "Pete, I just got a text saying the FBI chopper just left the sheriff's office five minutes ago."

"Good, have them tell the pilot to head due west. That should get them in the right area. Apex Valley Road goes east off Upper Apex Road and intersects with 119. That's the best place to block the road. I'll take off now, head that way, and let you know if I spot them."

"Thanks." I clicked off the call, texted Matt, told him where to send the pilot, then told Tommy where to go. "Take 119 south. It's the fastest way to get to the general area, otherwise, we'd have to backtrack through Central

City. We need to block the intersection of Highway 119 and Apex Valley Road in case he's heading that way."

"On it."

I leaned forward between the seats as Tommy sped down the highway. "Hurry, Tommy. The intersection is about four miles southwest of here. If we get there first, it'll block Gary's route if he actually goes that way."

Tommy barreled down the road as fast as he safely could while Renz and I updated everyone about the general area Gary was in. Another text had come in from Pete saying he saw a blue truck about a half mile ahead on North Clear Creek Road and that it had just turned right onto Silver Creek Road. The chopper could block Gary's car if he landed where Silver Creek and Road 15A intersected. He would be trapped with no road to turn onto. I passed that text onto Matt as we sped on. Another text from Pete hit my phone.

"Damn it! He said to turn north on Missouri Gulch Road. We can block Gary in right there if the chopper doesn't find the right road in time."

Tommy cranked the steering wheel right, and the tires squealed. He pressed the gas to the floor, and the SUV lurched ahead.

My phone rang. That time Tyler was calling.

"Agent Monroe, I think we have him heading east on Silver Creek Road."

"Yep, and we're heading north on Missouri Gulch. Road 15A is between us. We can block him in if we or the chopper get there in time. I have a local friend directing us."

"I see the chopper above us. I think this will work if you can get to Road 15A before he does."

I tapped Tommy's shoulder. "Faster. Tyler thinks we can get to Road 15A before Gary does if we speed up." I glanced at the speedometer—Tommy was going seventy five already.

I looked out the window when I heard the chopper above us. The squeeze play was going to work. Tommy made a hard left onto Road 15A, and we saw a car barreling toward us. The chopper zoomed over our heads and hovered right in front of the gray Accord. Gary had no place to go—he was trapped.

The Accord came to an abrupt stop, and the driver's-side door flew open.

"No! Son of a bitch, he's going to make a run for it into the tree cover."

We sped up, got nose to nose with the Accord, and leapt out of the SUV. The chopper took to the sky and tried to find him as he scurried through the trees.

Tommy yelled out to Fay to check the car for Melanie. Renz, Tommy, and I dove into the woods, likely several hundred feet behind Gary. I pictured myself as the fastest runner, so I yelled out that I was going to get around him and push him toward the guys. Seconds later, I heard yelling from behind. Tyler and Pearson had arrived. We would box Gary in if we could. I plowed through the trees and undergrowth as I moved along at a good clip.

Seconds later, I saw movement ahead. I prayed that it was Gary and not a wild animal, then I saw him. Between the trees, a flash of color caught my eye. He wore a red T-shirt and a tan hoodie. I stepped up my pace cautiously, not wanting to be in his direct line of fire in case he was armed.

Finally, I was parallel to Gary, and with another quick push ahead, I would be in front of him and would have the ability to catch him off guard. He hadn't seen me, and he appeared to be watching the approaching agents at his back. At last, I was a hundred feet ahead of him and found a giant pine to stand behind with a clear view of him heading my way. With my gun drawn, I waited until the perfect moment to spring out. I heard twigs snap with every step as he moved closer to me. I was ready and bolted out from behind the tree.

"Gary Rhodes, get down on your knees, now!" The business end of my Glock was pointed directly at his chest. I could see he was weighing his options. "Don't do anything stupid, or you'll die trying. Now get on the ground with your hands behind your head!"

He knelt then lunged at my legs, knocking me backward.

"You son of a bitch." I scrambled to my feet and tackled him before he had a chance to find my weapon in the ground cover.

Renz and Tommy were on him in a flash, and who I assumed to be Tyler and Pearson were right behind them. Renz cuffed Gary's hands then jerked him to his feet as he read him his Miranda rights.

"We finally have you back where you belong—in custody. Take a good look around, Gary, since this will be the last time you see wide-open spaces. Your forever home, as I'm sure you recall, is going to be a six-by-eight-foot cell." Renz gave him a shove toward the road. "Now, get moving."

I picked leaves out of my hair as we walked back to the road. Fay stood at the trunk of the Accord and removed Melanie's bindings. Although Melanie looked rattled and had a few scrapes, she appeared uninjured. To my right, I saw Pete leaning against his truck.

He grinned. "Looks like you got your man, Agent Monroe."

I walked up to him and shook his hand. "I couldn't have done it without you, Pete. You have no idea how much you've helped us, and I truly appreciate it."

He swatted the air. "No biggie."

"Um, yes it is. I owe you."

He grinned again. "Okay, then how about you folks meet me and Ted at the Gold Nugget for coffee and doughnuts tomorrow morning? Say like nine o'clock? They really do have the best food in town."

"It's a deal, but for now, we need to have that woman checked for injuries and notify her husband that she's safe." With a nod of gratitude to Pete, I crossed the road to Melanie, pulled my phone from my pocket, and handed it to her.

Chapter 53

We were back at the ranch by seven o'clock. Charlie's home was not only the holding area for victims of human trafficking. The task force was sure his computer held a wealth of information as far as names of every kidnapper, the buyers' names, prices girls were sold for, and where the girls went. It would take time to track down people up and down the chain of command and involvement, but it would get done, and we would get those criminals off the streets across the nation, one disgusting cell at a time.

I crossed the building to Matt. "Nice work, Agent Weston."

He let out what looked to be a happy sigh. "Likewise. Your entire team was awesome, and nothing would have gotten accomplished without the team effort."

"Or the help of a local friend."

Matt nodded. "I heard about him."

"Why don't you join us tomorrow morning at the Gold Nugget Café? You can personally thank Pete and his best friend Ted. They were both instrumental in this case right out of the gate."

"I think I'll take you up on that. We aren't leaving the area until all the criminals are interviewed. We'll need our bus to come in from Denver and transport those perps to the federal lockup until their court dates."

"Where are the girls that were found here? I'd like to check on them."

"We took them to the building directly behind this one when the EMTs arrived. Each one needed to be checked out and assessed for injuries. They'll all get their opportunity to speak with us and to call loved ones soon."

"Thank God. Okay, I'm going to see how they're doing."

I excused myself and waved Fay over to join me, and we headed to the building to our south.

Inside, we saw a group of girls sitting together on the floor with two deputies watching over them. We would have to decide where they would sleep that night and how the interviews would take place. We would likely conduct them right there since the sheriff's office was already bursting at the seams with cops and criminals.

"Holy shit!" I cupped my hand to my mouth and whispered to Fay. "Go back to the other building, and get Renz and Tommy. Hurry!"

Minutes later, the three of them met up with me in the building's doorway.

"What's going on?" Renz asked.

"Look at the group of girls in there. The second one on the left is Hope. Apparently, she hasn't been sold off yet. She needs to be taken into custody, and I sure as heck don't mean protective custody."

"You're positive that's her?" Tommy asked.

I pulled her picture up on my phone. "What do you think?"

"It's her. Guess there's no time like the present." He jerked his head, and the four of us approached her.

"Hope Daniels?"

She instinctively looked up.

"You're under arrest for murder, kidnapping, and trafficking underaged girls across state lines. Stand up, and put your hands behind your back," I said.

"But I'm a vic—"

"Victim? Hardly. Get on your feet right now."

She stood and began sobbing. She was so much like Claire it was ridiculous. I cuffed her and asked one of the deputies to take her to their station, then told him she was part of the human trafficking ring and was under arrest. I didn't want to spend another second listening to her whining for sympathy.

We listened to each girl as, one by one, they told us the heart-wrenching stories of how they'd been abducted and what had happened to them since.

It was after eleven p.m. by the time we'd finished the interviews and documented every name, age, home location, and story the girls told us. It turned out that all of them in that group, other than Hope, had been sold to Charlie by other kidnappers. The ring was likely much larger than we had thought, but with the evidence in the house, on the computers, and with the statements from the girls, we would get warrants out for them all and bring them to justice. I was sure taking that ring down would only be a blip in the enormous industry of human trafficking. The thought of it saddened me because I knew the statistics, and they were overwhelming. What saddened me even more was that none of those girls were Tracy Bast or Jillian Nance, and I didn't know if we would ever find them.

We began the process of contacting families and gave each girl several minutes to speak with their loved ones before moving on to the next. The families would be allowed to pick up the girls that next day, after noon, at the ranch. We would designate an area where we would speak with each family first then reunite them with their loved one and wish them well. I imagined we would be in the area for another full day before we would leave everything and everyone in the capable hands of the Denver FBI task force team.

"I guess we should call Hope's and Claire's parents and tell them we have the girls in custody and where they are. It'll be their only chance to see them before Hope and Claire are processed into the jail system in Denver and locked up while they await their arraignments." I found a quiet place to sit down and made the calls.

It was two a.m. by the time I dropped down into the welcoming bed of the hotel room Tory had booked for me. I was sure my colleagues were equally exhausted and probably climbing into their hotel room beds too. Tomorrow would be a busy day, then we would head back to Rapid City, board our jet, and fly home. It had taken a week of chasing Gary and Leon through multiple states in order to solve that case and arrest the people involved, but it was well worth it. Unfortunately, victims had died in the process, but every criminal would face murder charges for those crimes, whether their actual hand was on the victim or not. They would all be held accountable.

Just before I turned off the light, I fired off a text to Amber, apologized for the late hour, and told her only that I would be coming home in the next day or so and asked if she'd ever made homemade doughnuts. I knew that was just enough of a taunt to whip her into action. With a grin, I sent off the text and turned off the light.

Chapter 54

We gathered around the longest table the Gold Nugget Café had. Plenty of us were in attendance that morning, and we had plenty of reasons to celebrate. That particular human trafficking ring had been dismantled. The culprits would all go to prison, likely for life, with or without the chance of parole—but that would be up to a jury to decide, when the time came.

Matt brought along Tyler, Pearson, and their pilot, who were all instrumental in capturing Gary and rescuing Melanie. Renz, Tommy, Fay, and myself were there, along with Sheriff Dorfman, Pete, and Ted.

I couldn't be happier to get better acquainted with our new allies and enjoy the café's signature assortment of doughnuts, Danish, and crullers. The carafes of coffee were constantly refilled, and their coffee as well as the breakfast treats were delicious.

We spent that hour getting to know each other and keeping the conversation light. We would resume our FBI personalities once we returned to the sheriff's office to wrap up our part, fill out paperwork, and review the charges brought against Gary, Claire, and Hope. With Leon deceased, we couldn't do anything about his participation in the crimes. The other three would carry the weight of the charges against them—and there were plenty.

We parted ways with Pete and Ted at a few minutes after ten. Hugs, handshakes, and contact cards were passed among us.

Back at the sheriff's office, I was shocked to see Diane and Mike Daniels as well as Laura and Adam Usher. Hope's and Claire's parents were sitting in the lobby, waiting for us to show up. They leapt to their feet when we entered.

Diane huffed and tipped her wrist. "It's about time. We've been sitting here since eight thirty."

I wrinkled my brow, already irritated by her behavior. "Excuse me?"

"Where's Hope?"

"In lockup."

"Oh my God!"

Laura crowded in and took her turn. "And Claire?"

"The same. Let's go find a room where we can talk."

We were led to an unused conference room, and we all took seats.

Diane began again. "When can we take Hope home? I'm sure she's traumatized."

Renz immediately shut her down. "It's apparent you don't understand that your daughter"—he looked at the Ushers too—"both your daughters, are criminals."

"Hope is a victim of horrible violence against her."

"No she isn't. Hope is a kidnapper, a human trafficker,

and a murderer, and she will be charged as such. Claire will be charged with the same offenses, and neither of them will see the light of day for many years. That goes for Gary Rhodes too."

Mike Daniels shouted, "You can't—"

Tommy raised his hand in Mike's face. "We absolutely can and did. Your coddling not only created spoiled brats but criminals who thought the law didn't pertain to them. This was your wakeup call, but it's too late to do anything about it. Your daughters will remain in the custody of federal agents and locked up in the jail facility in Denver until their day in court. They weren't out on a cross-country joyride with Gary and Leon, for God's sake. As a matter of fact, Claire murdered Leon in cold blood, and she will be held accountable. You can see your daughters for ten minutes, then they're going to board the federal prison bus along with the other criminals involved in these crimes and sit in the Denver jail until their arraignment. I'd suggest you accept their fate, spend the next few minutes telling them that you love them, then go home. There's nothing else you can do since both girls are legal adults. You'll be notified of their court dates when they come up."

I stood. "We'll take you to separate interview rooms and bring the girls in so you can talk to them. That'll be the only time you'll see them until their court date, and that's only if you sign up for notifications. Ready?"

They walked with us down the hallway, where a deputy showed Hope's parents to one room and Claire's to another.

"They get ten minutes with the girls, and that's it. Agent

Weston is getting the transport bus ready as we speak."

We left them there and joined Sheriff Dorfman and members of the task force to finish our paperwork.

It was early afternoon by the time we were ready to leave Colorado in our rearview mirror. We said our goodbyes for the time being but not forever. We'd made new friends and colleagues in law enforcement, and they would be relationships we would always appreciate. I loved that state and vowed to return during one of the vacation weeks I actually took advantage of. I promised to stop and visit with them all the next time I was there, whether it be for work or play.

We had a long drive ahead of us and wouldn't arrive in Rapid City until nearly ten that night, where we would board our jet, take to the sky, and land in Milwaukee around midnight.

Tomorrow was Monday and a new work week would begin. Where it would take us, we didn't know, but I'd enjoyed and appreciated the new experience of working side by side with Fay and Tommy.

As we settled into the car and drove away, I checked my phone for calls and texts and saw that I'd missed a text from Amber. I laughed out loud when I read it.

Renz looked over his shoulder. "You can't laugh without telling us why."

I grinned. "It's a reply from Amber. I asked her last night if she knew how to make homemade doughnuts."

"And?"

"And she said she could rival anybody's 'best' recipe, even the Gold Nugget Café's."

"Guess you'll have to make her live up to that challenge since we all know how good the cafés doughnuts are," Tommy teased. "Just make sure you tell her to make a quadruple recipe since it'll be all four of us who'll be judging her work."

THE END

Thank you!

Thanks for reading *Blood Trail*, the second book in the FBI Agent Jade Monroe Live or Die Series. I hope you enjoyed it!

Find all my books leading up to this series at http://cmsutter.com.

Stay abreast of my new releases by signing up for my VIP email list at: http://cmsutter.com/newsletter/.

You'll be one of the first to get a glimpse of the cover reveals and release dates, and you'll have a chance at exciting raffles offered with each new release.

Posting a review will help other readers find my books. I appreciate every review, whether positive or negative, and if you have a second to spare, a review is truly appreciated.

Find me on Facebook at https://www.facebook.com/cmsutterauthor/.

Made in United States
Orlando, FL
01 May 2022

17391219R00183